Sour Crime Donuts

Books by Ginger Bolton

SURVIVAL OF THE FRITTERS

GOODBYE CRULLER WORLD

JEALOUSY FILLED DONUTS

BOSTON SCREAM MURDER

BEYOND A REASONABLE DONUT

DECK THE DONUTS

CINNAMON TWISTED

DOUBLE GRUDGE DONUTS

BLAME THE BEIGNETS

SOUR CRIME DONUTS

Published by Kensington Publishing Corp.

Sour Crime Donuts

GINGER BOLTON

Kensington Publishing Corp.
kensingtonbooks.com

KENSINGTON BOOKS are published by

Kensington Publishing Corp.
900 Third Avenue
New York, NY 10022

Copyright © 2025 by Janet Bolin

All rights reserved. No part of this book may be reproduced in any form or by any means without the prior written consent of the Publisher, excepting brief quotes used in reviews.

Without limiting the author's and publisher's exclusive rights, any unauthorized use of this publication to train generative artificial intelligence (AI) technologies is expressly prohibited.

All Kensington titles, imprints, and distributed lines are available at special quantity discounts for bulk purchases for sales promotion, premiums, fund-raising, educational, or institutional use.

This book is a work of fiction. Names, characters, businesses, organizations, places, events, and incidents either are the product of the author's imagination or are used fictitiously. Any resemblance to actual persons, living or dead, events, or locales is entirely coincidental.

To the extent that the image or images on the cover of this book depict a person or persons, such person or persons are merely models, and are not intended to portray any character or characters featured in the book.

Special book excerpts or customized printings can also be created to fit specific needs. For details, write or phone the office of the Kensington Sales Manager: Kensington Publishing Corp., 900 Third Avenue, New York, NY 10022. Attn. Sales Department. Phone: 1-800-221-2647.

The K and Teapot logo is a trademark of Kensington Publishing Corp.

ISBN: 978-1-4967-4964-2 (ebook)
ISBN: 978-1-4967-4963-5

First Kensington Trade Paperback Printing: September 2025

10 9 8 7 6 5 4 3 2 1

Printed in the United States of America

The authorized representative in the EU for product safety and compliance is eucomply OU, Parnu mnt 139b-14, Apt 123
Tallinn, Berlin 11317, hello@eucompliancepartner.com

Acknowledgments

Ever since I was very young, I wanted to write books. Many thanks to everyone who has helped make that happen.

Deputy Donut Mysteries exist thanks to my agent, John Talbot, and my editor, John Scognamiglio.

Using something like magic, the team at Kensington Publishing Corp. transforms my manuscripts into real books. I thank the magicians Carly Sommerstein and Kristine Mills, who also recruited the talented artist, Mary Ann Lasher, to create the cute covers and make the reader wonder what mischief Dep might get into next.

Larissa Ackerman works wonders publicizing Kensington Cozies. Watch for her fabulous cozy mini-conventions and plan to attend every one of them that takes place near you. Readers and authors getting together—what could be better?

Also, thank you to my writer friends who are always ready to talk about writing, even if it means taking a break from writing (we don't call it procrastinating)—Catherine Astolfo, Allison Brook, Melodie Campbell, Laurie Cass, Krista Davis, Daryl Wood Gerber, and Kaye George.

Thank you to booksellers and librarians who help us discover books and authors.

I'm glad my family and friends understand my love of writing, even when deadlines loom.

As always, my sincerest thanks to you, the reader. I hope you enjoy the book that you now hold in your hand.

Chapter 1

The young woman striding into Deputy Donut threw me a tentative grin as if she expected me to recognize her.

I felt like I should. . . .

We could almost have been sisters. We were both petite, and her hair was short and curly like mine, but while mine was nearly black, hers was mid-brown, and her eyes were hazel. Mine were so blue that people sometimes thought I wore royal-blue contact lenses.

On this morning in late August, the woman was dressed for the heat in faded denim cutoffs, a pale-yellow T-shirt, sneakers, and no socks. Her fresh-faced innocence almost shouted that she was from rural northern Wisconsin, perhaps not far from our village of Fallingbrook.

She walked through our dining room to our serving counter and looked across it at me. Tilting her head to one side, she asked, "Are you Emily?"

Her smile was contagious. I returned it. "Yes."

"I can tell you don't remember me. No wonder. I was little and you were, I don't know, in your late teens, I guess. I was totally in awe. We spent only part of one day together, at a campground at Fallingbrook Falls."

I mentally transformed her features into rounded, childish ones, and her name came to me. "Isabella?"

She twined her fingers through her curls, pulling at them. She let go, and the curls sprang back. "I go by Izzy now. I was a little pest back then."

"No, you weren't. You were imaginative and creative. I had fun that day, but I don't remember seeing you again after that, until now."

"That was the only time my folks ever took me there. We were visiting the people camping across from you. You showed me all of the places you liked when you were little. We went hunting for treasure, and I actually found some. Years later, I realized that you had somehow snuck those stickers and beads into tiny rock caves when I wasn't looking."

I touched my fingers to the Deputy Donut logo embroidered near the top of my apron. "Who, me?"

She grinned. "Hardly anyone else was around. You and I explored together, like hiking past this immense waterfall, and the mist made me think I understood the word 'mystical.' You were kind and gentle. Patient, too."

"You were bubbly and adventurous, ready for anything."

Izzy slid onto one of the rotating stools next to our serving counter. "And now we're both grown up, and you have this darling donut shop. What do you serve here?" She glanced over at the display case. "Lots of beautiful donuts."

"And things to drink with them. We always have a rich Colombian coffee available, and a special coffee for the day. And all sorts of teas and other beverages. Peaches are in season, so lately we've been making peaches-and-cream donuts. They're sour cream donuts split in half, covered with fresh sliced peaches, and topped with whipped cream. They'd be messy if we didn't serve them with spoons."

"Peaches are my favorite fruit! I'll have one of those. And some coffee."

"Are you sure you're old enough?" I winked to show I was teasing. "Today's special is a slightly fruity medium roast with hints of honey and chocolate from a small farm in Ethiopia."

"I'd love to try that." Izzy didn't seem to have outgrown her enthusiasm. She was almost bouncing on her stool.

I walked around the half-height wall to the kitchen. From there, I could see over the wall and watch for customers who might need something.

Our full-time assistant Olivia was frying a batch of plain raised donuts, and our summer assistant Jocelyn was dipping cooled donuts into a bowl of vanilla glaze.

Jocelyn nodded toward Izzy. "I overheard your conversation. I'll make your friend a peaches-and-cream donut."

I poured Izzy's coffee, took it to her, and watched her take the first sip. "To die for," she said.

With a flourish, Jocelyn placed a donut mounded with peach slices and whipped cream in front of Izzy. "You were talking about Fallingbrook Falls. I've spent a lot of time there, too."

Izzy's face relaxed into dreaminess. "I remember it as being an otherworldly, magical place." She stared down at the confection Jocelyn had brought her. "And this looks almost as magical."

The café's front door opened. Five women and one man, all in matching green T-shirts with the word TWIG printed in big white letters in front, started inside.

Jocelyn and I were facing the door. At the sound of voices, Izzy turned around.

A sturdy, ruddy-faced woman in front of the group looked toward us, stopped walking, and said in a voice that carried through our crowded dining room, "We can't hold our meeting if she's in here."

Chapter 2

The woman who had made the peculiar and very rude announcement herded the other five people outside to our patio. The door closed behind them. They marched to the sidewalk and stood in a row, looking up and down Wisconsin Street as if trying to decide where to go for their meeting.

Jocelyn tilted her head in obvious confusion. "What was that about? Some of those people looked familiar, like I've seen them around Fallingbrook, but not in here. Do you know any of them, Emily?"

"Maybe I've seen them in town, but not dressed alike. I don't know what I could have done to make them react like that."

Jocelyn called toward Olivia at the deep fryer, "Maybe they were afraid of Olivia and her boiling oil."

Olivia gave Jocelyn a side-eye. "Dream on. They were probably afraid you'd do a backflip and kick them in their chins."

Izzy spun her stool and faced us again. She was examining Jocelyn's face the same way she'd stared at me earlier, as if she knew her. I explained, "Jocelyn is one of Wisconsin's top gymnasts."

Jocelyn corrected me. "Was. I've retired from competition."

I defended my statement. "You're still one of the best ever."

Izzy placed her hand on her heart as if she were about to swoon. "No wonder you look familiar, Jocelyn. I was terribly disappointed when you didn't make it onto the Olympic team."

Jocelyn's nearly black eyes flashed. "So was I. But I'm doing something even more fun. I'm about to start my teaching career, with a kindergarten class at Fallingbrook Elementary."

Izzy clapped her palms together. "Lucky kids!"

I agreed and added, "Jocelyn's going to help us here on weekends, and she also coaches gymnastics part-time. You can see why we think she might intimidate strangers in green shirts." I was only partially joking.

Izzy shook her head. "It wasn't Olivia's boiling oil or Jocelyn's backflips or your imagination and empathy that scared that group away, Emily. I'm sorry, but I'm afraid I did it." She slipped a peach slice into her mouth and sighed, either because the peach was delicious or because the woman had upset her.

Izzy couldn't have changed much from the sweet and bubbly child I remembered. How could she have frightened anyone? I asked her, "What makes you think they left because of you?" Behind me, I heard Olivia remove a basket of donuts from the oil and hook it onto the side of the deep fryer.

Jocelyn inserted her own question. "Who were they, besides a bunch of random people wearing matching T-shirts with TWIG on front?"

Izzy answered Jocelyn's question first. "They're an environmental group, Toward Wisconsin in Green, and they hate me."

I spluttered, "Hate?" She had to be exaggerating. Olivia came to stand between Jocelyn and me. We must have been quite a sight, the tall, chestnut-haired woman standing between two short women, Jocelyn with her straight black ponytail and me with my short, dark curls. All of us were wearing our Deputy Donut hats, fake police caps with fuzzy donuts in front. Our uniforms matched in other ways, too. We all wore white polo shirts, black knee-length shorts, and white aprons. A cat wearing a hat like ours was embroidered on our aprons and shirts.

Izzy gazed down toward her donut. "They thought the property I'm buying should be turned into a park, with not even the tiniest blade of grass to be touched. But I'm planning to cut down trees, and they know it." She looked up at us. "I won't cut down more than I have to, but I have the opportunity to fulfill a dream." With her spoon, she mashed the tallest peak of whipped cream.

Olivia glared toward the street where we'd last seen the group wearing green shirts. "Maybe those TWIG people should buy the property you're talking about instead of spending money on T-shirts." Having raised a much younger sister who was now almost as old as Izzy, Olivia was going into mother mode. And so was I, even though I had never raised a child.

Izzy pointed at her chest. "I'm buying the property. It's too late for them. The sales contract is signed, and the lawyers are working on it." A dimple showed beside one corner of her mouth. "Besides, it would take a lot of T-shirts. I can't imagine any group of volunteers raising enough to buy the property."

Jocelyn let out a low whistle. "Wow."

Izzy blushed. "I didn't win a lottery, but that's what it feels like. About two months ago, out of the blue, my grandfather sent me money. I'm supposed to report back to him in a year about what I did with it. I could have invested in stocks and bonds or something, but what do I know about those things? What I do know is that here in northern Wisconsin, fresh produce is hard to find, especially during colder months, so I plan to do my part by growing veggies in greenhouses. When the year is up, I want to be able to say that I've started a viable business that will, before long, be profitable."

Olivia asked her, "Did you major in agriculture or something?"

Izzy ran fingertips along the marble counter. "Biology. But I've read lots about growing in greenhouses, and I even have a tiny greenhouse of my own. Imagine fresh, green, leafy lettuce, still crunchy because it doesn't have to be trucked long distances."

I took a deep breath. "That would be amazing. I grow a few veggies, but the season is short."

Olivia cautioned, "We're pretty far north here. It's cold during the winter, and we don't always get a lot of sunlight."

Izzy gazed toward the window into our office, though she seemed to be focusing beyond that, probably through the office's back windows and glass door toward trees lining the far side of the parking lot behind our building. "That's why we need someone to grow produce in the winter, and that someone can be me."

My business partner Tom and I had planned carefully before opening Deputy Donut, and I knew a few things about starting and running a business. I didn't want to crush Izzy's spirits, but I thought I should remind her, "You'll need power for heat and extra light. And water. Will you be able to recoup your costs for those plus your original outlay, not to mention maintenance and staffing costs, through sales?"

Izzy stirred the peaches and whipped cream over the donut. "Maybe not the first year or the second, but after that, yes. I've figured it all out. I'll be able to do most of the work myself, except for building the greenhouses, and maybe I can do some of that, too. Also, the property I found is perfect. It's on a south-facing hill. It will get lots of sunshine. I'll have to add light and heat during the colder and darker seasons."

Jocelyn leaned to one side as if she were about to topple over. She was good at defying gravity. "I don't think I've ever heard of greenhouses on slopes."

Izzy's laugh was still charmingly girlish. "That does conjure up a funny image. But my greenhouses won't tip, tilt, slide, or go downhill. Because of the bedrock underneath it, the hillside is naturally terraced, with nearly flat, level plateaus." She moved her hands, palms down, above the counter as if she were smoothing the tops of shelves. "I can put the greenhouses on those flat sections without having to blast into rock. Well, not much. The place even has a great water supply—a spring-fed stream runs down between man-made, dammed-up ponds on each plateau—there will be tons of water that I can capture, clean up, and pump back into the stream."

I jerked my head back in surprise. "How big is this property?"

"Acres and acres. It's huge."

Olivia was looking as surprised as I felt. "It sounds like it."

"It's fabulous." Izzy ate another slice of peach. "Peaches are so good! I love them. I'm going to start out small, with one or two greenhouses where I'll grow salad greens. I'd like to work my way up through tomatoes, peppers, and cucumbers, and someday I'd really like a greenhouse where I can grow fruit trees. Especially peaches. The trees don't have to be tall. Maybe I'm going overboard in my dreaming. Do you three think I am?"

Olivia thinned her lips into a serious expression that was not quite a frown. "Maybe."

Jocelyn straightened her hat. "I know about dreaming big and following your heart. You just keep doing it." Apparently, Jocelyn could also go into mother mode, Jocelyn-style. She added, "Not all of my dreams came true, but I don't regret trying."

Olivia did know how to be encouraging. "You accomplished much more than most people do, Jocelyn."

I gazed out at the charming donut shop that Tom and I had created. Tom was the father of my late first husband, Alec. With the help of Tom's artistic wife, my mother-in-law Cindy, Tom and I had painted one large donut on each of our tabletops. We'd covered the paintings with glass. Our almost white, peach-tinted walls featured art for sale by local artists, and our floors were rock maple, a lovely honey-like shade. In addition to offering welcoming surroundings, we carefully prepared the drinks and food we served. I was proud of what we'd accomplished, and our growing numbers of customers loved our shop. I took a deep breath. "With vision, enthusiasm, and persistence, you can aim for your dreams."

Olivia pointed out, "And hard work. You and Tom worked seven days a week in the beginning."

"And now we don't have to, because you and Jocelyn do." Tom and I enjoyed our two days off each week, while Jocelyn and Olivia wanted to put in as many hours as possible. Jocelyn had educational debts, and Olivia was helping put her sister, who had earned great scholarships, through college. And maybe, someday, Olivia would continue her own education, which she'd halted to look after her sister.

Izzy raised her fork like a flag. "Hard work and money. I don't mind hard work, and my grandfather sent me gobs of money. Also, I wrote and told him all about the property and my plans, and he wrote back, 'Go for it!'"

I rested my palms on the smooth, cool, marble counter. "Money helps. My first husband Alec hadn't been a detective for very long when he was killed on duty. His life insurance paid for my share of Deputy Donut and helped with the mortgage on the house that he and I bought."

Izzy studied my face. "I'm so sorry, Emily." She glanced at my left hand. "You're still wearing your wedding and engagement rings."

I straightened the rings on my finger. The sapphire on my engagement ring sometimes slid around as if trying to hide. "I recently married again."

Olivia stood up straighter. "Her new husband Brent is Fallingbrook's detective. We all have to behave."

Jocelyn's fake cough made it clear that Izzy wasn't supposed to take Olivia seriously.

Izzy spun her stool in a complete circle. "Is that why you called your shop Deputy Donut?"

I pointed at the window into our office. "See the small, short-haired cat lounging on the back of the sofa? Her full name is Deputy Donut. We call her Dep for short. Tom and I fitted out the office for her so she can spend her days here when I'm working. She has food, water, a litter box, toys, and an entire playground near the ceiling, with ramps and stairways going to and from it."

Izzy placed her right hand over her heart for a second. "A tortoiseshell tabby! She's adorable. I just want to kiss that cute orange stripey patch on her forehead. Is her name because your husband is a detective?"

"Actually, it's because Alec was. If Dep turns a little, you'll see the circles on her sides. They're sort of like donuts. When she was a tiny kitten, Alec called her his deputy, and we named her Deputy Donut. Tom and I opened this shop shortly after Alec was killed, long before Brent and I became a couple. Tom and I stole Dep's full name for our shop."

Olivia bragged, "Tom used to be Fallingbrook's police chief."

Izzy grinned. "You all really do have to behave."

Olivia folded her arms in an obviously phony attempt to look stern. "We would anyway."

Jocelyn pretended to hide another cough.

Izzy cut into her donut with the edge of her spoon. "Me, too."

I joked, "Except you might cut down trees that environmentalists want you to keep."

Jocelyn defended Izzy. "Those environmentalists will just have to find another park. Where is this sunny, terraced hillside you're buying?"

Izzy waved a hand. "Northwest of here. About the same distance from Fallingbrook as it is from Gooseleg, where I live, but west, so if you draw lines between the three places, you make a triangle. Would you three like to see my gorgeous hillside?"

I said I would. "It sounds as magical as Fallingbrook Falls."

Olivia asked, "Didn't you say you haven't taken possession yet, Izzy?"

Izzy's bouncing made it difficult to focus on her. "That doesn't matter. The land is vacant, and the owner said I could go out there anytime and look around. You know, bring an architect or contractor or whoever to help me plan. Meanwhile, I'd love to show it off if any of you want to go admire it with me. I know you'll love it, Emily. I remember how you felt about all those hiking trails around Fallingbrook Falls and how good you were, and obviously still are, at imagining and envisioning things. My new property isn't as forested, and the waterfalls aren't dramatic, but . . . well, you'll like it for sure. When do you finish work?" Her look embraced all three of us. "Want to meet me there?"

We looked at one another, and all of us said we would like to. I had many reasons for wanting to see her property. Mainly, I was curious, but I also wanted to give Izzy emotional support. However, if Olivia, Jocelyn, and I didn't think Izzy's plan was likely to succeed, we might be able to dissuade her before she locked herself into major problems.

I asked my two assistants, "Shall I drive? I'll bring you both home afterward."

Olivia protested, "You live north of here. Bringing us home

would be out of your way, and you like spending your evenings with Brent. I could go get my car, and after we tour the property together, I could bring Jocelyn back to Deputy Donut for her bike."

I made a sad face. "Taking you two along will be more fun for me than going separately. And Brent's at the event that Tom's attending." Ordinarily, Tom worked on Saturdays, but he and Brent were two of the organizers of an all-day event where citizens, especially kids, could meet Fallingbrook's first responders and tour their vehicles. And there would be hot dogs and ice cream. And donut holes, thanks to Tom. "Brent won't be home until after he helps clean up the fairgrounds."

Olivia gave me a high five. "Okay. Let's."

I turned to Izzy. "We finish here around five."

Izzy drew directions on a napkin. "It should take you about a half hour to get there from here."

We exchanged phone numbers and agreed to meet Izzy at the property around five thirty.

Olivia returned to the deep fryer, Jocelyn arranged donuts in our display case, and I served other customers.

Izzy finished her donut and coffee. Passing me on her way to the front door, she told me she'd never eaten a better donut or drunk better coffee. "They were perfect!" She waved goodbye and left.

I cleaned the serving counter. Izzy had left a ridiculously high tip. Frowning at her extravagance, I took her dishes to the dishwasher in the storeroom.

Something clanked behind our building.

I peeked through the glass window in the storeroom door that led to the parking lot.

The lid of the large, bright green metal container where we put food scraps and other compostable materials, like brown paper bags, was raised, hiding the person holding the lid except for the tips of three fingers. The lid lowered slowly.

Izzy turned away from the bin. She glanced left and right and then, with her head down, she scurried south between vehicles shimmering in the hot August sunshine. I didn't think she'd seen me.

She'd been carrying a brown paper bag. When she left Deputy Donut, she'd been empty-handed.

Chapter 3

I was almost certain that I recognized the brown paper bag that Izzy was carrying. Our peaches had come from the farmers' market in that bag or one like it. After we'd peeled and pitted the peaches, I'd put the peels and seeds in the bag. Dampness had soaked through it even before I took it out to the compost bin, and the bag Izzy had been carrying looked even wetter. She'd held it away from her body as if to avoid getting peach juice on her clothes.

I might have thought that someone carting away compost might have been hungry enough to eat fuzzy peach skins, but that hardly seemed to be the case with Izzy. She'd told us she wanted, in the future, to grow peach trees in greenhouses. She must have noticed that the peaches topping our sour cream donuts were fresh and extra delicious, and maybe she hoped to grow peaches that were as good. I could easily imagine that in her excitement, she'd decided to plant the stones from peaches immediately.

I returned to the kitchen. Standing at the deep fryers, Olivia squinted toward the dining room. "Here's another new customer. Could he be your new tenant?"

A short-term tenant was supposed to be moving into the Victorian cottage that Brent and I owned a few blocks from Deputy Donut. The tenant should have everything he needed, including the code for unlocking the doors. Still, I wouldn't be surprised if he came to Deputy Donut to meet me. The man Olivia had pointed out was little more than a tall, thin silhouette near our glass front door. Behind him, sunshine spilled over the street and our patio.

Olivia asked me, "Are you happy about renting out your house?"

I took a deep breath. "Yes and no. It's a great way for Brent and me to keep that house so we can use it during the winters to stay within walking distance of our jobs, but being a landlord is new to me, so I'm nervous, too. What if the guy doesn't like the place?"

With a wooden rod, Olivia deftly turned donuts in the boiling oil. "Your house is darling. How could he help loving it? I'd be more worried about him damaging things."

"There's that, too. But he comes with good references. He's a chef. He liked the photos of our kitchen."

She gave me a sly grin. "Is he single?"

Now that Olivia's sister was away at college, Olivia had time to think about herself, and maybe even to consider romance. I smiled at how much she'd lost her shyness since she first started working at Deputy Donut. "As far as I know, he is."

She rippled her shoulders. "Single, and he can cook. I can't wait to meet him."

The man came farther into the room. "That's not my new tenant," I concluded. "It's . . ."

From near the front of the dining room, Jocelyn sang out, "Good afternoon, Your Honor."

I finished my sentence. "It's our mayor, Jerry Creavus."

With a rude noise, Olivia focused on the donuts in the deep fryer.

I added, "He's single."

"*Pfffft.* He's old, over fifty. Plus, his ex-wife probably had a good reason for tossing him out."

The mayor bent toward Jocelyn. "Call me Jerry."

Jocelyn laughed, showed Jerry to a table, and came into the kitchen with his order. He wanted to try one of our peaches-and-cream donuts. He thought that green tea would go with it. "I agreed with him," Jocelyn said.

I spooned green tea leaves into a small teapot. "It does sound perfect."

Jocelyn and I headed toward Jerry's table. Before we got there, though, he dragged his chair to where the retired men, one of our two groups of morning regulars, sat. "Mind if I join you?" he asked them.

They said they didn't mind. I couldn't tell if they meant it or were being polite.

Jocelyn and I set Jerry's donut and tea in front of him.

Charles, one of the retired men, asked Jerry, "What's this about you opposing a new resort?"

Jerry poured pale, barely steeped tea into his cup. "We don't need a flashy resort in Fallingbrook."

As always, the Knitpickers, our other regular morning group, were paying attention to everything going on at the retired men's table. The two groups had originally come in only on weekday mornings, but they'd expanded their visits to include Saturdays. I figured it was only a matter of time before they decided that they needed our coffee and sweet treats on Sundays, too. The men's and women's groups each had their own regular tables and never sat together, but they might as well have, considering the cheerful bickering they tossed at one another.

Priscilla lifted an index finger high. "According to the news report I saw, the resort wouldn't be in Fallingbrook."

Jerry had his answer ready. "We don't need one anywhere near Fallingbrook. It will attract the wrong sort of people."

Priscilla barked out a laugh. "You mean tourists with money."

Jerry waved a hand and almost knocked his teacup off its saucer. "They wouldn't spend it here."

Priscilla raised one eyebrow. "So, you'd rather have the resort here in Fallingbrook."

Jerry nearly exploded. "No way! It would ruin the town's homey, Victorian vibe."

Cheryl, the most grandmotherly Knitpicker, suggested, "New buildings can be designed to look Victorian."

Jerry clapped his right hand against his jaw and then quickly dropped his hand from his face as if the argument were giving him a toothache, but he didn't want anyone to notice. "Trust me. They wouldn't do that, and even if they did, everyone would be able to tell the difference. They'd raze perfectly good buildings and destroy a block or two. And who goes to resorts in the middle of towns?"

"Jobs," Charles argued. "There'd be more summer jobs for students. And there'd be full-time, year-round jobs, too. Fallingbrook might grow." He winked at me. "Emily and Tom would need a bigger place. Look how crowded it is in here this morning."

I clamped my teeth together to prevent myself from laughing aloud. Although nearly every table inside and on the patio was occupied, the only crowded table was the retired men's table now that Jerry had squeezed his chair into the circle around it.

Cheryl made a horrified grimace. "No. I like this place just the way it is, and you should, too, Charles."

As if Cheryl hadn't spoken, Charles went on with his argument, "More businesses increase our tax base."

Jerry pointed out, "And end up costing us more for servicing those businesses than the taxes they contribute. Besides, we couldn't increase our village budget with taxes from the resort if the resort isn't in Fallingbrook, which it really can't be."

The retired men and the Knitpickers never minded a verbal

squabble. They kept baiting Jerry, forcing him to restate his views.

Jerry didn't want a "flashy" resort in Fallingbrook, which was understandable, but he also didn't want one outside the village limits. He didn't seem to be able to express a solid reason for that opposition, though. Did he have an agenda he was trying to hide?

Jocelyn and I glanced at each other and then split up to go to other tables, both inside and out on the patio, to ask people what else we could bring them.

Usually, the Knitpickers and retired men stayed until shortly before the lunch crowd arrived, but Jerry's repetitive and circular attempts at reasoning must have bored them. By an apparently silent agreement, they stood and claimed it was time for them to go. Jerry left, too. Although we always wanted new customers to discover us, I wasn't sure that our mayor was good for business.

Probably because it was August, locals and tourists kept us occupied, though we had time to take turns eating quick lunches in the office. I sat on the couch. Purring, Dep curled up next to my thigh. I ran my fingers through her short, soft fur. Smaller than average, she really was cute. And cuddly.

Late in the afternoon, Olivia and I were again in the kitchen, and Jocelyn was chatting with diners. A man I'd never seen before came in. Like Jerry, this man was tall, but he was younger and more muscular. Although not conventionally handsome, he had a pleasant face. Olivia murmured so that only I could hear, "I hope this is your single chef tenant."

He appeared to ask Jocelyn a question. She pointed at me.

Right hand outstretched, the man came to our serving counter. "Emily? I'm Glenn Sitherby. I came to tell you that I love the house."

I shook his hand. "Great! Do you have any questions?"

"None. The manual you left on the kitchen counter answers more questions than I'll probably ever need to ask. And speaking of the kitchen—it's even better than it looks in the photos on the website. And this place looks great, too. You obviously love cooking. I'm surprised you're willing to give up that house and that kitchen for a day, let alone a month."

"Brent and I each had our own houses before we were married, and his is out in the country, so we're happy to spend our summers in the woods. And I love the kitchen in that house, too."

Glenn quirked up one corner of his mouth. "I'm beginning to believe that northern Wisconsinites know how to live."

"We certainly know where to live."

"That's why I'm here. I'm deciding where to open a restaurant. Do you think this area can support a fine dining restaurant? Can you suggest a good place for one?"

"Selfishly, I'd love one in Fallingbrook's center, if you can find an appropriate building. We have pubs and coffee shops, and we all serve good food, but we have to go to out-of-town resorts and dinner clubs for a white tablecloth, china, and crystal experience. And if you could come up with a name that references first responders or law enforcement like our Deputy Donut, or the Fireplug pub, you'd really fit in. Our bookstore is called Booked, our yarn shop is On the Lamb, and new funny names keep popping up."

"I'd like to refer to food, like one good ingredient that nearly everyone loves. I'm thinking of 'Sweet Pepper.'"

"That sounds welcoming, and it would also fit in. A few blocks north of here, just beyond the town square, you'll find casual dining at Frisky Pomegranate."

Glenn's light blue eyes were almost flirtatious. "I seem to have come to the right place. And I don't mean only the area. Your shop is charming."

"Let me bring you today's special donut and coffee, on the house. The donut is a sour cream raised donut topped with fresh peaches and whipped cream, and the day's special coffee is—"

He held up one hand. "Could I have tea?"

"Sure. Our mayor was in here this morning, and he thought that green tea would go with the donuts."

"That sounds good."

I was apprehensive about a chef's reaction to our donuts, but I reminded myself that taste was subjective. I knew they were good. I watched him take his first bites of peaches and cream, and then I almost held my breath while he tasted the donut underneath the other goodies.

I needn't have worried. "Just right." He looked and sounded sincere. "Your cooking matches the kitchen in your house."

I cocked a thumb over my shoulder. "Our assistants do a lot of the cooking and decorating, and we all—along with my business partner Tom, who isn't here today—devise and tweak our recipes."

"I'm not surprised that you're organized and a team player, not after I saw the manual you put together. And thank you for leaving tea, coffee, sugar, milk, and eggs in the house."

"It's only a few days' worth, until you can shop."

"It's much appreciated." He finished his donut and tea, and then asked me to point him toward Frisky Pomegranate. "You recommended it in your manual. It's walking distance from here, right?"

"Yes. The street out front is Wisconsin Street. Turn left and walk north on that to where Oak Street ends at Wisconsin Street. Oak Street and our village square will be on your right. You can cut through the square. It's actually a rectangle, and a rather large one, with so many trees you might think you're in a forest. Well, almost. At the north end of the square, there's a bandstand. Beyond that, you'll see Frisky Pomegranate across the street."

He stood. "I'll tour your downtown on my way, get a feel for the place. I walked here from your house. Fallingbrook is picturesque, just the sort of place I imagined for my restaurant."

He tossed a smile and a wave toward the kitchen, where Jocelyn and Olivia were undoubtedly pretending not to listen to us, and then he sauntered outside and turned north.

On the way to the dishwasher in the storeroom, I said to Olivia. "He isn't wearing a wedding ring."

Olivia blushed.

Jocelyn teased, "You could have taken a break from making dough for tomorrow and talked to him."

Olivia retorted, "Maybe I didn't want to. Besides, he's renting Emily's house for a month, right, Emily?"

"And maybe more. At the moment, it's open-ended, though if someone wants to rent it starting near the end of September, I'll need to find out if Glenn wants to stay longer."

Olivia gave the dough she was kneading a solid thump with the heel of her hand. "I'm sure he'll be back for more of our donuts."

At four thirty, the other customers left. We locked the front door and tidied. During the night, four retired police officers, the Jolly Cops, would clean thoroughly, including the deep fryers.

We took off our aprons and hats and went into the office. Dep stood up from snoozing on the couch and stretched. I asked her, "Would you like to wait for me here or come with us to see the property that Izzy's so excited about?"

Chapter 4

Dep must have forgotten that coming with us meant one of those dreaded rides in a car. She purred and twined around my bare ankles. I put her harness and leash on her.

We locked the doors, set the alarms, and left through the office to the back porch and the parking lot behind it.

Dep walked nicely on her leash but did not want to go near my small white SUV. I opened the door behind the driver's seat. Olivia helped me remove Dep's leash and put the suddenly stiff-legged cat into the carrier that I kept tethered to the rear seat belt.

Like her younger sister, Olivia had a magic touch with Dep. She ran around the car and took the seat next to Dep's carrier. Jocelyn sat in front with me. Dep wailed, but before I pulled out of the alleyway from the parking lot and onto Wisconsin Street, Olivia unzipped the carrier enough to reach inside and pet Dep. The little cat's cries diminished to grumbles, and we three humans were able to hear one another, as long as we spoke loudly. I told the others about Izzy removing peach skins and pits from our compost bin.

Jocelyn reached a conclusion similar to mine. "She's going to grow trees from the peach pits."

Olivia pointed out, "The plants from seeds don't always

come out like the parent plants. She could end up with hard and bitter peaches. But I admire her passion and optimism."

Not very far north, we left Fallingbrook behind, and Wisconsin Street became County Road C. We traveled through sparsely populated, rolling countryside. Jocelyn consulted the map that Izzy had drawn on a napkin. "County Road H should be the next intersection."

It was. I turned left, and we headed west. Still high in the sky, the sun wasn't in our eyes. Meandering streams crossed former pastures, and then forests crowded against the road. Although it was still August, some maples already displayed bouquets of red leaves in their bright green crowns. The road dipped and curved, then gradually rose, and the forests bordering the road were composed mostly of pines, their needles dark.

We rounded a curve. An older, burgundy-colored compact sedan was parked on the right shoulder between the road and a ditch. Izzy was sitting on the car's trunk.

I slowed and put on my turn signal.

Izzy slid off the car, jumped up and down, and waved both hands above her head. Her smile was huge. She pointed toward a pine-covered hill rising beyond the ditch.

I parked on the gravel shoulder about two car lengths behind her car. She ran to us.

I helped Olivia make certain that Dep couldn't flee while we unzipped her carrier and snapped her leash onto her harness. Hugging the slightly ruffled cat, Olivia scrambled out of the car.

"Awww," Izzy cooed, "what a darling!" She let Dep sniff her hand and then ran gentle fingers through the fur on Dep's shoulders. Dep purred. Izzy exclaimed, "She likes me!"

I pointed at the hill beside us. "Is this the property you're buying?"

Izzy waved her arm as if encompassing the entire hill. "Yes."

Olivia stared up into the masses of needle-covered branches. "I see why people are worried that you'll cut down trees. There's nothing but trees."

Izzy lifted Dep out of Olivia's arms. "Not as many as it looks like from down here on the road. I'll carry the kitty to keep her little paws off the gravel. Come on, I'll show you." Almost dancing in her excitement, she led us several yards past her car, and then she turned, faced back the way we'd come, and pointed with her left elbow toward the slope above us. A gap between trees was visible, just barely. No one driving quickly from the east, as we had, would notice it, but someone coming from the west might.

"See?" Izzy asked. "Years ago, there must have been a homestead up there. This is the beginning of the lane the settlers carved out of the hill for their horses and carriages. The original house and outbuildings or whatever are long gone, but the current owner maintained trails for ATVs so he could hunt here. I'll need to have the former driveway repaired and widened, but for now, it's an easy trail for walking. I won't cut down the trees near the road, and the driveway will always be mostly hidden. I also won't widen the driveway much, like not enough for transport trucks, just enough for things like small cube vans. Here, take the kitty. I'll leap across the ditch, and then if she doesn't want to walk, I can carry her again."

I accepted my purring cat. "She'll probably prefer to explore the ground." I ran down the slope and leaped over a sluggish rivulet in the bottom of the ditch. Hanging on to Dep's leash, I set her gently on the grassy ground. "I hope she won't slow us down."

Jocelyn grinned down at Dep, already investigating the stem of a milkweed. "If we get tired of her dawdling, I'll carry her."

Olivia joined us. "Or we can take turns."

Walking backward, Izzy started up the trail in front of us.

"We don't have to explore the entire acreage, but I want to show you some of the level spots and the ponds." We followed her more or less northeastward. The trail, stony but mostly carpeted in past years' fallen pine needles, gradually ran uphill between towering pines and rocky outcroppings. After making a wide curve between boulders, the trail turned northwest. The pine needle carpeting thinned, the trees ended, and a huge sunlit meadow spread in front of us. Izzy made a sweeping gesture with one outstretched arm. "See? I know it's rocky, and I'll probably need to have some blasting done. But look over there near those trees." A forest bordered the western edge of the meadow. "From here, you can only see the cattails on this side of it, but there's the lowest pond."

Olivia asked, "You're buying all of this, from the road up to here and all the way to that pond?"

A mischievous dimple danced in Izzy's cheek. "And more, a few yards into those woods over there. I won't touch those trees. And I have more acres higher up, and more flattish meadows and ponds. And the spring that feeds the ponds."

My mouth was probably gaping open. "And waterfalls, you told us. This is really impressive, Izzy. I understand why you're excited. I don't know much about the price of land out here, but after you buy this, are you sure you'll be able to do everything else?"

Izzy put a finger to her lips. "Don't tell anyone, but I'm buying this land below market value. The owner wants to get rid of it, and undeveloped like this, it's not worth a lot. The price of the land is only a fraction of what my grandfather sent me. I can make it work. I know I can."

If determination, exhilaration, and persistence were enough, Izzy would succeed.

Her enthusiasm must have infected Jocelyn. She turned a cartwheel.

Izzy applauded. "I never expected a private gymnastics show from the great Jocelyn Portsmouth!"

Jocelyn brushed her hands together and shrugged. "I couldn't help it." She twirled, taking in our surroundings, and then announced, "Even if you didn't want to build greenhouses, Izzy, this would be a great spot for a home."

Izzy looked toward a red-winged blackbird taking off from cattails near the pond. "That could happen, too, if the business goes the way I hope, I mean, the way I plan. I feel sorry for the first homesteaders, though. It's too stony for farming or even for grazing more than a few sheep or goats. And for now, I'll continue renting a tiny home and living frugally. If I have to, I can sell the land. There's at least one other person who wanted to buy it, but my bid won." Looping her thumbs through imaginary overall straps, she strutted in a happy half circle. I couldn't help smiling. And also wondering if I'd encouraged her imagination a bit too much when she was a little girl...

No, Emily, I told myself. *There's nothing wrong with following your dreams.*

Olivia gazed southward. The road was down there, but the pines hid it from us. "Aren't you afraid that the pines will grow too tall, and shade any greenhouses you put here?"

Izzy remained undaunted. "The TWIG people will see only the trees nearest the road, so if I lop off a few up here, they shouldn't know. I'll gate the driveway and"—she gazed toward the trail we'd taken—"uh-oh, speaking of intruders. What's going on?"

Men shouted. Maybe they were down on the road, but they sounded closer, like they could have been on the trail leading up to where we stood.

Chapter 5

One man's voice became higher, almost shrill as if squeezed by anger. Another voice was deep. It carried, seemingly without effort, up through the piney woods toward us. A loud dispute was an odd thing to hear in this isolated spot. Who had suddenly shown up here, and why were they yelling?

Izzy had mentioned that the current owner hunted on this property.

I picked up Dep. Cuddling her protectively, I gazed around. The sunny plateau offered no shelter. Hunters wouldn't shoot because they saw something move before they knew what the something was, would they? We were probably safe.

Izzy obviously thought so. Shoulders back, she marched toward the sounds.

I breathed, "Wait!"

Izzy kept going.

Jocelyn tossed me a worried look and sprinted after Izzy. Beside me, Olivia gasped.

Shrugging, I turned toward Olivia. "We might as well all stay together."

With a grim nod, she strode toward the other two.

Izzy and Jocelyn ran toward where the trail curved. They kept going. Trees blocked my view of them.

Izzy yelled, "Stop that!"

Olivia took off toward the shouting match and Izzy's attempts to end it. Still clutching Dep, I sped my pace. Behind Olivia, I trotted around the uppermost wall of pines. Now the stand of trees completely hid the sunlit meadow from me. Pines also covered the downhill slope between me and the road, and I was in a canyon between rows of trees. The shift from sunlight to shade was so abrupt that I had to stop to distinguish shadows on the ground from obstacles that could have sent me sprawling, kitty and all, onto the needle-covered but rocky ground. As my eyes adjusted, I noticed that one of the shadows was actually a cave-like niche at the base of a boulder just below the outer edge of the trail's curve, and I again remembered that day with Izzy at Fallingbrook Falls and the fun of sneaking treasures into similar places when she wasn't looking, and then watching her find them.

On the trail not far below me, the man with the shrill voice yelled, "Get off my property!"

Izzy and Jocelyn were close to the angry man and a taller man who, I guessed, was the one with the deep voice. Olivia pelted down the trail toward them.

Worried about what she, Izzy, and Jocelyn might be getting into, I hurried down the trail.

A middle-aged, slightly balding man stuck his index finger up, nearly into the face of the twenty-something man. "I told you. Get out!"

The men were dressed almost alike, in khakis, white polo shirts, and unscuffed leather loafers. The older man wore a casual but beautifully tailored navy blazer. The younger man wasn't wearing socks, but the older man's pants were longer, covering his ankles.

I had never seen these men before.

Neither of them appeared to be carrying a gun or a knife or even a fishing pole. With one hand, the older man held something that resembled a walking stick with a wheel at its base or a unicycle with no seat. Whatever it was, it could, I supposed, be used as a weapon. The clipboard under his other arm looked more benign.

Izzy stomped right up to the blustering older man. "This is not your property, Adam Nofftry."

Now that my eyes had completely adjusted to the shade among the pines, I became alarmed at the color of Adam Nofftry's heavily jowled face—red, verging on purple. He turned to Izzy and scowled. "Back off, Isabella Korinth. It's not your property, and never will be."

Izzy planted her fists on her hips. "Yes, it will. In fifteen and a half days. I have a contract."

Adam shook the cane-like thing, lifting its wheel off the ground. The wheel spun in a lazy circle. "There are holes in that contract you could drive a bulldozer through. It's illegal and you know it. My lawyers can flatten petty scammers like you. I will be the owner of this property, and I will develop it the way I want to." Was Adam the developer our mayor was trying to stop? If so, I was beginning to understand Jerry's motivation.

Izzy's face was becoming disturbingly red.

The tall man seemed to notice. He ignored the rest of us, gazed at Izzy as if memorizing her features, and said calmly, "So, if no one in this group owns this property, then maybe we're all trespassing." His voice was gentle and so deep and almost musical that he could have been an actor or radio announcer. Or a singer. He had the earnest look and thin face of . . . I wasn't sure what. A medieval scholar?

Izzy looked up at him. "I have permission to be here." She had become, if anything, even redder, but her tone had softened. She waved to encompass Jocelyn, Olivia, and me. "And I'm allowed to bring friends and advisers."

In my arms, Dep yawned.

Adam scoffed, "And a cat."

The tall man asked Izzy, "Who does own this place?"

Izzy opened her mouth as if to tell him but seemed to

change her mind. She folded her arms and thinned her lips. A sunbeam, softened by filtering pine branches, lit her blushing face, reminding me of the charming child at Fallingbrook Falls.

The younger man continued to stare at Izzy. "It's beautiful. These woods, I mean. This whole hillside. At least, I guess it is, from what I've seen."

Adam growled, "It's none of your business, and I'm telling you that I'm going to own it."

Izzy looked away from the tall man, shook her head, and repeated softly, "I've signed a contract."

Again, Adam argued, "Not a legal one. It's worth nothing."

Izzy might have been about to contradict him, but the tall man sent her a concerned and apologetic look. "I'm sorry. I meant no harm. I saw other cars here and . . ." He waved a gnat or something away from his face. "I'm from . . . I came from Duluth and was just looking around. I thought I, um, was in a state forest, and this was a trailhead or something. I'll go." Blushing was apparently contagious, or maybe the day's earlier heat had affected Adam, Izzy, and the tall man. To me, the shade beneath the sharp-scented pines was almost cool.

The tall man turned and started down the track. With his arms looking stiff and swinging only slightly, he walked with straight-backed dignity.

Watching him go, Olivia muttered so that only I would hear, "No flames!"

Confused, I cast a questioning look at her.

She grinned and whispered from one corner of her mouth, "Pants on fire."

Silently filling in the beginning of the taunt, *Liar, liar*, I nearly lost my serious expression. The man striding away from us had sounded like he was making up a justification for being on the property Izzy was buying. Why had he really been there, and why didn't he want to admit it?

Adam Nofftry began to look only marginally less like he was about to suffer a heart attack. All of us who worked at Deputy Donut kept our first aid certification up to date. I hoped we wouldn't need to administer CPR to him. He snapped at Izzy, "I also have permission to be here."

Izzy stared toward the rapidly fleeing tall man but addressed the balding man. "Fine, Adam. We'll leave you to it. Come on, ladies and cat." She turned her back on Adam and strode down the hill.

The younger man was about to disappear beyond the pines closest to the road. Izzy started running. Jocelyn quickly caught up with her. Olivia and I rushed down the trail behind them.

Dep mewed a complaint, probably about being jostled in my arms as I negotiated the uneven ground.

Before I reached the base of the trail, I looked over my shoulder.

Adam still stood where he'd been when we left him. He was watching us.

I didn't like his scheming smirk.

Chapter 6

I hurried down the trail with Olivia. We stopped between the lowest rank of pines.

Izzy and Jocelyn had not crossed the ditch. Standing on our side of it, they watched the tall man fold himself into a new-looking gray sedan.

Olivia admitted grudgingly, "The sun is glaring off that car, so it's hard to see, but I think that his front license plate does have those greenish swaths at the top and bottom like Minnesota plates have, so maybe he didn't lie when he said he came from Duluth."

He pulled away slowly and then did a cautious U-turn, backing up once as if to make certain he didn't roll the car down the slope on the south side of the road. I squinted, trying to see past the reflected sunshine. "I think I see a sticker that could mean it's a rental car. Maybe he only came from Duluth today."

"Aha! Pants on fire."

This time when she said it, I laughed aloud. "Could you read the license number?"

"No. Could you?"

"I was too busy looking for a rental sticker." Still carrying Dep, I charged down through the weeds to Izzy and Jocelyn.

Izzy watched the gray car head eastward, away from us.

She placed her hand on her heart. "Doesn't Mr. Mystery have the most beautiful voice you've ever heard? And did you notice how kind and caring he was? Not to mention superhot?"

I admitted, "He does seem to have a certain quiet strength." I wanted to warn Izzy not to trust him.

Olivia beat me to it. "There's something off about him."

Izzy looked genuinely perplexed. "Like what? I'm tempted to follow him and see where he goes."

Olivia warned, "Don't. Not by yourself. C'mon, Emily and Jocelyn, let's get Dep into the car. Mr. Mystery's going east, like we will to get back to Fallingbrook. And, Izzy, didn't you say you lived in Gooseleg? Drive west, the way your car is pointing, and then take the road curving northeast."

Izzy gazed toward the gray sedan. It wasn't going fast. "Okay, I do have plants to water at home, but if you three learn anything about him, let me know, okay? I'll see you in Deputy Donut."

Jocelyn, Olivia, and I said goodbye and then hurried past the enormous, black, and very shiny SUV that Adam must have parked between Izzy's and my cars.

Olivia placed Dep into her carrier and sat beside her in the rear seat. Jocelyn and I got into the front. When everyone was buckled in, I made a tire-squealing U-turn, with no backing up, and accelerated toward where we'd last seen Mr. Mystery in his ponderous gray sedan.

Jocelyn checked the passenger-side mirror. "Izzy's not coming this way."

"Good." I floored the gas pedal.

Jocelyn turned toward me. "What's wrong, Emily? You always want people to be in love and live happily ever after, and romantic sparks were flying between those two."

Olivia called toward us, pitching her voice above Dep's grumbling, "Izzy doesn't need to fall for a fake."

I told Jocelyn, "I thought he was making up stories about why he was there. What if unscrupulous people heard about the money Izzy says she received from her grandfather? She certainly wasn't shy about telling us, who are basically strangers, about it. Mr. Mystery could have learned about her windfall and also about her intended purchase of that land. He could have gone there so he could meet her and eventually help himself to some of her money. Or maybe he's working with that Adam guy, who definitely gives con-man vibes, and their argument was staged to make Izzy trust Mr. Mystery. Olivia and I didn't read his license number. Did you, Jocelyn?"

"I didn't think of it."

Olivia asked us, "And did you two notice Mr. Mystery's accent? He didn't sound like he was from around here or Duluth. I watch lots of movies and shows, and even though his car has Minnesota plates, I swear he talks like someone from the Northeast. And Emily thought she spotted a sticker from a rental company on his car."

Jocelyn concluded, "Maybe that explains why he's driving a geezer car. Except, he kind of drives like a geezer, too, the way he turned around back there." She made a show of leaning forward and grasping the dash with both hands. "Emily doesn't drive like a geezer. I'd tell you to drive faster, Emily, so we could check his license number, but you're already approaching warp speed."

I pointed ahead. "There he is, still driving cautiously and slowly. Hang on! And tell me if you see any police cars."

The only one who complained was Dep. Maybe my suddenly increased speed was making Jocelyn and Olivia too scared to speak. Jocelyn, scared? That would be a first.

I didn't manage to pull close to the sedan. Spewing gravel, it swerved onto the right-hand shoulder and then made a sharp left turn onto a one-lane country road that was little more than a cow path. I slowed and watched the car skid and fishtail through the dirt. "I'm not following him down that."

Jocelyn poked fun at me. "Chicken!"

Olivia commented over Dep's complaints, "He doesn't appear to have driven much, at least not on country roads. Either that, or he's purposely trying to keep us from getting a good look at his license plate. I don't see that as a geezer move. Izzy's right that he's a mystery."

Dust ballooned behind Mr. Mystery's car. I couldn't read the plate, and I definitely couldn't tell if the car was a rental.

"Someday, Emily," Jocelyn warned in ominous tones, "you'll regret not following him."

I pushed down on the gas and continued along the highway. "I doubt it."

Olivia called from the back, "What I regret is those men coming along when they did and distracting Izzy from our tour. I wanted to see more. Waterfalls and ponds? It has to be beautiful."

Jocelyn agreed. "I wanted to, too. Maybe she'll invite us back."

I glanced into the rearview mirror. As far as I could tell, no one was following us. "I think we can almost depend on that, maybe after she takes possession. She wants to share her excitement."

Olivia asked, "But what if Adam is right, and he can stop the sale? If he's the developer the mayor was talking about, he might know more about real estate than Izzy does."

Turning south on County Road C toward Fallingbrook, I suggested, "He also might know more about using any means to get what he wants. I hope Izzy has a good lawyer."

The conversation changed to donut flavors and recipes. We came up with an idea for unraised sour cream donuts containing fresh, chopped peaches. "Baked donuts," Olivia suggested, "so that we don't lose the pieces of peach in boiling oil."

I dropped her off at the store below her second-floor apartment, took Jocelyn to her parents' home, and headed north up County Road C again. Several miles beyond the intersection with H, County Road C entered Chicory Lake State Forest and started down a hill. Near the top, still high above Chicory Lake, I turned right, onto our nearly straight driveway. It ran almost a quarter of a mile between strips of lawn separating it from forests on both sides. Sunlight gilded the tops of pines on the land slanting down toward the lake to the left of the driveway and up toward the state forest to the right.

As always, our log chalet appeared like an enchanted home from an Alpine fairy tale. The golden-brown peeled logs almost glowed, and cheerful petunias and impatiens nodded in flower boxes hanging from the railing on our wide front porch. Brent had bought this place when we were already spending lots of time together, but I'd still been in denial that he and I were more than friends. I loved our lakefront hillside and the chalet.

I took Dep into the great room and freed her from her harness. With its log walls, wood floors, high ceilings, and huge windows overlooking forests, the room was both awe-inspiring and comfy. Dep dashed to the kitchen end of the room and checked on her bowls of water and kibble. I let her outside into the catio that Brent and Tom had built on the eastern side of the house. They had built a roof over an existing deck and surrounded the new outdoor room with two kinds of screens, one that was insect-proof and a stronger mesh one that would keep a little cat inside and wild animals out. Dep could climb up to perches and safely watch the woods for wildlife. In the kitchen, I marinated chicken pieces and made aluminum foil pouches of potatoes, onions, garlic, seasonings, and olive oil. I went out to our vegetable garden beside the catio and picked big, ripe, red tomatoes. I cut them in half, sprinkled them with olive oil, and put them in a grillable wire basket.

Whistling, Brent came in through the front door. He was wearing navy-blue shorts, a navy-blue Fallingbrook Police Department T-shirt, sneakers, and no socks. I ran to my tall, handsome, muscular husband, whose warm gray eyes always sent me messages of love, and threw myself into his arms. He picked me up and twirled me around. We shared a long kiss. He set me down. "Where's Dep?"

"Apparently, she finds the catio more interesting than you. Your fault for building it. How was the Lights and Sirens Fair?"

"Great. The kids loved it. And who knows? Maybe we inspired some of them to become first responders."

In the kitchen, he picked up the bowl of marinating chicken and the basket of tomato halves. Whistling again, he took them out to the barbecue in our catio's outdoor kitchen. He grilled the chicken and tomatoes, and I made a salad from our homegrown cucumbers and red peppers. We ate at our catio dining table.

I described Izzy, her plans, and our too-short tour of the land she was buying. I also told him about Adam Nofftry's threats about preventing Izzy's purchase of the land and about the man who Izzy nicknamed Mr. Mystery.

Brent cut off a bite of chicken. "That acreage has been on and off the market. I considered it before I bought this place, but I fell for this one. And I was sure you'd like it."

"We weren't together yet."

"I know."

"But I did fall for you before you bought this place."

"I know that, too."

Purring, Dep came down from a kitty hammock and inserted herself into our hug.

By the time we cleared the dishes, it was completely dark outside. Brent asked, "Want to check for remnants of the meteor shower again?"

"Sure!" The annual August sky event known as the Perseid meteor shower had mostly ended a few days before, but we'd discovered that we might still see a few falling stars if we went out onto our lawn, stretched out on lounges, and watched the sky. I leashed Dep and took her with us. The night was nearly silent except for her purring and the chirping of insects. I don't know how many meteors Dep saw. Brent and I saw three.

Chapter 7

The next day was Sunday. Brent had the day off, but since he was always on call, and we didn't want to possibly leave our sociable cat at home alone for hours, I took her to Deputy Donut.

Tom was back at work. Olivia, Jocelyn, and I described the peach donuts we'd mentally devised in the car the evening before, and Tom joined us in experimenting with them. We added bits of delicious fresh peaches to our non-yeast recipe for baked sour cream donuts. We topped them with thick sour cream frosting flavored with peach extract. We decided to feature the peachy sour cream donuts that day along with a coffee from Costa Rica, a medium roast with hints of plums and dark chocolate.

Izzy came in after lunch. Her brand-new leather briefcase contrasted with her slashed jeans and her cropped and boxy green cable-knit cardigan. She was also carrying a long cardboard tube like the kind used for mailing posters. She chose a table for two, ordered one of our peachy sour cream donuts and a mug of the Costa Rican coffee, and then she pulled a roll of paper out of the cardboard tube, unrolled it, and rolled it backward until it lay flat on the table. She explained, "I'm working on plans and drawings for where to put my greenhouses." She'd had a drone operator take aerial photos of the property, and this enlargement showed the entire acreage. She'd also cut out shapes representing greenhouses, sheds, and barns, and was positioning and repositioning them on the photo. "It's still in the dreaming stage."

I studied the photo. "Four ponds?"

"Four mostly level plateaus, four ponds, four dams, a meandering stream, and here are the little waterfalls." She traced a sinuous line between the plateaus. "With a driveway connecting the plateaus. But I won't own the top of the hill. Yet." She looked up at me. "Did you see where Mr. Mystery went after we left?"

"He turned north onto a dirt track off County Road H."

She asked wistfully, "Did you follow him?"

"That track looked bumpy."

"Do you think he lives there? No, I guess he doesn't. He said he was from Duluth."

I reminded her, "Didn't he correct that to 'came from Duluth'?"

"I guess so, maybe."

"I think he was driving a rental car."

"He seemed too caring to subject a rental car to a bumpy track." I didn't say anything, but I probably showed skepticism. She asked, "Didn't you think he was caring?"

"I couldn't tell."

She repositioned one of the greenhouse-shaped rectangles on the photo. "I suppose I'll never see him again."

"Be cautious, Izzy, about going alone to that isolated property. Maybe it's a coincidence, but it seems like too many people seem to treat it like it's theirs, and they might not like your showing up there, too." I was probably being overprotective.

"It was only two people."

"Only two people in a short amount of time."

"I'm not worried about those two. Adam Nofftry is all bluster, and Mr. Mystery is all"—she wriggled her shoulders in a fake shiver—"intriguing."

"Do you have a boyfriend, Izzy?"

She bit into a donut and gave me a saucy grin. "Not yet, but if I ever see Mr. Mystery again . . ."

I made a show of shaking my head in a way that implied I had no hopes for her. Behind me, the front door opened. Heavy footsteps approached us.

Izzy gazed at the remains of the donut in her hand. "These are delicious. Can you pack a half dozen of them for me to take home?"

A gruff voice came from, it seemed, only inches from my left shoulder blade. "You know, young lady, TWIG is going to stop at nothing to prevent you or anyone else from cutting down trees on that land."

Izzy dropped the half-eaten donut onto her plate and cupped both hands over the greenhouse shapes she'd been moving around like paper doll furniture. "I'm not going to cut down many trees."

The woman who Izzy had said was an environmentalist and the head of TWIG snapped, "One is too many. Why don't you build your greenhouses farther south in a better area for raising crops? Maybe on some barren wasteland."

Izzy remained calm. "Ramona, people around here deserve fresh produce in all seasons, and I mean fresh, not something that has been wilting for days in a train or a truck. Or in a container on a ship."

With a disdainful sniff, Ramona marched toward our serving counter.

I gave Izzy an apologetic smile and followed Ramona. She stood expectantly near the cash register. I asked her, "What can I get you?"

"Six of the kind of donuts that Izzy ordered." Ramona

seemed to bite down on a triumphant smile. Did she hope that by buying those donuts, she'd deprive Izzy of hers?

"We're calling them peachy sour cream donuts. They have—"

Ramona waved a hand to stop me. "Just box them up for me."

I opened the display case and told her, "We have only three of those peachy sour cream donuts at the moment." I started to tell her we'd have another batch ready in a few minutes.

Ramona interrupted me again. "That's fine. Just throw in three other donuts."

I selected three of our consistently popular donuts—a raised donut with vanilla glaze, an old-fashioned cake donut dusted with cinnamon and sugar, and a chocolate cake donut with chocolate icing. I showed Ramona the open box. She nodded a curt approval. I taped the box shut.

She paid me and pulled a sheaf of flyers from a green tote bag with TWIG printed on it in white. "You can give these notices about our next TWIG meeting to your fellow workers and to customers." She shot a quick glance toward the front of the dining room, where Izzy was again poring over her enlarged photo and cutouts. "But not *her*. We don't need protesters disrupting our meeting."

I placed the flyers on the counter next to the cash register. Carrying her box of donuts, Ramona stomped past Izzy and left.

Izzy shot me an impish look. Admiring her spirit and gumption, I smiled.

Our mayor came in. He spotted Izzy, saluted, strode to her table, and boomed, "There's the young entrepreneur who is going to bring fresh food and prosperity to Fallingbrook!"

It was Sunday afternoon, so the Knitpickers and retired men weren't in Deputy Donut. Jerry found a different group of people and tried to convince them that a flashy resort would not be good for the community. He went from table to table. Some of our customers agreed with him, some argued that the resort would provide jobs and attract tourists, and others pointed out that Fallingbrook and the area around it could support and benefit from both a resort and a business supplying produce year-round.

Finally, I began to understand Jerry's objection to the resort. Standing in the middle of the dining room where everyone could hear him, he announced, "When the election comes around, remember that people need to eat. A vote for me is a vote for wholesome fresh food and permanent jobs, while a vote for a newcomer like Adam Nofftry is a vote for money to flow out of the area."

A man called out, "Is Nofftry running for mayor against you?"

Jerry shook his head sadly. "I'm afraid so. You know me. I've been your mayor for a long time. I know the people of Fallingbrook, and I work hard for you."

First, Ramona from TWIG had requested that we hand out her flyers, and now we had a politician making speeches. He even had a handful of leaflets. When he seemed to run out of things to say, temporarily, at least, I joined him in the middle of the room and asked him, "Would you like a table, or would you prefer to sit at our serving counter?"

His face reddened. "As delicious as your coffee and donuts are, I don't have time to stay. Can I buy some donuts to take out?"

I led him to the display case. "How many, and which ones?"

"Six. You choose them."

A new batch of peachy donuts was ready, cooled, and frosted. I told him, "I'm putting in four of today's special sour cream donuts with chunks of peach in them, and two chocolate donuts with fudge icing."

"Excellent. Mind if I leave some of my brochures here?"

Without waiting for my response, he set his leaflets on top of Ramona's. He paid me and left with his box of donuts.

Later, in the kitchen, Olivia sidled to me. "Izzy must be lonely. She's been here for two hours already. I know lonely when I see it, though she's extroverted, and I was introverted and hardly ever got out to meet people. Mind if I go talk to her?"

"Go ahead!" I cocked my head back toward Tom. "We're happy when people feel comfortable enough here to treat Deputy Donut as a second home. That is, when they're not delivering speeches."

Olivia laughed and went off to sit at the table with Izzy. With their heads bent over the photo, they chatted together and moved pieces of paper around.

The front door opened, and Mr. Mystery came in.

I was standing at the serving counter. In the kitchen behind me, on the other side of the half-height wall, Tom was mixing dough for the next day, and Jocelyn was frosting the latest batch of our peachy sour cream donuts.

Walking toward the serving counter, Mr. Mystery glanced at me and then past me toward Jocelyn. He seemed to freeze for a second, and then he turned his head as if considering running away. Izzy and Olivia were now in his view. He probably recognized them, too. With a visible gulp, he continued to the serving counter.

"I saw your sign outside," he told me. "And I developed a craving for donuts."

"For here or to go?"

"I, um, to go, I guess. A half dozen?"

I pointed. "Come over here to the display case and tell me what you'd like. Our special donut today is baked, not fried. They're sour cream donuts with chunks of fresh peach and peach-flavored sour cream frosting."

"Sounds good. And do you have anything with chocolate?" He blushed and smiled. "I see that you do."

He chose four peachy sour cream donuts, a chocolate-glazed maraschino cherry donut, and a peanut butter donut with chocolate fudge frosting.

I smiled. "Are you planning to eat these all yourself?"

His blush never seemed to quite go away before he needed to blush again. "I don't . . . well, yes, probably." His laugh sounded uneasy.

A woman I'd never seen before strode into Deputy Donut. She was small, with dark hair sleeked back from her heart-shaped face. She wore a perfectly tailored black business suit, the kind with an above-the-knee skirt, in a rich-looking fabric that was probably a blend of silk and wool. Her black high heels struck down hard on our rock maple floor.

Mr. Mystery paid me and turned around.

Izzy stared expectantly toward him.

The woman who had just come in stopped walking. "Landon! What are you doing here?" I couldn't quite place her accent. Izzy lowered her head as if again studying the enlarged photo. Beside her, Olivia watched the two newcomers.

Mr. Mystery—Landon—held up the box. "Buying donuts." His voice sounded slightly strangled.

The woman let out a brittle laugh. "All for you?"

"Maybe you'd like to share them?"

She inserted her wrist into the crook of his elbow. Her fingers were elegantly long and perfectly manicured. "Ugh. No, thanks. I detest gooey sweets. Let's go."

They walked out, turned right, and headed south.

Jocelyn and I hurried to Izzy's table.

Izzy pushed her mug aside. "So now we know Mr. Mystery's name. It's Landon, but we don't know if that's his first or last name. Did I manage to look like I couldn't care less who he is or what he does?"

"Welllll . . ." Jocelyn began.

I finished for her. "Yes. You ignored him when he was leaving with that woman."

Izzy let out a dramatic sigh. "How disappointing that he already has a girlfriend."

I edged one of her greenhouse cutouts away from one it was overlapping. "She seemed surprised to see him."

Izzy straightened both cutouts. "But he blushed like he was interested in her. I wonder if he planned to meet her here. Do any of you know who she is?"

We all said that we'd never seen her before.

Izzy gazed toward the front door. "The funny thing is that she reminded me of my cousin Hope. I haven't seen Hope since I was about ten and she was in her mid-teens."

I suggested, "Maybe it is Hope, and she's here to see you."

Izzy scrunched one of her small rectangles of paper. "Hope wouldn't come to Wisconsin to see me. The last time we were in touch, I lived in Chicago, but I went away to college and then moved to Gooseleg, and our families haven't been close since our fathers, who are brothers, stopped communicating with each other after my father refused to work any longer for their father, the grandfather who sent me the money, and my parents moved to Spain. The last I knew, Hope's father was an executive in at least one of my grandfather's companies, and Hope works for our grandfather, too. She would never venture this far from New York City."

Olivia pointed an index finger toward the ceiling. "Aha! I'm sure the woman who was in here had a New York accent." She looked at Jocelyn and me. "Remember, yesterday, I guessed that the man, Landon, had an accent from the Northeast? He could be from the New York City area. I doubt that he's actually from Duluth."

Izzy looked down at the piece of paper she'd wrinkled. "Maybe he recently moved to Duluth." She smoothed the paper. "He's a mystery, but I'll probably never see him again, and that's totally okay." She rolled up the photo and inserted it into the tube, and then she gathered her cutouts and drawings and put them into her briefcase. "If you still have a half dozen of those donuts, I'd like to buy them to take home."

We'd sold all but four of the peachy sour cream donuts. Izzy pointed into the display case. "They all look yummy! Give me a strawberry donut with strawberry frosting and strawberry-shaped sprinkles and one of those chocolate-walnut donuts with fudge frosting."

I joked, "That's a lot of donuts for one person. Maybe you should run out there and try to coerce Landon's friend to try some of the 'gooey sweets' she claims to detest."

"Nope. She doesn't deserve to find out how wrong she is. Maybe I'll be like Landon and eat every single one. Not all at once." Calling a cheerful goodbye, she left.

Olivia looked at the clock on the wall. "I thought she was going to stay until we locked the door."

Jocelyn cleared Izzy's dishes. "If her greenhouse project doesn't work out, maybe she'd like to work here. Not now, but after I start teaching."

I threw my hands up in mock horror. "Which is all too soon."

She gave me one of her brilliant smiles. "But I'll be working here weekends and summers."

Later, serving our last customers, I thought that the shop, now that Izzy was gone, seemed especially quiet. Her enthusiastic and friendly personality would make her a wonderful employee if she ever wanted to work for someone else, which seemed doubtful. Then again, drama seemed to follow her, and maybe we could do without drama at Deputy Donut.

After work, I put Dep into the car and started north toward home. I was on County Road C when a call from Izzy came through my car's speakers. "Emily, I'm at the road beside my property, and I'm afraid that something's wrong. Adam Nofftry's car is here, and it's covered in dust as if it's been here ever since we left last night. You said I should be cautious about coming here by myself, and I'm freaking out. I gathered from something Olivia said that you live north of Fallingbrook, so I wondered, if it's not too much to ask, well, could you come here and help me try to figure out what's going on?"

She sounded close to panic.

Chapter 8

Feeling guilty for possibly ruining Izzy's carefree confidence about visiting the acreage she was buying, I told her, "I'll be there in a few minutes." I had my car call Brent. He didn't answer. Dictating a message that I would be home a few minutes later than expected, I raced to County Road H, turned west, and drove past the dirt track that Mr. Mystery—Landon—had veered onto the previous evening. The dust his car kicked up had settled. Surrounded by browning grasses, the packed-earth track baked in the late-afternoon sunshine. I sped on, around curves and up the gradual incline.

Izzy's dark red sedan was on the right shoulder behind the black SUV that Adam Nofftry appeared to have driven the previous evening.

This time, Izzy wasn't jumping up and down and waving her arms. Where was she? Had she decided to explore the hillside by herself, after all?

My tires crunching on gravel, I pulled up behind her car. Dep let out a wail. I got out, snapped her leash onto her harness, and carried her toward Izzy's car.

Its driver's door inched open. Peering back toward me and then checking the road in the other direction, Izzy edged out onto the shoulder. She was still in the slashed jeans she'd worn in Deputy Donut earlier, but now she had unbuttoned the boxy green sweater. She wore a white cropped top underneath it. She met Dep and me between our two cars. "Sorry to bother you, Emily, but do you see what I mean? His car doesn't look like it moved, and he doesn't seem like the type to camp out on vacant property."

I could barely see beyond the sunlight shimmering off the top of Izzy's car, but I understood. "My husband has a black SUV similar to that one, but not as huge. Even small amounts of dust show up. But that SUV does look like it's where it was when we left yesterday. Maybe Adam's a creature of habit."

"Creature," Izzy repeated, making a disgusted face. "He probably left his SUV here as a show of ownership, for all the good that will do him."

We started up the former driveway between the walls of evergreens. I took a deep breath. "What a great place. I love the smell of the pines and the way their branches whisper in the breezes."

"Don't worry. Except for needing to widen the entrance to the driveway, I'm not touching a needle of the trees between the driveway and the road. I love them." High up, a woodpecker hammered into wood. Izzy laughed. "Woodpeckers have to eat, so they can do whatever they want to the trees. Ramona and TWIG can't complain about that." By the time we neared where the driveway curved into the meadow, I didn't know whether to be relieved because we had not yet encountered Adam Nofftry or worried that he might be hiding and planning to ambush us. I murmured, "I'm glad you called me. Both of us, with Dep's help, can watch for Adam in case he means you harm."

"I'm not going to let him intimidate . . ." Her voice dropped off. She stared at the base of the rocky outcropping on the outer edge of the curve. "Ugh. Just because he thinks he's going to own this property is no reason for him to leave litter here. He's carrying his territory marking too far."

The previous day, I'd noticed that the outcropping hovered

over a cave-like niche. Now something was in that tiny cave. A pinch of white cardboard stuck out beneath recently piled-up pinecones and pine needles. Pulling at her leash, Dep strained toward the debris. I followed her and squatted for a closer look.

A box? It was like someone had attempted to hide it but had not quite succeeded. Dep reached a tentative paw toward the box as if she wanted whatever was inside it. Catnip? I swept debris off one corner of the lid.

And uncovered our Deputy Donut logo.

I rocked back on my heels and laughed up at Izzy. "Did you hide treasure here like someone did years ago at Fallingbrook Falls, and then you called me so that I could be the one to find it?" If so, she'd been a good actor when she'd sounded scared.

"No. Are you sure you didn't hide it for me to find?" Instead of returning my teasing tone, she sounded tense.

"I couldn't have. I just got off work."

"Then Adam Nofftry must have put it there. Like he already owns the place."

"I don't think he could have. As far as I know, he has never been inside our shop."

Izzy's eyes were wary. "I certainly did not put it there. And I'm sure it wasn't there yesterday. I glanced at this boulder as I ran down the hill during the quarrel between Adam and Landon, and I remember thinking that this tiny little cave was darling. I could almost see elves inside it."

"I noticed it, too." Still half expecting to find glittery stickers or gaudy beads, I opened the box.

Two of our peachy sour cream donuts were inside, along with smudges of frosting, both chocolate and the peach-flavored sour cream frosting from the peachy donuts.

Neither Izzy nor I would have put food out where wildlife might find it, and we wouldn't have heaped dirt and dead leaves over an unsealed box containing food. I flicked an ant out of the box. "Today was the first day ever that we made these donuts, so this box landed here today. I'm sorry that litter from Deputy Donut is marring this beautiful spot. Here, take Dep's leash, and I'll get rid of these"—I made a phony tragic face—"*sob, sob*, unwanted gooey treats and the box."

"Thank you. Why would anyone throw out your donuts? They were delicious. Mine are already gone. I shared them with the neighbors, and then I ran out to the road and put the box in the trash only seconds before it was collected. But thank you for getting rid of this. C'mon, Dep, let's look around while we wait for your mother to come back. Maybe we'll find actual hidden treasure."

I closed the box. The tape on it held, mostly. I carried the unwanted litter down the trail, jumped over the water-filled ditch, and locked the box with its contents in my car. Heading back toward the property's former driveway, I took a few seconds to peer as well as I could through the tinted windows of Adam's SUV. Nothing seemed out of place. Although tempted to try the doors, I didn't touch anything.

On the hill above me, someone let out a piercing and prolonged scream.

Chapter 9

"Emily! Help!" Izzy's voice was both shrill and quivering. And she had my precious kitty....

I leaped over the ditch and dashed up the trail.

Izzy and Dep weren't near the elfin cave. The scattered remains of the pile of pine needles and cones showed where the box had been. I kept going.

"Emily!" The frantic call came from higher up and farther west.

I sprinted up to the meadow. I didn't see Izzy and Dep. I shouted, "Where are you?" I was nearly out of breath.

"Here! Come here!" A hand waved beside cattails near the pond on the far side of the meadow.

Had Dep fallen into the water?

I ran.

Stumbling over stony and uneven ground, I called, "Are you okay?"

Izzy came out from behind the curtain of cattails. She was clutching Dep in her arms. "Hurry!"

Dep was okay, wasn't she? Fifteen or so feet from Izzy and Dep, I could see that neither of them was wet. Dep blinked. She looked fine.

Izzy, however, was a peculiar shade of grayish-green. I ran to her, plucked Dep out of her arms, and guided her to sit down on a rock. "Put your head between your knees. You're about to faint."

She protested, "I'm okay." But she obeyed.

I felt Dep's legs and around her ribs. She wasn't purring, which was just as well. Cats sometimes purred when they were injured. Holding her in one arm, I bent and rubbed Izzy's back. "What's wrong?"

She raised her head but didn't look at me. She seemed to be staring at where an ATV trail ran up the hill toward the next plateau. She whispered, "It's Adam Nofftry. He's over there by the pond, and he looks dead. But maybe you shouldn't go look, or we'll both faint." She hadn't entirely lost her sense of humor.

I took a deep, steadying breath. "I'll check."

"Want me to come? Or hold your kitty?"

"Just stay there with your head down."

Carrying Dep underneath one arm, I stepped gingerly past the cattails.

In his khaki pants and tailored but casual navy blazer, now rumpled and muddy, Adam Nofftry lay unmoving at the edge of the pond. One of his loafers had fallen off. His socks were navy and khaki in an argyle pattern.

He looked dead to me, too.

I yelled to Izzy, "Call 911. Ask for police and an ambulance."

"Okay." Her voice had strengthened, but it still wobbled.

I made my way to the man lying with one navy-blue sleeve in the water. Still clutching Dep, I felt the wrist that wasn't in the pond. I couldn't find a pulse, but his skin was not as chilly as I'd expected. Was that because it was a warm day? Or because I felt suddenly about to freeze? Dep struggled as if wanting to be set down to do her own investigating. I tightened my grip on her and returned to Izzy.

She calmly gave the emergency dispatcher directions and

described the three cars parked on the shoulder. "There's a former driveway, but I don't think anyone should attempt to drive up it unless they have an ATV." She had again buttoned the green sweater.

Grasping Dep's leash tightly, I set her on the ground and squeezed Izzy's shoulder. "Tell the dispatcher that Adam has no apparent pulse and that I'm calling my husband, Brent Fyne, Fallingbrook's detective. I hope he's at home and can get here faster than other Fallingbrook first responders."

Izzy relayed that information, and I called Brent. He had just come in after an afternoon of kayaking on Chicory Lake, where there was no phone reception. From his own search for real estate, he remembered where the property was. I told him, "Adam looks like he just keeled over, a heart attack or something. He's on the edge of the lowest pond. It's near the western end of the property. We're beside a stand of cattails."

"I'll be there in a few minutes. Stay on the line."

It hadn't occurred to me until Brent told me to stay on the line that Adam might have been attacked. It was possible that he had signs of trauma that I couldn't see. I had no intention of returning to his body or rolling it over to check.

If he'd been attacked, could his attacker still be in the area? Even though I'd seen no vehicles down at the road besides mine, Izzy's, and the SUV that had to be Adam's, I glanced nervously toward the woods west of the pond. From where my car was, a curve hid the road below those woods. Could someone have parked down there? Considering where we'd found the box with a couple of donuts still in it, and that Adam had not been in Deputy Donut that day, I suspected that whoever had tried to hide the litter had parked near where Izzy, Adam, and I had. Maybe the litterer hadn't even known that the owner of the SUV was on that hill.

Naturally, I pictured Landon. I didn't know if, yesterday, he'd arrived before or after Adam, but if it had been after, he wouldn't have known for sure who had driven the black SUV. He might have thought that Olivia, Jocelyn, and I had arrived in it. Or Izzy.

Maybe, today, he had come back and had brought his donuts up to the hill while he tried to find Izzy. To do... what?

With her phone against her ear, Izzy sat despondently on the rock. Dep jumped into her lap. Izzy gasped and then breathed a laugh. Hanging on to Dep's leash, I stared at our surroundings and listened. The cattails swayed, rustling. A red-winged blackbird called from the other side of the pond. Insects sang and buzzed. Through my phone, I heard the quiet thrum of Brent's car, and then in my other ear, I heard a vehicle on the road, approaching quickly from the east. "About to park," Brent told me. "Is everything okay where you are?"

"Except for Adam Nofftry, yes. Izzy, Dep, and I are fine."

His car door slammed. The sound was instant through my phone and delayed slightly through the air. Moments later, in the shorts, T-shirt, and sneakers he must have worn kayaking, Brent appeared on the far side of the meadow. He ran to us.

Barely out of breath, he pulled his police-issue notebook and pen out of his back pocket. Izzy and I disconnected our calls. I introduced Brent and Izzy to each other and then sent Brent around behind the cattails. Their leaves brushing against each other could have been conspirators whispering. Could someone be hiding in the thicket of plants?

Brent returned to us. "Who found the body?" His face did not reveal his thoughts, even to me.

Izzy gently put Dep on the ground between us, stood, and brushed at the seat of her jeans. Her face was no longer green. "I did. Emily and I saw some litter." She pointed toward the eastern end of the meadow. "Over there. Emily took it away. While she was gone, Dep and I wandered around, and that's when I saw it. Him."

Brent repeated, "Litter? What was it?"

I touched the Deputy Donut logo on my shirt, "It was a Deputy Donut box that still had two donuts in it, a new kind that we started making only today. As far as I know, Adam has never been inside Deputy Donut, and he didn't buy any of those donuts today."

Brent gave me one of his piercing detective looks. "Could someone else have bought them and given them to him?"

"It's possible. But I'm guessing that someone in addition to Adam was here today. Whoever it was might have had no idea that Adam was here."

Izzy admitted, "I bought some of them today. I shared them with my neighbors. They have two teenaged boys. We ate all of the donuts in minutes." She gave me a weak smile. "My neighbors loved them, too." She looked up at Brent, and her expression was earnest. "Adam's SUV might not have moved after the rest of us left here yesterday. He was alive then."

I confirmed that I'd probably been the last one to turn around and see him. "He was watching us leave. But just now when I checked for a pulse, I thought his body was too warm to have been there long. I think he's wearing the same outfit he had on yesterday, though."

Brent grunted. "Emily, Izzy said you removed the box with two donuts in it. Why?"

"I felt responsible. It was litter with Deputy Donut's name on it, so I thought I should clean it up."

"Where is it now?"

"In the back of my car."

Brent gazed toward an immense dragonfly perched on the tip of a cattail. The dragonfly's delicate, veined wings glistened in the sunshine. "How long did that take?"

"About five minutes, I guess. Maybe seven. What do you think, Izzy?"

"Seven sounds about right."

Brent turned to Izzy. "What made you come to this particular spot while Emily was gone?"

Izzy waved toward the water beyond the cattails. "Birds hang out here. I thought Dep might like to see them. And the pond, too. I really like the ponds here. Liked them." The corners of her mouth twisted up in a mostly unsuccessful attempt at a grin. "Also, as Emily can tell you, I was here, I mean down at the road, before Emily got here. When I saw Adam's car looking like he hadn't moved it since yesterday, I got scared that he might want to argue with me again about which of us was going to succeed in buying the property. I didn't want to face that again, so I called Emily and asked her to check the place out with me. I didn't come up here, not then. I locked myself inside my car and waited for Emily. She got here in about ten minutes, but it seemed longer." Again, that attempt at a smile. "Seeing Adam's car still here freaked me out, but I never thought it would amount to anything as horrible as him being dead." She took a tremulous breath. "I know it maybe looks bad, since he and I disagreed about this property, but I didn't come up here before I called Emily or while I was waiting for her to drive here, I swear. And besides, I wasn't worried about Adam buying this place out from under me. My contract is good. I just didn't want to argue with him about it." She bit her lip and then blurted, "I wish I hadn't come here today! Or that I'd gotten here sooner. Maybe I could have gotten help for him in time."

Brent said gently, "Maybe not. I'm not positive, but he might have had a health crisis. It probably happened too fast for anyone to have saved him."

Shared grief flashed between Brent's eyes and mine. Brent had been with Alec, both of them detectives, when Alec was shot. I'd been a 911 dispatcher, but I'd taken that one crucial evening off, and a new operator had been on duty. Both Brent and a witness had called for help immediately, but it had been too late. Brent and I knew that neither of us could have saved Alec, but that didn't prevent us from feeling survivor's guilt and agonizing moments of *if only*.

Brent looked down at Izzy standing in the sunlight and spoke quietly. "I'll need to talk to you some more, Izzy."

She gulped. "Okay."

He stared into my eyes. "You can go home, Emily. The box with donuts in it probably has nothing to do with the man lying back there, but don't touch it, okay? I'll deal with it when I get home."

Izzy cupped her elbows in her palms and hunched her shoulders forward. "Can't she stay while you talk to me?"

He shook his head. "I'm afraid not."

She raised her chin. "Do I need a lawyer?" She hiccupped. "I can afford one."

"Call one," he said, "if you like."

Izzy bent her head over her phone.

I scooped Dep into my arms. Carrying her across the sunlit, deceptively innocent-looking meadow, I heard nothing except grasshoppers whirring and clicking and the woodpecker attacking the tree. The sun was still hot enough to warm the backs of my shoulders. Above me, a distant jet painted a white streak across the vivid blue sky.

Before I rounded the curve, I glanced back. Brent and Izzy were still side by side. My husband stood at ease, his feet apart. My young friend looked down toward her phone. I waved. Brent waved back, and I started down the trail through the tunnel of trees. A mile or so away, sirens wailed. Hugging Dep, I strode down to the road.

Brent's SUV was in front of Adam's. Again I peeked through Adam's windows and saw nothing unusual. I hurried past Izzy's car to mine and eased Dep into her carrier.

The sirens were closer, but no vehicles were in sight. I made a U-turn and headed east, the way I'd come.

Lights flashing, an ambulance sped past me in the westbound lane. A police car followed the ambulance. I glanced into my rearview mirror. Both vehicles disappeared around a curve, heading toward the dismal scene on the hillside Izzy was buying.

Although Dep was mimicking a siren too well to hear me, I was glad to have a living thing to talk to. "It's sad," I told her. "He didn't seem like a nice man, but he was probably in his fifties, too young to die. But there's one good thing, I guess. He took his last breath in a gorgeous place that he wanted to own. But has his death ruined Izzy's excitement about owning that property?"

Dep groaned.

We were approaching the dirt lane that Landon had veered onto the previous evening. I'd seen him since then, but where did that road go, why had Landon decided to take it, and what had he done there before I saw him again? He'd bought donuts from us only hours before Izzy and I found that box with a couple of donuts still in it. Had he been back in this area since then?

I skidded to a stop.

Chapter 10

Both Brent and I had guessed that Adam died from natural causes. Even if he'd been attacked, how likely was it that his attacker would have fled down this dirt track? Landon had to know that we'd seen him turn here the day before, and if he had attacked Adam, he probably wouldn't have escaped down this desolate farm road afterward. Just the same, I was not heading down there alone. I would tell Brent that Landon had suddenly turned onto this track while Adam had, I believed, still been alive.

I took my foot off the brake and drove home.

Hoping that Brent would discover that Adam's death had not been the least bit suspicious, and that Brent would be home soon, I took Dep inside and changed into cutoffs and a T-shirt. It was a perfect evening for Nicoise salad. In the vegetable garden near our catio, I picked grape tomatoes and green beans. I hard-boiled eggs, boiled whole white potatoes, blanched the beans, and sliced the potatoes and a red onion. I made the dressing and stirred the beans, potatoes, and onions into it. I washed the lettuce. Finally, I quartered the grape tomatoes and put everything except the tomatoes into the fridge.

It was almost dark when Brent came in, picked up Dep, and hugged us both.

As soon as I could speak, I asked, "How's Izzy?"

"Shaken. I'll interview her first thing tomorrow morning in my office when her lawyers can come with her. I sent her home shortly after you left."

"Lawyers, plural? And she was able to reach them on a Sunday?"

"She has friends in Gooseleg, sisters. Both are lawyers, and in their small town, they do a bit of everything. They're handling her purchase of that property, and they have taken on criminal cases when necessary." He pulled his notebook and pen out of his back pocket. "Do you mind if I take more notes now for your statement? Or would you rather wait until after dinner?"

"Now's a good time. Nearly everything's ready, and I can do the rest while we talk." I headed back to the kitchen section of the great room. "I hope her lawyers are good. But I believe she's innocent of anything criminal. Do you still think Adam died of natural causes?"

Brent followed me. "Probably."

Knowing that the police had to treat any unusual or unexpected death as suspicious, I asked, "Do you suspect Izzy of anything?"

Brent turned the question back on me. "Do you?"

I started peeling an egg. "No. She was sure that Adam wouldn't be able to prevent her from buying the property, so she didn't have a motive to harm him. And besides, she's . . . enthusiastic and optimistic about everything, too happy, or at least she was happy before this happened, to do anything that might curb her spirits. I don't think she knows how to be mean. But it does look bad because she was near the property alone before she called me about seeing Adam's car, and she was up in the meadow alone with Dep when she found Adam's body."

"Do you believe her story about staying in her car until you got there?"

"Yes. She's either a very good actress, or she was truly shocked when she found the body. She screamed, and when I reached her, she was almost green."

Brent gave me one of his solemn and silent detective looks. He didn't have to remind me that things could often be interpreted in different ways. I sighed and admitted, "I suppose that a person who had just killed someone, even accidentally, might feel faint." The word *accidentally* echoed painfully through my brain. Could Izzy have caused Adam to have a fatal accident?

"You say Izzy was usually happy and optimistic. Does that fit with her phoning you because Adam's car was where it had been the day before?"

I cut the eggs into wedges. "Maybe, if only because, just today, I warned her about going to that property alone because of other people showing up there. Did you see anything else that didn't seem to belong on that property?"

"Farther up the hill, we found a clipboard and one of those measuring devices that's like a wheel on a stick. Izzy had already left by then. I'll ask her tomorrow if they're hers."

I ripped the lettuce into bite-sized pieces. "Adam had things like that there yesterday."

"What do you think about Izzy's honesty?"

I frowned down at the lettuce. "She seems honest to me. Young, innocent, and maybe a little naive, but basically honest. But she could be fooling me, and I could be thinking she's almost exactly like the child I remember. Why? Did she say or do something that made you wonder?"

"It seems a little too convenient that she claims to have seen the man she referred to as Landon driving west, away from the property, when she was driving east, having come from Gooseleg, to it."

"This evening? Before she called me?"

"Yes. Didn't she tell you?"

"She was probably too distracted." I added tuna to our

salads. "Yesterday, after all of us except Adam left the place, Landon drove east. We encouraged Izzy to head west, the shortest way back to Gooseleg. Olivia, Jocelyn, and I were in my car behind Landon. He suddenly swerved onto the right shoulder, and then made a sharp left onto a dirt road. We guessed that he didn't want us following him. But now I wonder if he's camping up there."

"I think I know which road you mean. Is it more like a farmer's lane?"

"Yes. Maybe he was with Adam today when Adam died, and then Landon fled west afterward, in time for Izzy to see him." I waved my hand in a circle. "He could have eventually circled back to the dirt road to pick up his tent and camping gear before he left the area. Or maybe he'd already packed up his belongings and was on his way back to Duluth."

Brent reminded me, "If Izzy actually saw him."

"She seems too enamored to make up a story that would make him appear guilty of something, even to save herself from being suspected. But . . ." I sighed. "She might be a little less attracted to Landon than she was at first. She thought that the woman who came into Deputy Donut today and called him Landon might be his girlfriend."

"Is Landon his first or last name?"

I spooned the dressing-soaked veggies over the tuna in our bowls. "It wasn't clear. The woman seemed surprised to see him, and he blushed, something he's good at. They left immediately, together. He had already bought some of today's new peachy sour cream donuts, and there was chocolate frosting on some of the other donuts in his box. He offered to share the donuts, but the woman announced—to everyone within hearing—'I detest gooey sweets.'" I said it with my nose pointed upward and my lips pinched and prissy.

Brent laughed. "That must have made her popular with your staff and customers."

I rolled my eyes. "Very. I don't know why she'd come to a donut shop if she didn't like gooey sweets. Maybe she'd wanted a coffee, but when she saw the man she called Landon leaving, she clung to his arm and went out with him. She didn't interact with anyone besides him. Strangely, Izzy said the woman resembled Hope, a cousin Izzy hadn't seen since Izzy was about ten. Hope was older, and Izzy thought Hope lived in New York City."

Brent turned to the next page in his notebook. "How many donuts did this Landon buy?"

"Six."

"How many donuts would the box you found hold?"

"Six big ones, maybe eight smaller ones."

"Are you sure that the box wasn't beneath that rock when you were there yesterday?"

I arranged kalamata olives on our salads. "Positive. Yesterday, Izzy and I both noticed that rock and the niche under it, and that space was empty."

"And you're sure that the donuts in the box you found under the rock were from a recipe that you never made before today?"

"I didn't taste them, but they looked like them, and I thought I smelled the peach flavoring we used in today's frosting. Do you think the donuts have something to do with Adam's death?"

"Possibly not directly, but we might be able to collect fingerprints or other evidence that could tell us who else was on that property today. I took the box with the remaining donuts in it from your car and put it into an evidence bag to send to the forensics lab."

I arranged the quartered grape tomatoes on our salads. "They should definitely find my fingerprints on that box."

"Maybe we'll find someone else's also, and that person can tell us if they saw Adam there and whether or not he appeared to be struggling with a health issue. Or if his car was beside the road when they were there. Or if they noticed anything unusual in the vicinity. It's a long shot. Izzy said she bought six donuts from you today, and four of them were your new peachy sour cream donuts. Can you remember anyone else who bought those donuts today that you put into boxes that size? Plus any donuts with chocolate or fudge frosting that would account for the smears that were inside that box?"

"Jerry Creavus also bought a half dozen donuts, and some of them were like the ones still in that box you took as evidence, and some had chocolate or fudge frosting. Adam is, I mean was, running against Jerry for mayor, and Jerry was loudly opposed, at least when he was in Deputy Donut, to Adam's plans for a resort. Jerry claimed to favor Izzy's project."

"I'll talk to him. Anyone else?"

"The woman who heads Toward Wisconsin in Green, TWIG, bought a half dozen donuts, and some of them were also like the ones in the box I found, and at least one of them was frosted with chocolate or fudge. Izzy called the woman Ramona. Apparently TWIG wanted that property for a park. Ramona threatened Izzy with dire consequences if Izzy cuts down even one tree."

Writing in his notebook, Brent whistled. "That must have gone over well with your feisty young friend."

"She takes it in her stride."

"And you're sure that Adam Nofftry didn't buy a box containing some of your newest donuts today?"

"Not unless he came in during my lunch hour or when I was in the storeroom. Tom, Olivia, or Jocelyn might know. Possibly, one of those other people I mentioned gave Adam a box of donuts."

"Any guesses which of those people might have done that?"

I drizzled the rest of the dressing over our salads. "Not

Izzy. She didn't like him. Maybe Jerry. A politician might do things that other people wouldn't do, like give donuts to his opponent. Landon, the mystery man, didn't seem to have known Adam before Adam started yelling at him to get off the property yesterday. And Ramona, the TWIG lady, probably didn't like Adam, either, or she wouldn't if he had managed to buy that property and cut down a tree or two. She seems too grouchy to be going around handing out sweets to people she doesn't like."

"So, we have Izzy and Jerry, who had problems with Adam, and Landon who might not have known Adam well but might have been annoyed by Adam's yelling at him, and Ramona the environmentalist, who probably wanted to prevent Adam from opening a resort in the area if it meant cutting down trees, but wouldn't give him one donut, let alone a half dozen."

I placed the wedges of hard-boiled egg around the edges of the salads. "And Ramona is only one member of TWIG. The others probably also oppose resorts and developments. Plus, there are probably lots of other people who disliked Adam, and anyone could have been visiting that property, with or without donuts. From what I saw of Adam, he was a bully."

Brent set down his notebook and then, sure that I wasn't pregnant, he poured each of us a glass of dry rosé. We toasted each other, and then he went back to his questions. "Did you tell Izzy the license number of the car Landon was driving?"

"I didn't get a close look at it, so I don't know what it was."

"Could she have memorized it yesterday?"

"She could have. She and Jocelyn ran down that trail before Olivia and I did. The sun was reflecting off the car, and all I noticed was that the plates were from Minnesota and that the car looked like a rental. Jocelyn and Olivia didn't memorize the plate number. Landon had said that he 'came from Duluth.' However, Olivia thought that Landon's accent was more northeastern US than Minnesotan. The woman who resembled Izzy's cousin Hope might have had a New York accent, so maybe Landon is actually from New York."

Brent pocketed his notebook and pen. "I'll have a statement typed tomorrow for you to sign, though I expect to spend most of the day at the site where Adam died." He picked up cutlery and napkins. "It's a perfect temperature outside. I'll turn on the fairy lights in the catio, set that table, and let's enjoy our dinner there. For now, let's forget the unfortunate Adam Nofftry."

The salad was delicious, and the wine complemented it perfectly.

We didn't discuss Adam Nofftry again that night. I was certain that neither of us actually forgot about him.

Chapter 11

The next morning, Izzy came into Deputy Donut. Her curls were neatly combed, staying in place better than mine ever did. Instead of her usual sneakers, T-shirt or sweater, and cutoffs or jeans, she wore black patent heels, a neatly tailored black linen dress, and a jean-style jacket made of black-and-white–striped linen. Her leather briefcase seemed extra bulky next to her slim black shoulder bag. She looked great, mostly because the green cast was gone from her face and her smile had returned. She sat at the table where she'd spent most of the previous afternoon.

I hurried to her. "How are you doing today?"

"I'll get over the nightmares. How about you?"

"Your scream prepared me, so I wasn't as shocked as you probably were. I slept okay." I always felt safe with Brent. "What would you like today?"

"Coffee. I just came from your husband's office. He offered my lawyers and me coffee, but he also told us that the coffee in the police department wasn't very good. So I said I was coming here."

I kidded, "You didn't bring your lawyers? We welcome new customers."

She slumped her shoulders. "So sorry." She straightened and winked. "They're friends of mine, but I wanted to keep some distance between the business we do together and our social life. Like, we might need to switch gears a little, you know? And this is a place for relaxing."

"Would you like our usual Colombian or today's special coffee? It's a medium roast, slightly chocolatey and almost spicy. It's from Java."

"As my grandfather—not the one I told you about, the other one, my mother's father—would have said, 'a cup of Java.' How can I resist that?"

"No one can. And would you like anything to go with it?"

"A donut?" She made it into a question, as if she hadn't decided.

"Do you like apricots?"

"Of course. And I hope to grow some of them in my greenhouses, too." Remembering what had happened the day before where she planned to build those greenhouses must have caused the flicker of pain that crossed her face.

"We made apricot fritters today, from fresh apricots."

"I'd like two of them. Three if they're small."

I brought her the coffee and two plump fritters. "If this isn't enough, we have lots."

She gazed down at the plate of golden fritters. "It might not be enough. Giving a statement at the police station made me hungry."

"How did it go?"

"Fine. I said that Adam might have had a heart attack or stroke or something like that. Do heart attacks and strokes make people thirsty?"

"I hope I never find out."

"I wonder if Adam felt terrible and thought that water would help, so he went to the pond for a drink but collapsed there. Or maybe someone scared him to death. Like Ramona from TWIG. She'd be enough to scare anyone. Well, not me."

I suggested, "Maybe Mr. Mystery returned and frightened him."

"How could the mysterious Landon scare anyone? Didn't you see how gentle and kind his eyes are?" Without apparently noticing that I didn't respond, she asked, "Has he been back here since he left with that woman who looked like my cousin?"

"I haven't seen him."

She looked down at her fritter. "This is as delicious as I'd hoped it would be. I wonder what Landon's doing in Fallingbrook. And if he's still around. He wasn't wearing a ring when he was in here yesterday, but that woman will probably set a trap for him."

"Maybe you shouldn't trust him so much. He seemed to struggle to come up with a reason for exploring your property the day before yesterday."

"He thought it was a public trail."

"But there are no signs that would have given him that impression."

"Maybe he got the idea from maps? The former driveway could show up as a trail. And the ponds would show up, too, and the stream. Anyone might think it was a public area."

It appeared that she wasn't going to mention seeing him near her property shortly before she—and I—arrived there, so I told her, "Brent said you saw him driving away from the property when you were on your way to it yesterday."

She sipped at the coffee, and then set her mug down on the table. "Your coffee is worth waiting for. I didn't say that Landon, if that's his name, was coming from the property. I don't know where he'd been, only that he passed me going the other way. I wish I'd turned around and followed him and had not gone back to my—soon to be mine—property. Maybe someone else could have discovered Adam's body before I ever returned. Maybe the mayor, who seems to like my project and didn't like Adam's plans, could have decided to check the place out. Or Ramona and her gang could have gone there to count trees, and they could have found him. They could have been the ones talking to your husband today."

"Even though Adam Nofftry is no longer a threat to you, I wonder how safe you'll be on that property after you buy it."

She patted the black-and-white–striped jacket. "Luckily, I'm young and have a good, strong heart. No one is going to scare me to death." She grinned up at me. "Don't tell anyone, but I have a black belt in karate."

I wasn't surprised, given how intrepid Izzy had been the day we spent together when she was little. Still, I felt myself going pale. "Did you tell Brent?"

"Should I? I'm not ashamed of it, but it seems like an odd thing to brag about."

"If it turns out that Adam hit his head on a rock or something, it might be best if Brent heard about it from you sooner rather than later."

"He gave me his number. I'll call him." With one last bite, she finished an apricot fritter. "I wonder if Landon is Mr. Mystery's first or last name. Whatever, I like it. Don't you?"

"I suppose so."

"You've already landed yourself a kind and handsome husband, or you'd be more excited about Landon."

I had to laugh. "Maybe not. Landon's sort of young for me."

"Well, you'd be excited for me." She gazed at the north wall of the dining room as if she could see through it all the way to wherever Landon was. "I wonder what it would take to get him to stay in Fallingbrook. Or move to Gooseleg, which might be even better."

I teased, "You're impossible." I became serious again. "How many people have you told about your grandfather giving you money?"

"I don't keep it a secret, but I don't go around telling everyone."

"Maybe you told someone who told someone who told Landon. Or he heard about it somehow, and he's come to this area to find you. Maybe he's hoping to scam you out of some of your cash."

"I'm not scammable."

I corrected myself. "Or charm you out of it."

"I don't see how he would have heard about it way off in Duluth."

I reminded her, "Olivia and I weren't sure he was telling the truth about where he was from."

"Why would he lie about that? He looked honest."

"Did he? Don't you think that a successful scammer might look honest?"

"I'll worry about that if I ever encounter him again. Which I probably won't." She gazed around our crowded dining room. "And don't start thinking that I come here in hopes of seeing him. It's you folks and your delicious coffee and donuts that keep bringing me back."

"That's what we hope people will think."

"Is this your dream career?"

"I love it."

"So, you understand being passionate about what you really want to do. I'm glad I came down to Fallingbrook and rediscovered my old friend from years ago."

I thanked her. "I'm glad you did, too."

But after she left, I wondered how glad I should be. Yes, it was great discovering that the adventurous little girl had turned into a self-possessed young woman focused on accomplishing her goals, but why had she called me to meet her at the property yesterday? Two sisters who were not only Izzy's friends but were also her lawyers might have been a more likely choice to help her figure out why Adam's car was parked on the road beside her property. And then after I got there and was putting the mostly empty donut box in my car, Izzy suddenly became brave enough to explore by herself with only my cat as company.

And brave enough to let out an earsplitting scream that had sounded totally authentic.

Could she possibly have known, before she asked me to join her, where Adam's body was? Maybe she'd been afraid she couldn't believably fake a case of shock and horror if we "discovered" the body together, so she'd hidden debris, knowing that I would probably want to remove the litter immediately. And then Dep played into her hands by noticing the box of donuts before Izzy had to pretend to find it.

She'd been a sweet little girl, and she still had an endearing air of naivete that I wanted to trust.

I knew what Brent would say about that.

Wondering if Izzy would check our compost bin for apricot pits, I positioned myself in the storeroom behind small appliances on wire racks where I wouldn't easily be seen from the bin, and I watched through the window in the door to the parking lot. Minutes passed, and Izzy didn't appear, maybe because she hadn't been dressed for rooting through food scraps. I returned to the dining room, cleared her dishes, and cleaned the table.

Late in the afternoon, Jerry Creavus came in. He stopped in the doorway and seemed to survey the room. He walked to a table of tourists. In a booming voice, he welcomed them to Fallingbrook, and then he moved to a table of townspeople, shook their hands, clapped them on their backs, and asked to join them. Some of them nodded. He pulled an extra chair to their table and beckoned to me.

Tugging at the collar of his short-sleeved shirt, he said, "It's hot out there! Do you have anything cold to drink, Emily?"

"Iced tea or coffee? Juice, water, lemonade?"

"Iced tea."

"How about iced green tea with a hint of lemon and honey?"

"That sounds good. I'll try it."

"And to go with it, how about a raised, glazed donut with raspberry sorbet filling the hole?"

"Ooh-la-la, you're getting fancy. Sorbet, these days, not good old-fashioned sherbet. Sure, I'll try one of those."

I took him the iced tea and his donut, mounded with sorbet and served in a bowl. He poked his spoon into the sorbet. "This is the type of thing I expected Adam Nofftry to serve in one of his restaurants at one of his fancy resorts. Well, Emily, I don't know if you heard the terrible news, but you won't be getting competition from him."

I didn't admit that I'd been the second—or possibly the third or fourth—person on the scene after Adam died. "It's sad," I agreed. "He was relatively young, I think."

Jerry nodded. "A tragedy. Competition is actually a good thing. Did you know that?" Although Jerry faced me as if he were talking only to me, he spoke loudly enough to be heard by everyone else at his table and at several of the surrounding ones. He pointed an index finger upward. "Nofftry, now, while I didn't want him to build that resort anywhere near here, his heart was in the right place. He was a good man, and I'm sure he'd have tried to help Fallingbrook by sending some of his clientele into town. They would have discovered the businesses here, including your cozy little donut shop. Who could resist a place like this? And while Nofftry didn't have a chance of winning the election, his competition with me was good for Fallingbrook." Jerry's right hand tapped his jaw. "I would have collaborated with him on setting new policies going forward. Also, simply by running against me, he forced me to become a better candidate. I endeavored to be more in tune with my constituents, and you can't expect that to change now that he has, sadly, passed away. He left a legacy, and his passing is a blow to us all."

The other people at Jerry's table murmured in agreement,

and I left him to his politicking and returned to the kitchen to make fresh coffee. It was four o'clock, almost our closing time, but someone was sure to want a refill.

Grinding Colombian coffee beans to the medium coarseness we liked for our drip coffee, I thought about Jerry and the speech he had just delivered. Two days before, Jerry had acted like Adam Nofftry was his enemy. Now he claimed that Adam's death was a tragic loss. His sudden appreciation of Adam made me wonder more, not less, where Jerry had been after he left our shop with his half dozen donuts. Maybe Jerry's reaction was simply the common one after a death.

Pouring water into a coffee maker, I had my back to most of our dining room.

Behind me, Jocelyn said, "Look who's here." Her usually upbeat voice had gained a pinched and ominous tone.

Chapter 12

I turned around.

Brent, who almost never came to Deputy Donut except on business, was just inside our front door, along with Misty, a tall blond police officer who had been one of my two best friends ever since junior high. Both Brent and Misty seemed to avoid meeting my gaze. Brent glanced toward our office and gave a nearly imperceptible nod. As far as I knew, Dep was the only one in our office at the moment, but Brent's face lacked his usual tenderness for her. I sidestepped toward our display case and peeked through the window between the kitchen and the office. Misty's temporary patrol partner Tyler Tainwright stood on our back porch looking in through the glass door. Like Misty, he was in uniform.

And a man in a well-tailored brown suit was beside him.

The hairs on my arms stood on end. The man was Vic Throppen, a detective from the Wisconsin Division of Criminal Investigation.

That meant that Brent had learned enough during his investigation to suspect homicide, and he'd asked for help from the DCI. Vic would now take the lead on Adam's case.

If anything, Vic looked thinner and more drawn than the last time I'd seen him, and his nose seemed even pointier, as if sniffing out clues had sharpened it. Vic could be fair, and I hoped that he would be this time. But he was about as empathetic as a slab of concrete.

Brent and Misty stood unmoving until conversation and clatter in the dining room died down. Brent announced, "We have to ask all of the customers to take your personal belongings and leave through this door, please." As always, his voice was deep and warm, but now it held authority that no one would want to ignore.

Finally, he stared toward the kitchen where Tom, Olivia, Jocelyn, and I stood as if turned to our own form of concrete. "Deputy Donut staff, please remain where you are."

Jerry Creavus was one of the first people to stand. "Detective Fyne, what's going on?"

Brent's answer was curt. "We'll explain later."

Customers gulped down the last of their drinks and donuts, grabbed purses and bags, and filed out, good-naturedly enough. Holding the door for them, Misty smiled. As always, she was beautiful, but now distress showed in the set of her jaw and the wrinkle between her eyebrows.

Jerry told her consolingly, and in his booming voice, "Police business, Officer Ritsorf, we understand." He stood back and let the other customers file outside, and then, as if he himself had rounded them up, he followed some of them north on Wisconsin Street toward the municipal offices, which were in the same building as the police station.

I fiddled with my apron strings. I always looped them around and tied them in a bow in front, with the apron folded over the strings to shorten the apron and keep it from twisting around my knees when I walked.

Tom stood at attention and watched Brent.

Olivia reached for the marble counter of our kitchen island as if to steady herself.

Jocelyn folded her arms and raised her chin in an unspoken question. Or a challenge.

Brent singled her out. "Jocelyn, can you come here and

lock the front door?" He tapped the table beside him, one of our two largest ones. "Then I'd like to talk to you here."

Jocelyn dropped her arms to her sides. "Okay." She started toward the front.

Brent came closer. "Olivia, will you please let Tyler and Detective Throppen into the office and lock the door behind them? Misty will interview Tom, and Vic Throppen will interview Emily. And Olivia, stay in the office. Tyler will interview you there. We have only a few questions for each of you."

Biting her lower lip, Olivia started toward the office.

Near the kitchen, Brent picked up two of our dining chairs, one in each hand. "Emily, mind talking to Vic in the storeroom?"

"Of course not. Here, let me take one of those chairs."

Carrying the chair through the kitchen, I nodded toward the window into the office and then turned and asked Brent, who was behind me with the other chair, "Is Dep going to be a problem?"

Finally, Brent smiled, though it was strained. "She seems quite happy to be shedding all over Tyler's uniform."

I took a better look through the window from the kitchen to the office. Blushing, Tyler seemed to be listening to Olivia while he cradled Dep like a baby in his arms. I suspected that Dep was purring so loudly that we almost should have been able to hear her through the glass. Tyler reached into a pocket of his armored vest, took out a notebook, and passed Dep to Olivia. Then they both sat down, and I could see only the sides of their faces. Olivia was blushing, too.

Leading Brent toward the storeroom, I smiled.

Olivia.

Although I was fond of matchmaking, I hadn't come up with any ideas of who in Fallingbrook might suit Olivia. And there he was, Tyler, the quiet, serious officer who sometimes patrolled with Misty or her regular partner Hooligan, who was taking time off to be with his and Samantha's baby. Samantha was the other one of my best friends since junior high.

Brent brought me back to the somewhat unnerving present. "Let's set these chairs near the back door, and Vic can interview you there."

"Okay."

Vic hadn't yet followed us into the storeroom. Brent placed both hands on my shoulders. "Sorry to close your shop early and worry you folks."

"It's okay."

Brent always had good reasons. Which was why I tensed with alarm.

He pulled me closer and kissed my forehead. "And Em?"

"Yes?"

"Don't look so worried."

I gave him a bleak smile. "I'll try." I reached up with both hands, stroked the sides of his face, and whispered, "You're good at your job and I love you for it."

He gently kissed my lips. "Thanks for understanding. You know how much I love you, and I hope to be home before daybreak."

Brisk footsteps approached us through the kitchen.

Brent let go of me and headed toward the kitchen. Vic came around the corner. The two men nodded at each other, and then Brent went out of my sight. I hoped Vic didn't hear my too-loud sigh.

Gesturing for me to sit on one of the chairs, Vic took the other. Unlike Brent, he didn't apologize for the disruption. He handed me a pen and a stapled set of papers. "Brent asked me to have you read your statement, make any necessary corrections, and sign it when it's satisfactory."

Brent had summarized everything I'd told him the night before. I signed the statement and gave it to Vic along with the pen. He tucked the statement behind his back and balanced his notebook on his knee. "And now I have some questions for you, Emily. Can you tell me the ingredients of the donuts you made for the first time yesterday, the ones you folks call 'peachy sour cream donuts' and that you told Brent were in the box you found last evening underneath an overhang of rock?"

"I can give you the recipe."

He lifted a hand to stop me. "I want to hear your version."

I listed the ingredients in the donuts and then the ingredients in the frosting.

When I was done, Vic asked, "Anything else?"

"Not that I can think of."

"Are you certain you haven't forgotten anything?"

I recited the ingredients again. "Did I miss an ingredient one of the times?" I was sure I hadn't.

"No." As if he doubted me, he drew out the word. "You listed the same ingredients, and in the same order."

Why was he hinting that I'd forgotten something? I eased forward a little on my chair and guessed, "Did the forensics lab find something in the donuts that I didn't mention?" Maybe we had different names for the same ingredients.

Vic didn't exactly answer my question. "Did you put any nuts in your batter?"

"There were no nuts in our peachy sour cream donuts, but some of the other donuts that people bought yesterday when they bought our peachy donuts contained nuts. And we always have an inventory of nuts of various types."

"You said 'flour.' What kinds of flour did you use in your peachy sour cream donuts?"

"Unbleached all-purpose wheat flour."

"Did you mix it with other flours?"

"No."

"Do you have almond flour on the premises?"

I smoothed my apron over my knees. "Yes, but we haven't used any this week, and we didn't put any in those donuts."

He scowled. "You don't need to jump to conclusions." He pulled a folded document out of the chest pocket of his suit jacket. With a flick of the wrist, he gave it a shake that unfolded it. "I brought a search warrant."

Although he didn't hand it to me, I was able to read it. "You're searching for almonds, almond products including almond flour and ground almonds? We have almonds and almond flour. I can show them to you."

"The forensics investigators will do the searching, thank you. Could someone have added almond products to those donuts accidentally?"

"Unlikely, and I'm almost sure that we didn't. All four of us worked together to create the first batch of batter, and then whoever was available mixed up the later batches. I didn't notice anyone looking for other ingredients besides the ones we'd started using early in the day."

"Didn't notice." He emphasized the second word.

"I'm sure they would have asked the rest of us before they changed the recipe we'd all agreed on. We took notes as we went along and wrote down the final version."

Vic asked again, "Could someone have added different ingredients by accident?"

"Anything's possible, but I doubt it." I looked off into the distance. "Some almond flour in peach-flavored donuts might be a good idea, though."

Vic tucked the top of the search warrant underneath the notebook, clamping the open search warrant to his knee and making it easy for me to continue reading it. I looked at it again, and then raised my head in surprise. "And you're searching for cardamom?"

Without answering, he stared steadily at my face.

I told him, "We have some with our other spices, but none of that was in those donuts, either."

"Are you sure?"

"Yes, though it would be a good addition. We didn't think

of it when we were concocting the recipe." I read more of the search warrant. "Okay, peaches. Those were definitely in those donuts, and we might still have some. You'll probably also find fresh apricots." I read more. "You're also going to search for peach products. Yes, peach extract was in both the donuts and the frosting. I don't understand why you'd be looking for the stones from peaches, both whole and separated. What does that mean?"

"What it says." Vic was writing in his notebook, but I gave him what I thought might be as piercing a look as any of his. "Are you saying that peach pits were in the donuts in that box? I'm sure we didn't put any of those into our batter. For one thing, they're big, and we would have noticed."

Vic put down his pen and met my gaze. "What were the solid, crunchy bits in those donuts?"

"Crunchy like sand? Whoever put the box under the overhanging rock piled dirt and dead leaves on it. Some of that stuff might have gotten into the donuts, especially in the frosting."

"Not as gritty and solid as sand, and not dirt, and not crumbled dead leaves. This was like nut pieces, ground small, but not as small as in almond flour."

"You're hinting that we put ground-up peach pits in our donuts. We don't have anything that could grind up peach stones. Those are hard." I thought a second. "But they do crack open sometimes, and the interior kernels resemble almonds, but aren't those kernels toxic?"

"You tell me."

"I forget, but none of us would have ground up those kernels and put them into anything, and I'm sure that none of us did."

I leaned toward the search warrant again. There was one more set of things that the police were entitled to search for—appliances used for chopping or grinding nuts. I told Vic, "We have lots of things that can be used to grind or chop nuts—knives, nut choppers, spice grinders, and coffee grinders. We didn't use any of those things for grinding peach kernels, and we didn't chop them up with knives, either."

"Were you watching all of those appliances at all times yesterday? And all of your knives?"

I had to admit that I hadn't been. I frowned toward some of the storeroom's shelves, covered with many of the bowls, pans, and other things we used, like nut choppers and spice grinders. "I don't see how ground peach pits, almond flour, and cardamom could have been in our donuts. Even though the box I found was ours, the donuts in it must have come from somewhere else."

"As I understand from Brent, you were the one who saw the donuts, and you told him that the donuts in the box were some that you and the others made here yesterday."

"They certainly looked and smelled like them, but I didn't try one."

He squinched his lips together as if he'd just sucked on a sour peach.

I suggested, "Could one of the people who bought the donuts yesterday have adulterated them? That would be hard to do after they were baked, but anyone could have scraped the frosting off, added things to it, and refrosted the donuts, I suppose." I slapped my hand across my mouth. "Oh!"

Vic leaned forward. The search warrant started to slide out from between his notebook and his knee. "Did you remember something?" He caught the search warrant before it could land on the floor.

I dropped both hands into my lap. "The day before yesterday, I heard a noise out there." I gestured toward the window in the storeroom door. "Do you know who Izzy is? Isabella Korinth?"

"The person who found the body." The words came out in a rapid monotone, as if he couldn't wait to be done with them.

"The day before yesterday, she was in here. She told Jocelyn, Olivia, and me about the greenhouse project she planned for the land where Adam Nofftry later died. After Izzy left, she removed a paper bag from our compost bin, and I'm almost certain that it was a bag I'd thrown out that had contained peach skins and stones. She took the bag of whatever it was away with her."

"Why would she do all that?" His tone made it clear that he believed Izzy had intentionally used the insides of peach pits to poison Adam.

I explained as calmly as I could, "The peaches we'd served her were especially delicious. I figured that she wanted to start seedlings. She does want to grow peach trees in greenhouses, eventually."

Vic said in a dry tone, "Starting trees from seeds now for some unknown eventual date is planning ahead."

"She's very enthusiastic and optimistic about her project. I'm sure she wasn't taking them with the idea of poisoning anyone. I . . . I had met her before, when she was a little girl. I spent an entire day with her then, and I can't imagine her attempting to poison anyone. Besides, she took that bag in full daylight. She had to have known that anyone could have seen her." I didn't think it was necessary to tell Vic that, after she closed the compost bin, she'd appeared to look around as if to see if anyone was watching. She'd been next to a parking lot that people often cut through. It was natural to check for speeding vehicles. I added, "Plus, she seems to like me and to have happy memories of the day we spent together years ago. If she truly does like me, inserting poisons in donuts from my shop would be strange."

"Didn't you tell Brent that she seemed to be attracted to a man who was on that property arguing with the deceased?"

"Yes. And the attraction appeared to be mutual."

"But then she told Brent that she saw that same man near the scene shortly before she discovered the deceased. Would it also be strange for her to try to cast suspicion on a man she liked?"

"She's very direct. Honest, I believe, and young and innocent. And I think she lost some of her interest in the man after she saw him in here with a woman."

"Maybe she realized she needed to provide us with a suspect besides herself. And, as you told Brent, Isabella Korinth was one of the people who bought your peachy sour cream donuts yesterday." Vic shut his notebook and put his pen and the search warrant in pockets. "That's all I need from you now. You won't be able to open tomorrow, and probably Wednesday, too."

"Okay." Other than missing out on some revenue, closing for those two days wouldn't affect me much. I usually took Tuesdays and Wednesdays off, but Olivia and Jocelyn liked to work every day that they possibly could. Would being closed for a police investigation damage our reputation and cut our future revenue? I managed not to groan.

Vic stood and picked up the statement I'd signed. "We'll let you know when you can open." He walked to the door leading to our loading dock. "Meanwhile, do not discuss this case with anyone. You can go out this way. I'll lock the door behind you."

"I need to collect my cat from the office. And my purse. It's actually a backpack."

"Is your car in the lot behind the building?"

"Yes."

"Wait out there. One of the officers will let you know when you can come to your other back door for your cat and your purse."

So, Vic didn't trust me to simply walk through the shop. I took off my apron and hat, hung the hat on its hook, and tossed the apron into the container our laundry service provided.

Outside, the afternoon was still hot. My car was in the

shade of a tall tree. I got into the driver's seat, rolled down the windows, and stared at the back of Deputy Donut.

Our kitchen had no windows to the outdoors, but the office had windows on all four sides. Olivia sat in the desk chair with her back to me. She must have been the one talking. Using her arms and hands, she gestured widely. In breaks from taking notes, Tyler reached out and petted Dep, curled on the sofa and crowding his thigh. He kept nodding and giving Olivia encouraging looks. Maybe after the interview, she would offer Tyler the use of the lint roller we kept in the office.

Tom must have been let out the front door. He walked up the driveway, spotted me in my car, and came to my open driver's window. "Emily, let's pay Jocelyn and Olivia—"

I interrupted. "For the days they have to miss? I was thinking the same thing."

"It's going to be okay, Emily."

"When do you think we'll be allowed to talk to one another about our interviews?"

"Probably after they compare what we all said. Don't worry. As if you could help it. As if either of us could. Meanwhile, I'll head off. Neighbors are having a barbecue and pool party, and many guests, including Cindy, will already be in the pool."

"Have a great time, and give my love to Cindy."

"I will." He patted my car door, turned, and strode toward his SUV. Like Brent's and Adam Nofftry's, Tom's SUV was black. It hadn't collected much dust in that parking lot since early morning, but thanks to the afternoon's fierce sunshine, it was probably stifling inside.

Tyler disappeared from the office, leaving Olivia alone. She scooped Dep off the couch and stood holding her and staring toward our dining room.

Minutes later, Tyler joined her in the office, talking as he stroked Dep, who was still in Olivia's arms and had to be purring. Brent entered the office. The three of them put Dep into her harness and leashed her, and then Brent came out to the parking lot with my backpack and Dep. I got out of the car and lifted Dep out of his arms. "Have you finished interviewing Jocelyn?"

Brent put my backpack on my passenger seat. "Yes, but she's still inside. Misty asked her how to lock the front door so we can make certain that it's locked until the forensics investigators get here, probably later this evening. And Tyler will probably dismiss Olivia soon. While I was enticing Dep away from them, Tyler and Olivia were discussing their favorite books and movies." Brent's smile hinted at what I'd been thinking. Olivia and Tyler might discover that they wanted to see each other more.

I asked suspiciously, "Are you the one who decided Tyler should interview Olivia?"

"It worked out that way." His eyes twinkled, and a grin pulled at the corners of his mouth.

"Am I allowed to talk to Olivia and Jocelyn about the case?"

"Yes. I had a quick conference with Vic, Misty, and Tyler. You all said basically the same things. And let me know if any of you remember anything else. Like if someone suddenly remembers adding an ingredient to those donuts that none of you think anyone added." He squeezed my shoulder and then headed back toward the office door.

I told Dep, "I think I'm sadder about Brent having to question people he likes than I am about having to close Deputy Donut during an investigation."

Chapter 13

Jocelyn came up the driveway from the front of our building at the same time that Tyler let Olivia out through the office door. "Thanks, Olivia," he said. He was blushing and smiling. So was Olivia.

Instead of heading toward her bike, Jocelyn came to me. "I'm glad I caught you before you drove away."

Olivia joined us.

I nodded toward the back of the building. "Brent said we're allowed to talk to one another about the case, even about what just happened in there. Apparently we all said the same things."

Jocelyn grinned and pulled a flyer out of her pocket. "Who wants to talk about flour and peach pits, anyway? I'm thinking of going to tonight's TWIG meeting. Want to come along? Maybe that Ramona person will confess to murdering the developer."

Hugging Dep, I asked, "When is it?"

Jocelyn opened the flyer. "Seven, in the town hall auditorium."

I scratched Dep's chin. "I'll come. And I even have time to take this little one back to Chicory Lake. It's too bad that I can't take her to our Maple Street house, but our rental agreement doesn't require our tenant to look after a cat on demand."

"The single chef," Jocelyn said in a fake dreamy tone. "Maybe he'd do it if Olivia asked him."

Olivia blushed. "It wouldn't need me. Who could resist Dep? But I have an idea. How about if Jocelyn and I put together a picnic dinner for the three of us, and Emily, you meet us in the square when you get back into town? We can eat there before the meeting."

I slipped one hand inside Dep's harness and felt her little heart beating inside that cute, soft-furred little body. "I'd love that. I'll be back in about an hour. Want me to bring anything from home? A bottle of wine?"

"Sure," Olivia said. "Sharing one bottle won't get us high enough to disrupt TWIG's meeting."

Jocelyn's eyes twinkled. "Then maybe she should bring two."

Olivia elbowed her. "Maybe not. How about if we meet at one of the picnic tables south of the fountain, Emily?"

"Perfect." I wrestled Dep into her carrier in my car's rear seat.

When I drove away, Jocelyn stood beside her bike with her hand on the seat. Looking at Olivia, she grinned mischievously. Olivia glanced up toward our office and blushed.

The music I played in the car on the way to Chicory Lake didn't calm Dep much, or me, either. Could the forensics team have gotten it wrong? I could imagine almond flour and cardamom accidentally being mixed in with wheat flour and spices, but ground peach pits? How could that be? And Izzy had not only taken peach skins and pits from our compost bin, but she had also bought peachy donuts from us and had, as the police would see it, a little too conveniently shared them with her neighbors and then rushed the box out to the road in time for garbage pickup. Could Izzy have two very different sides to go with her two different looks? First, she'd been the charming young woman in denim, T-shirts, and sometimes a sweater who reminded me of the child in play clothes, and then today, she was a sophisticate in tailored linen who could hire a couple of lawyers to accompany her to a police interview.

At home, I took Dep inside and gave her an early dinner and some fresh water. I changed out of my Deputy Donut uniform and put on jeans and a blue-checked shirt. A divided, insulated tote would keep the chardonnay cold and the Burgundy cool. I grabbed a light jacket and my backpack and headed for the door. Dep was curled on a couch. I blew her a kiss. "I won't be late." Locking her inside our chalet, I mumbled so that Dep wouldn't be able to hear and possibly become dejected, "But Brent might be."

Back in Fallingbrook, I parked east of the square, not far from the town hall, and then I strolled along meandering pathways between majestic old trees and manicured lawns and flower beds, bright with snapdragons, zinnias, and salvia, to the middle of the square. Above the sound of water splashing in the fountain, I heard shouts. Olivia and Jocelyn waved from a picnic table covered in a red plaid tablecloth. They had also changed out of their Deputy Donut uniforms into jeans.

Jocelyn pointed at Olivia's oatmeal-colored sweater and at her own plain, dark blue T-shirt. "We decided to try to blend into the crowd."

I set the insulated tote on the table and pulled out the bottles. "Me, too. It's probably not the best night to advertise Deputy Donut. I didn't detour to see what's going on at our shop. Do you know if there's police tape around it?" I shuddered dramatically.

Olivia set out three plates. "There isn't, but there's an ominous-looking black van parked out front and investigators in hazmat suits inside."

I opened my insulated tote. "Did you see Brent?"

Olivia and Jocelyn shook their heads. I figured he was either inside Deputy Donut or at police headquarters.

Jocelyn gave a shout of laughter. "Emily really did bring two bottles of wine!"

I defended myself. "I didn't know what we were eating, and I thought we should have a choice."

Olivia and Jocelyn had assembled a feast during the hour or so that I'd been gone. Olivia had put mozzarella cheese, halved cherry tomatoes, and sliced black olives on recently baked focaccia, broiled the focaccia pizzas in her oven until the cheese melted, and then had garnished the result with fresh basil leaves. Jocelyn had made a salad of blanched but still crisp green beans, green onions, and tomato slices from her parents' garden. We decided to open only the chardonnay. "For now," Jocelyn suggested.

Jocelyn and I sat with our backs to the nearest pathway, and Olivia faced us. The focaccia pizzas and salad were delicious, and the chardonnay was cool and brisk.

Olivia glanced toward the fountain. "Don't look now, but here comes Izzy's 'Mr. Mystery.'"

I wasn't good at obeying the words "don't look now."

Landon walked toward us, but his face was averted as if he were conscientiously studying the trees and the tall, red canna lilies on the other side of the path. Again he was dressed in business casual clothes, this time black slacks with a white dress shirt. He strode past, intent on anything but us. He wore black loafers and no socks.

As soon as he might have been out of earshot, Olivia clanked her fork down onto her plate. "He knew we were here. When I first spotted him, he seemed to be looking straight at us. Then he turned his head and kept walking."

I guessed, "Maybe he didn't recognize us. Or he wasn't wearing his contacts or something."

"He's guilty," Jocelyn announced. "He broke into Izzy's

place, stole the peach pits, ground them up, took off the donuts' frosting, mixed the ground kernels into it, spread it on the donuts again, and forced Adam to eat them."

Olivia squeezed her face between her hands. "And Izzy will be blamed."

I divided the remainder of the chardonnay between our glasses. "Only four donuts were missing from that box. Most likely Adam ate no more than four donuts, if that. And it's possible that Adam never saw or touched the donuts that came from that box. He died next to a pond, all the way across that lower meadow from where Dep found the donuts. Maybe Landon is merely shy. I wonder how he would have acted if Izzy had been with us."

Olivia laughed. "Probably the same, if he's shy. I'm guessing that he had nothing to do with Adam's death, or he would have long ago driven off to Duluth or wherever in his rental car."

Did Brent know that Landon was still in town? I sent Brent a text telling him where we'd spotted Landon and which direction he was heading. Brent thanked me.

For dessert, we ate Jocelyn's homemade ginger snaps and the chilled, super-sweet green grapes that Olivia brought.

We had finished and were tidying away our meal when I heard wheels on the paved walkway behind me. A soft voice called, "Emily!"

I turned around. A woman who was about my size and had pink streaks running through her dark, shoulder-length, wavy hair walked toward us. A wiry man, taller than the woman but not really tall, pushed a stroller. I leaped off the picnic bench. "Samantha! And Hooligan!" I checked the little face peering out from the stroller. "And Lainey!"

Lainey reached dimpled hands toward me.

Hooligan beamed down at his daughter. Samantha bent toward the stroller. "Want to hold her, Emily? She's kind of wiggly these days."

"Of course I want to."

Samantha lifted Lainey out of the stroller and handed her to me. Lainey had inherited her reddish hair from her father. Cuddling the warm little bundle of love, I sat on the bench with my back to the picnic table. Lainey turned toward me and laced her fingers into my curls. She barely pulled at my hair, and then she seemed to want to stand on my lap. Grasping her beneath her armpits, I let her rise to her feet. She was wearing cute little handmade leather shoes from The Craft Croft, the local artisans' co-op. Giggling, Lainey plunked down on my lap, then she wanted to stand again. We did this a few times until Hooligan swooped down and lifted her above his head, airplane style. "You're going to wear Auntie Emily out!"

"I don't mind. Even a short snuggle with my favorite pretend niece is worth it."

Hooligan lowered Lainey until her face was next to mine. She gave me a sloppy kiss on the nose.

I asked her, "Isn't it about your bedtime, Lainey?"

Samantha answered, "We were on our way home. But what's going on at Deputy Donut?"

I gave them a brief summary. If Hooligan were on duty, he would know more details than I did. Samantha had also been a first responder, an emergency medical technician, but she stopped working about three days before Lainey was born. Hooligan asked, "How's Misty doing without me partnering her, and how's Tyler doing?"

"They're morose." Both Samantha and Hooligan could tell I was joking. "Misty questioned Jocelyn, Tyler questioned Olivia, and Brent talked to Tom. I got to talk to DCI Agent Vic Throppen."

Samantha must have noticed Olivia's blush. "Tyler's single, Olivia. And he's a really nice guy, right, Hooligan?"

"Right. He's thorough, smart, and considerate."

Olivia's face reddened more, but she said only, "Maybe, as of today, he and I are on opposite sides of the law."

Hooligan buckled Lainey into her stroller. "Knowing all of you at Deputy Donut, I think you're on the same side of the law as Tyler." He kissed the top of Lainey's strawberry-blond hair. "Come on, princess, let's get you home, bathed, and into your crib." He put an arm around Samantha. Together, they pushed the stroller north.

I could almost feel Jocelyn and Olivia staring at my back. I stifled a sigh. Brent and I were afraid we would never have the two children we wanted, or even one.

My doctor suspected I had endometriosis. Symptoms varied, and no two women had the same set of them, but endometriosis sometimes interfered with the ability to get pregnant. My next step was to go to Milwaukee for tests and perhaps surgery to remove the troublesome cells. The surgery could be laparoscopic, which would reduce recovery time, but I'd still need to take time off work. If the endometriosis was causing inflammation, that could be treated.

Afraid of what might be found or not found, I had not made an appointment with the clinic. What if tests came up with nothing more than the advice we'd been hearing all along? "Stop worrying and just relax."

We tried to.

Chapter 14

I put on an unconcerned face and turned toward the others. "Shall we put the remains of our picnic into my car, or should we take them to the meeting? If we put the Burgundy into a paper bag, we can pass it between ourselves, and no one will notice."

Olivia folded the tablecloth. "We could take this and hide underneath it in case we're the only people who show up besides Ramona."

However, we put everything, including the unopened bottle of Burgundy and the tablecloth, into my car and then strolled back through the square to the town hall, a lovely, yellow brick building only a few years newer than the cottage Brent and I were renting to Glenn. As with our house, Victorian details had been retained and restored. Stone steps that were nearly as wide as the building led up to a deep stone porch, and stone columns supported the porch roof. I was more familiar with the eastern half of the building, which housed the police department and Brent's office, which he had once shared with Alec, than with the western half. Both sections of the building had identical, and identically heavy, oak front doors.

Jocelyn tugged one of the town hall doors open, and we

walked into the gloriously restored lobby. Red carpet covered the floor, ornate plaster decorated the ceiling, and gleaming glass and brass chandeliers and sconces lit the vast space. This half of the building had been set up to house offices and also a theater that had once been on the vaudeville circuit and was still used for plays, concerts, and meetings. Across from the outer doors, both doors to the theater stood open.

The meeting was scheduled to start in ten minutes, and only a smattering of people sat in the red plush seats. It was a cozy space, with about thirty rows of seats divided by two aisles sloping down toward the stage. We chose seats on the right side of the center section, about ten rows back from the stage. Olivia went in first, I followed, and Jocelyn sat in the aisle seat.

Olivia leaned toward us and whispered, "Maybe I should have brought that tablecloth. We're kind of conspicuous."

I joked, "Want me to run back for it?"

Jocelyn raised her hands, palms forward, up in mock dismay. "No, stay. You might miss hearing something that could prove that we didn't poison our donuts, and also that Izzy didn't do anything wrong."

Olivia removed a ball cap from her tote, slapped it onto her head, and pulled her russet-colored, wavy ponytail through the opening in back. "I'm staying, too." She waggled her eyebrows. "In disguise."

We'd all been making fun of the situation, but were any of the TWIG members murderers? And if so, what would they think about our attending their meeting?

By seven, about twenty more people had shown up. At five after, four people in green T-shirts marched down the aisle beside us, removed RESERVED signs from front-row seats, and sat where, by crooking their necks upward, they would get a perfect view of the podium at the edge of the stage in front of the closed red velvet curtains. Five more minutes passed. I heard people shuffle into seats behind ours. Finally, something nudged and poked at the other side of the red velvet curtains. After several struggles, Ramona slipped out from between the curtains and stood behind the podium.

She turned on a light and began speaking. People shouted that they couldn't hear her. A spry gent in a TWIG T-shirt scrambled onto the stage and fiddled with the microphone. It went live, the man ran down steps on the left side of the stage, and the house lights dimmed.

Ramona introduced herself. "I'm the head of the Fallingbrook chapter of a movement growing throughout the state—Toward Wisconsin in Green." The applause was, perhaps, embarrassingly scanty, but quite vigorous in the front row.

Ramona said she hoped we were all attending the meeting to support the cause of conservation, and that if we weren't already TWIG members, we should join. She gave a series of tips for helping conserve Wisconsin's greenery. She promised interesting lectures, meetings, and outings. "And protests," she added in decibels that would awaken anyone nodding off. "As you leave the room tonight, you'll have the opportunity to sign up to support us in various ways. You are more than welcome to participate in our protests, here and in other parts of the state. You'll notice that the protest we'd planned north of Fallingbrook on County Road H has to be delayed by a week due to an unfortunate occurrence necessitating a police investigation." Her widened eyes appeared almost gleeful.

Was TWIG postponing the protest at the property Izzy was buying because of the investigation, or because TWIG members hoped that the police wouldn't notice their strong opposition to Izzy's project and guess that one of their number might have done something to prevent Adam from developing the property if he had been able to buy it? Or in hopes of incriminating Izzy?

"Postponed," Ramona repeated. "Not canceled."

A couple of rows behind me and toward my left, someone stage-whispered, "Hallelujah."

I turned my head. A balding man and a white-haired woman in TWIG T-shirts gazed adoringly down toward Ramona.

I thought I recognized dark hair and a noble-looking forehead on a man all the way up in the backrow near the left aisle. I moved my head slightly.

How odd. Landon, Mr. Mystery, whose visit to Fallingbrook seemed almost random, was at the TWIG meeting. The door beside him opened, and the woman who'd left Deputy Donut with him slipped into the aisle seat beside him. He didn't acknowledge her. He continued focusing on Ramona. I wanted to text Brent that Landon was in the town hall theater, but wrestling my phone from my backpack could have disturbed some of the few people nearby. I returned my attention to the front.

Ramona shook a finger. "But we can't rest easy on the basis of one unfortunate incident, one police investigation, one possible end to a plan that would devastate our area. Wisconsin's forests are still under threat of decimation. Our grandchildren could inherit nothing but a windswept desert."

Several people around the auditorium responded with gasps and other comments, including Jocelyn, whose "Oh!" sounded a tiny bit sarcastic. I elbowed her. She turned what might have started as a laugh into a cough.

After long exhortations about contributing to TWIG's cause, the lights over the audience brightened, and Ramona asked if there were any questions.

Jocelyn stood and called out, "Are you carpooling to the protests or are you each going in your own vehicles?"

On my other side, Olivia slumped lower in her seat and pulled the bill of her cap down until it hid most of her face.

Ramona fiddled with papers on the podium. Finally, she

squinted into the audience. "When you sign up to accompany us on one of our protests, simply add a note that you need a ride, and one of us will try to accommodate you. Be sure to write down your contact information." She waved an index finger back and forth, aiming it toward the audience until she chose another questioner. "Next?"

Jocelyn sat down. I whispered, "Did that answer your question?"

She winked. "Yes, but probably not the way she hoped."

After a few "questions" that were more like rambling autobiographies, Ramona ended the meeting.

I turned toward the back of the room and told Jocelyn and Olivia, "Mr. Mystery is back there talking with the woman Izzy fears might be his girlfriend."

Our mayor leaned against the doorframe nearest them. That door was now open, but it had been closed after the woman who resembled Izzy's cousin came in. Had Jerry attended the meeting, or had he left his office to greet his constituents as they straggled out of the auditorium? He remained in the doorway, shaking hands and slowing everyone going up that aisle.

The three of us started up the other aisle. The older couple in TWIG T-shirts were in front of us. The woman leaned toward the man and said something.

He bellowed, "WHAT?"

"THAT GIRL SHOULD BE ARRESTED BEFORE SHE CUTS DOWN EVEN ONE TREE."

"WHY?"

"MURDER!"

"WHAT?"

"TELL YOU LATER."

Beside me, Jocelyn heaved a dramatic sigh.

Behind us, a woman asked someone, "Did you notice the police around that donut shop where Ramona wouldn't let us eat the other day?"

Jocelyn heaved another sigh. None of the three of us turned around.

A man answered, "What's that all about?"

"Probably something to do with that man's death. I've heard that donut shop is good, but now I'm wondering. Someone there might be up to mischief. Or, you know, they could be lax on food safety, and maybe they've caused a few cases of food poisoning. You just never know these days. You can't be too careful."

Olivia, Jocelyn, and I all let out hefty sighs.

We made it to the lobby as Landon and the woman who resembled Izzy's cousin headed outside.

I looked at my two assistants. Jocelyn whispered, "Of course we're following them."

Outside, the sun had set, but the sky was still light. The woman with Landon was dressed for a night out, in a sleek black sundress and high heels. Landon was dressed as he had been earlier, in black slacks and a white shirt, also dressy enough for a date. They turned left on Oak, toward Wisconsin Street.

Olivia suggested, "Let's hang back until other people get between them and us."

I texted Landon's location to Brent, and then we headed west on Oak behind Landon, the woman, and two groups of people who walked so slowly that I expected Brent to catch up with us. He hadn't answered my text, however, and might have been too busy to read it.

Landon and the woman crossed Wisconsin Street and headed south, toward Deputy Donut. The other people stayed on the east side of Wisconsin, so we did, too. The first group, two couples, went into the Fireplug. We dawdled near the pub's crowded patio. As if totally uninterested in Landon and his friend, Olivia stared toward the pub's front door.

Jocelyn pointed south down Wisconsin Street. "Is that

Mr. Mystery's rental car parked down there, on the other side of the street, just this side of Deputy Donut?"

I stared toward the dark sedan. "I think it might be."

Landon and the woman stopped on the sidewalk beside the car. He opened the passenger door. After she was inside the car, he walked out into the street, got into the driver's seat and drove south, the direction the car had been facing.

I asked my companions, "Could either of you read the license number? I couldn't."

Olivia shook her head. "It was too far away."

Jocelyn peered down Wisconsin Street. "I couldn't read it, either. He turned right. I'm going to follow them." She took off, running.

Sending Brent another text, I sauntered with Olivia down the street after Jocelyn. We slowed when we were across the street from Deputy Donut.

A black police van was outside in front, and there were probably more police vehicles in the lot behind the building. Lights were bright inside, and we could make out several figures in white hazmat suits behind the half-height wall separating the dining area from the kitchen.

I muttered, "Great. Our reputation is probably done." But I couldn't blame Brent and Vic for doing their jobs. Also, we had loyal customers. They wouldn't stay away.

We'd gone barely a block beyond Deputy Donut when Jocelyn ran back to us. "I was too slow. I don't know where they went. Maybe west, or they could be heading north through the parking lots. Maybe he's taking her to that dirt road we saw him turn onto Saturday evening."

Olivia suggested cheerfully, "Police vehicles could be blocking the lot behind Deputy Donut. Maybe they'll run into the detectives there."

I texted Brent an update. He thanked me. I put my phone away and suggested to Jocelyn and Olivia, "Your picnic things are in my car. How about if we go there, and I'll take you both home? Or to your bike, Jocelyn."

"I left it at home this time."

We turned around, walked back up Wisconsin Street, crossed Oak, and cut through the village square. We were close to where we'd eaten our picnic when a car sped north on Wisconsin. I asked, "Is that Landon?"

It wasn't quite dark yet, but because of the square's trees and flower gardens, none of us caught more than a glimpse of a car's gleaming dark finish and red taillights.

We all got into my car, and I dropped Olivia and Jocelyn off.

Jocelyn grinned. "I bet you can't wait for Brent to come home and tell you everything he's allowed to."

I laughed. "You're right."

Chapter 15

I had to wait until morning to find out more. Over breakfast in the still-cool catio, Brent told me, "The medical examiner concluded that Adam died of anaphylactic shock. A card in his wallet warned that he was allergic to almonds. He'd eaten donuts with almond flour in them. And ground-up peach kernels, but the peach kernels aren't what killed him, and they probably wouldn't have, by themselves. But they couldn't have helped."

My coffee, which had been delicious, became suddenly bitter. "How awful. Didn't he have one of those injection thingies that can pump adrenaline into the thigh?"

"We didn't find an autoinjector near him or anywhere on that property. People sometimes forget to carry them or don't have a new one on hand."

"How foolhardy. But I don't understand why he would eat donuts. As Tom, Olivia, and Jocelyn told me, and probably told you, Adam didn't buy donuts from us, so he didn't get a chance to ask if they contained nuts. And our boxes say right on them that the contents might include allergens. The print might be too small for some people to bother reading. However, I'm positive that the peachy sour cream donuts we made didn't contain almonds or ground nuts of any sort, especially not the kernels from inside peach pits. Isn't there something about poisons in peach pits and some other seeds? I asked Vic, but he didn't answer."

"They contain a toxin that if ground and ingested can combine with enzymes in the digestive system to create cyanide compounds. However, Adam probably only ate one donut before he succumbed, not the four that we might have guessed. No one could hide enough peach pits in four donuts, let alone in one donut, to kill an adult man. The medical examiner determined that it was definitely the allergy that killed Adam."

"Did you find anything incriminating in Deputy Donut?"

"I stayed out of the search, and so did Misty and Tyler, who were busy on other calls. Investigators found nothing in your shop besides the almond flour that you all told us was there. And you have cardamom on hand. As you folks told us, you'd sold all of the donuts you made from your peachy sour cream batter, plus you used up all of the icing, so we couldn't send any of those things to be tested. There was no sign of peach pits. Your coffee, nut, and spice grinders were taken away for analysis."

"We would never grind anything except coffee beans in our coffee grinders!" The thought horrified me. "But I hope they can analyze whatever crumbs they find in those grinders and prove that we didn't grind the kernels from peach pits in any of them. What else did they take?"

"All of the trash on the premises, including from the compost and other bins outside. If everything comes back negative, you can open. I'll let you and Tom know as soon as I can."

"I'm sorry we didn't have any of those donuts left over so they could be tested."

"We'll question everyone who bought boxes of them. I hope that at least one of them will still have a donut that forensics can analyze. Mayor Creavus bought some, you said, and Ramona from TWIG? And someone whose name might be Landon who is driving a car that he might have rented in Minnesota and who was still in the area last night. And Izzy."

"Yes. Ramona's last name is Schleehart."

"Could any of you read the license number of the car this Landon person was driving?"

"It was too far away." I speared a piece of bacon. "Didn't you say that Izzy told you what it was?"

"The one she gave us didn't match any records in Minnesota. But if he's hanging around Fallingbrook, we'll find him."

"Speeding, perhaps. But maybe the driver that zipped past the square last night wasn't him."

"Tyler might end up contacting every car rental agency in Minnesota."

"Lucky Tyler."

We shared a warm goodbye, and Brent left for work.

I spent the morning the way I spent most Tuesday mornings, doing chores. Brent did his share on weekends, when he usually wasn't working and I was. In the afternoon, I went kayaking on Chicory Lake. Wearing her life jacket with her leash attached to my life jacket, Dep rode on my lap. We startled one great blue heron into squawking flight and spotted two fish jumping. I was concerned that by being down on the lake where we had no cell phone reception, I might miss a call about getting Deputy Donut ready to open, but when Dep and I returned to the chalet, I checked. I hadn't missed any calls.

I made a pot of chili, ate a bowl of it, saved some in the fridge for Brent, and froze the rest in single servings.

I was still up when Brent arrived home. Dep and I sat with him in the kitchen while he ate his late dinner. "Thanks, Em, this is what I needed. It's a shame that you, Tom, Jocelyn, and Olivia won't be able to show off your cooking skills at Deputy Donut again tomorrow."

"I'm used to having Wednesdays off. Did you find any of

those peachy sour cream donuts to be tested and compared to the ones Izzy and I found?"

"Both Jerry Creavus and Ramona Schleehart said they'd eaten all of the donuts they'd bought at Deputy Donut. Jerry threw his empty box into the dumpster behind the town hall, but that dumpster was emptied before we knew we might need to examine its contents. Ramona tore hers up and composted it at a community garden. Investigators will sift through that compost. And we haven't tracked down this Landon character yet."

"Maybe when we saw him drive north last night, he was heading back to Duluth, but I'm afraid he's going to stick around in hopes of getting something from Izzy. Like all of her money."

"We'll find him."

"Has Tyler located where Landon might have rented that car?"

"Not yet. Vic will probably do the local interviewing, and I'll take over cold-calling car rental agencies in Duluth."

"As long as you don't have to dumpster-dive or sift through compost."

He put his dishes into the dishwasher. "Tyler and Misty might enjoy those jobs."

"You're terrible," I told him.

He hugged me. "I know."

The next morning after Brent left for work, I shopped for groceries and then went home and baked and froze cookies and mixed up enough bread dough for several loaves. I wrapped the dough tightly and put it in the freezer.

Cleaning up after lunch and then folding a load of laundry, I kept thinking about Landon veering off County Road H onto a dirt road. Where did that road go, and why had Landon turned down it? Had he merely been trying to prevent us from following him, or was he renting a cabin or camping along that road? When Izzy saw him the next day, had he been fleeing after forcing Adam to eat donuts containing almonds? Izzy had said he'd been going west. If he'd been in the process of returning to that dirt road, he'd gone the long way around, which was easy to imagine if he was leaving the scene of a crime.

Standing in the middle of the great room, I put my hands on my hips and looked down at Dep batting at a catnip mouse on the floor. "The afternoon's half over. Would you like another adventure today, or would you rather stay home by yourself and nap?"

She abandoned the toy and rubbed against my bare ankles. "Meow."

She probably expected to go kayaking again, but I fastened her halter instead of her life jacket on her and put her into her carrier in the car. "You can thank me later," I told my justifiably indignant furbaby. I drove south.

My turn from County Road H onto the dirt road was more graceful than Landon's had been. The road was rutted, riddled with dried mud puddles. I drove slowly, but dust, golden in the afternoon sunshine, rose behind my car. I didn't see anything other than tire tracks, weeds, and small shrubs. Nothing hinted that anyone had gotten out of a vehicle during the past few days. The road dwindled to two dirt tracks. Weeds brushed against the underside of my car. I muttered to Dep, "I hope I don't have to back out of here."

"Meow."

I checked my mirrors again. "I also hope that no one comes in behind us. Not that I'd see them or they'd see us with all that dust we're kicking up."

"Mer-ow."

"And I hope no one comes toward us."

"Ow."

Hemmed in by young, fast-growing aspens and poplars, the road curved and twisted. I reminded myself that Landon must have driven out of this narrow track, one way or another. Maybe the road was a shortcut leading to another county road, probably J. I didn't think there was a County Road I. The track widened slightly, mostly because something, vehicles, perhaps, had broken and bent the twigs, branches, and even some of the trunks of sumacs and wild roses beside the track. And then the road, such as it was, went downhill, in more ways than one.

I crept down the slope. Ahead, a puddle or stream blocked both tire tracks. I stopped several feet from the water and got out, leaving my driver's door open to give Dep fresh air.

The water turned out to be a stream, shallow but rocky, and not something I would consider fording. Level, sandy soil on both sides showed that the stream was wider and deeper in wet seasons, and there were tire prints of vehicles that had come this far and then turned around. I frowned down at the dirt. I couldn't make out individual tracks, but several vehicles must have been here since the most recent rain, over a week before. There was no litter, but there were lots of shoe and boot prints. I shaded my eyes and peered at the track rising on the other side of the stream. It appeared that the vehicles that had driven up that hill had narrow wheelbases, like ATVs, perhaps. At the top of the bank on my side of the stream, an animal trail ran through the grasses and wildflowers. If a similar trail ran along the other side of the stream, it was hidden behind shrubs and weeds.

Dep's plaintive mews reminded me that she was in the car. I returned, closed the driver's door, and opened the rear one. "I promised you an adventure, didn't I, sweetheart? How about a hike?"

"Meow."

"You poor baby. I understand. I'll get you out of there." I unzipped the carrier, fastened her leash on her, set her on the ground, and then let her lead the way. She headed down to the stream, sniffed at its edge without getting her nose or paws wet, and then walked daintily along the sand in the dried-up part of the streambed.

Beside us, water flowed slowly around stones. As if hoping to see fish jump, Dep watched water striders glide over the stream and dragonflies hover above it. Eventually, she headed up the embankment, and we continued east on the animal trail. Judging by the boot prints we were still following, it was also a pathway that humans used.

Had I locked the car? I told Dep, "It's time to turn around."

I had locked it, but Dep had no interest in getting into it, and Brent wouldn't be home for hours, so I let Dep explore in the other direction along the sand beside the stream. Dep was probably still hoping to see a fish. I wondered who owned this idyllic spot, where the stream came from, and where it went.

Dep stopped and stared toward the water.

I asked her, "Is that a fish?" My voice sounded loud among the clicking and chirring of insects. I stepped closer to the nearly silent stream. The "fish" was a mostly white plastic tubelike thing caught between stones. Rippling water distorted whatever was printed on the tube, and the colors on the endcaps had faded slightly, but I had taken first-aid courses every few years, and I recognized the object.

It was an autoinjector of the sort that Adam Nofftry should have been carrying but apparently had not been.

Chapter 16

The autoinjector in the stream probably had nothing to do with Adam Nofftry or his death, but I pulled my phone out of my shorts pocket and called Brent.

He didn't ask why I was exploring a dirt road. He merely said, "Misty and Tyler deserve a break from sorting through dumpsters and compost bins. I'll send them in one of the department's SUVs. They can be there in about twenty minutes. Can you wait for them?"

"Sure." I told him where Misty and Tyler would find me and then carried Dep higher on the bank and sat on the ground in the shade of a willow.

Clouds reflected on the surface of the stream, occasionally obscuring the autoinjector, but I kept my eye on where I'd last seen it, and the clouds drifted off, to be replaced by blue sky and then by other clouds. The autoinjector didn't budge. Dep snoozed in my lap.

Lulled by her warmth, quiet breathing, and the rise and fall of the cicadas' songs, I might have slept, too, but I stared toward that plastic tube and the reflections of clouds. My eyes stung and blurred.

Gradually, I realized I was hearing an engine, and then the squeaking of a vehicle's springs as it bumped over potholes and gullies. Those noises stopped. A car door slammed, and then another. And the back hatch of a sturdy SUV?

Minutes later, Misty came toward me on the animal trail. Carrying a small, short-handled fishing net, Tyler was right behind her. Misty was senior in the police department to her usual partner, Hooligan, and also to Tyler.

Holding Dep in my arms, I stood. "I heard that you two have been having a fun day with garbage."

Misty grinned. "Thank goodness for hazmat suits, gloves, and masks."

"Did you find anything?"

Misty gazed down toward the water. "That environmentalist woman didn't lie about tearing up one of your boxes and mixing the pieces with the compost. She was very thorough with her tearing and her mixing. I doubt that forensics will be able to learn anything from those bits of cardboard, but no one can say we didn't try. Forensics investigators get the fun of sorting through Deputy Donut's food scraps, and the dumpster behind the town hall had recently been replaced. There was hardly anything in it. Certainly no Deputy Donut boxes. Aha. I see why you called, Emily."

"Dep spotted it first."

Tyler lengthened his net's telescopic handle. "We should have brought her with us yesterday."

I asked, "Did Brent send you to search here?"

Misty started down the embankment. "He came, too."

Hmmmm, I thought. *Brent must have led a search here because I told him about Landon driving up this road. Maybe Brent suspects Landon more than he's been letting on.* I asked, "Did you two help with the investigation Sunday night after Izzy found the body?"

Tyler followed Misty to the edge of the stream. "No. We had three days off after working the night shift. We started working days again starting Monday at noon." They worked twelve-hour shifts for three days at a time, with three days off between changing to twelve-hour night shifts. "So, on Sunday night, we missed out on searching all over the meadows near where that man died. Misty's husband Scott and his firefighters pumped the water out of the pond, but they didn't find anything." Scott was Fallingbrook's fire chief. Most of his firefighters were volunteers.

Tyler pointed at the autoinjector. "That thing wasn't here yesterday." He aimed his net toward the stones. "I should have brought a grabber. This isn't going to fit between the stones the thing is lodged against."

I pointed at his feet. "You two are wearing leather boots and long pants. How about if I take off my sandals and wade in just below those stones. I won't touch the autoinjector, but I can move stones out of the way, and you can be downstream and catch the autoinjector in your net."

Tyler had a very nice smile. "If you don't mind."

Misty added, "And if you're careful. Want me to hold Dep?"

"You don't need to." Hanging on to Dep's harness with one hand, I unsnapped her leash, looped the leash around the willow's narrow trunk, threaded the leash through its handle, and reattached the leash to the harness. "This will keep her from wandering off, and you can rescue Tyler or me if one of us falls in. Or we both do." I let go of Dep's harness. She hunkered down in the weeds and pawed at a beetle.

"Great." Misty's tone implied that she'd rather hug Dep.

Avoiding possibly slippery stones, I waded into the water. Slow-moving, shallow, and heated by days of sunshine, the stream was almost warm. I didn't particularly appreciate the cooler mud oozing between my toes, however. I told myself to think of it as silky, not slimy. "Ready?" I asked Tyler, who was standing a yard or two downstream from me.

"Yes." The toes of his boots were almost in the stream. Bracing her feet in the dried-up, sandy mud near the edge of the water, Misty stood beside him.

I lifted one of the stones. The autoinjector edged away

from another stone and rolled along the streambed so lazily that Tyler had plenty of time to net it. Apologizing to a crayfish that had squirmed, churning up silt, to conceal itself underneath another stone, I gently put the first stone back where it had been.

Misty held out a plastic bag. "That thing's not dry enough for a paper evidence bag. We'll give it to forensics in this and let them decide how to handle and store it." Tyler deftly tipped the autoinjector out of the net and into the bag. "Bravo," Misty said.

I splashed to them. Standing on the sandy soil, they gazed at the bag in Misty's hand. She lifted it high and turned it around to see all sides of the autoinjector. "No name visible. I know that these things don't require specific prescriptions, but we could have hoped that whoever left it here might have labeled it with his name or initials."

I strapped my sandals onto my muddy feet. "Is it heavy, like it hasn't been used?"

Misty answered, "I can't tell. Water could have seeped into it. Forensics will check."

Tyler glanced at the weedy slope across the stream. "I'm not mistaken, am I, Misty? We did search this very spot, from both banks? And though we didn't wade into the water, we checked it visually, pretty thoroughly."

"We did, and for about a half mile in both directions from the track where we parked. Unless we were all dazzled by reflections or something, it wasn't here. Maybe it floated down from even farther upstream. Emily, you drive up and down County Road C all the time. Is there a bridge on it somewhere near the intersection with County Road H?"

I removed Dep's leash from the tree trunk. "It's more like a culvert, not far north of the intersection. It could be the same stream."

Tyler shielded his phone from the glare of daylight and scrolled through screens. "It's hard to tell from these tiny maps. We might get a better idea from the computer in the vehicle."

I offered, "I'm about to go past there. I'll let you know if it looks like it could be the same stream, though I'm not sure how I'll be able to tell."

Misty bent to pet Dep. "You don't need to check it by yourself. Unless we get called away, we'll have a look. Meanwhile, do you mind helping us keep an eye out for anything else that doesn't belong here?" She scratched Dep's chin. "You, too, Little Miss Eagle Eyes."

We took our time, letting Dep lead the way and set the pace. We didn't find a thing, either in the water or on land. I asked Misty and Tyler, "Did you collect possible evidence here yesterday?"

Tyler answered cheerfully, "We found nothing that hadn't been here less than several weeks or even months, and we gave forensics an entire trash bag of old cigarette filters and disposable cups, just in case they get bored."

"No wonder the place was so clean when Dep and I got here."

Misty steepled her hands underneath her chin. "We aim to serve. Speaking of which, how do you plan to get your car out of here? Want help?"

"I figure I can make a twenty-point turn on the sandy soil down by the water's edge. How do you plan to get out?"

She pointed up the track at the back of a police department SUV. "I already made that turn, but higher on the slope, at the expense of a few weeds and bushes."

I looked from the dried streambed to the broken-off bushes farther up the hill. "Your method looks safer. Is that what you did yesterday, too?"

"Yes, and we weren't the first."

Landon? "Thanks. I should be able to turn my car around by myself."

Misty and Tyler waved goodbye and started up the track toward the departmental SUV.

I put Dep into her carrier. "Okay, Dep, are you ready to ride backward uphill until we can turn around without bashing too many wild roses?"

"Rowr."

With help from the car's rear-facing camera, I backed up the slope to where the police department's SUV had been. Misty, with Tyler in the passenger seat, had already pulled ahead and stopped.

Using fewer than ten backups, I managed to turn around without, I hoped, letting broken-off branches scratch my car. Misty drove up the lane slowly, and I followed. Again, I didn't see signs that anyone had recently gotten out of vehicles along the dirt road. No campers or picknickers, and probably not Landon, either. Maybe he had driven up here, walked east, and tossed Adam's autoinjector where he thought no one would find it. Then the creek had rolled the cylinder westward, through the mud, stirring up silt that camouflaged the autoinjector until it lodged against stones, and the flowing water rinsed the silt off it.

Or maybe Misty's guess about someone tossing the autoinjector into a stream passing through a culvert underneath County Road C was accurate.

I didn't catch up with Misty and Tyler until I reached the shoulder just south of the culvert I'd told them about. I parked behind them, opened the windows all the way for Dep, got out, and joined the two police officers on the left side of the road.

Tyler waved back toward the police vehicle. "I'm still not sure, but I think this is a tributary of the stream we just explored."

Misty turned to me. "What do you think, Emily?"

I gazed down into the almost still, almost clear water. "It could be. I don't know how we could be certain unless we toss an autoinjector into the water. Not," I added quickly, "the same one."

Grinning, Tyler raised an index finger. "Poohsticks!"

Misty stared at him as if he'd suddenly sprouted a sunflower from his forehead. "*WHAT?*"

I laughed. "It's a game, invented by Winnie-the-Pooh. Everyone gets a stick and drops it on the upstream side of a bridge, then they all run across the bridge and watch the water. The person whose stick shows up first wins the game."

Misty pushed her hat back. "I see, I guess. But Winnie-the-Pooh isn't real. I mean, wasn't he named after a real bear? But neither a real bear nor a toy could have invented the game."

I asked her, "Didn't you read those books or have them read to you when you were a kid?"

"Apparently not."

I shook my head. "Poor Misty. A wasted childhood."

Misty readjusted her equipment belt. "Not completely. I was only about twelve when I met you and Samantha, and neither of you were exactly opposed to being childish."

I thought of the games we'd played around Fallingbrook Falls, and of the day I'd spent there with Izzy. "We called it adventuring, and exploring. And having fun."

Misty smiled. "And it was."

Tyler crossed the road to the side where our vehicles were. We followed him. With mini-howls, Dep reminded me that she was still inside my car. Tyler clambered down the mown embankment beside the shoulder, climbed back up, and solemnly handed us each a small twig. "It was the best I could do."

I laughed. "How will we tell them apart?"

"Easy," Misty answered. "Whichever one wins is mine."

Tyler held his stick over the edge of the culvert. "Drop them on the count of three. One, two, three."

We dropped our twigs and hurried across the road.

We hadn't needed to hurry. The water was, if anything,

more sluggish than in the creek where we'd fished out the autoinjector. Eventually, the first, and then a second twig emerged, both turning in circles. We waited another couple of minutes. The first two twigs—mine and Tyler's, he and I decided—spun slowly down the creek. The third stick didn't show up. Laughing, we returned to the SUVs.

I asked Misty, "When are your next days off?"

She opened her driver's door. "We finish tonight at midnight and will be back on duty Sunday at midnight."

"Have a great time. With luck, Deputy Donut will be open again tomorrow. You know, you can come in even when you're not taking a break during your on-duty days."

Misty told me, "I was just saying to Scott that we can do that, even though he's on call most of the time, like Brent is."

"Do you have any idea how late Brent's working tonight?"

Tyler answered that one. "Late. I called him when we were on the way here and told him we were bringing your find back to the office."

Misty added, "You know how Brent is when he's on a case. He doesn't want to let go until he gets every loose end tied up."

The two of us exchanged proud smiles. We and Samantha had married men who worked hard, helped others, and loved what they did. And Misty and Samantha were every bit as dedicated. I was the only one in the group who wasn't a first responder. That was fine with all of us.

Misty and Tyler climbed aboard their SUV. Misty drove beyond the culvert to a safe place to make a U-turn, and then, her strobes flashing for a second as a goodbye, she sped toward Fallingbrook.

Behind her, a woman driving a sedate sedan looked at me, shook her head sadly, and lifted both hands off the wheel long enough to brush one index finger over the other one in a shame-on-you gesture.

I told Dep, "She thought I'd been pulled over!"

Dep didn't seem to think it was as funny as I did. She let out a reproving wail.

At home, I took off her harness and opened the door to the catio. She streaked into it and ran up to one of her favorite perches.

Brent telephoned me. "Deputy Donut has been cleared. Officers will bring your coffee, nut, and spice grinders to your shop in the morning. I said someone would be there by six thirty, and you'd like your things then."

I thanked him and let Tom know. We agreed that Tom would ask the Jolly Cops to return to their regular cleaning of the shop during the night, and I would call Jocelyn and Olivia.

They were both eager to get back to work. "See you tomorrow morning at six thirty," I told them.

Chapter 17

Brent came home at some horrible hour, but he got up in the morning almost as soon as Dep and I did, and we prepared a red pepper and Wisconsin Colby cheese omelet for breakfast and packed a lunch for Brent.

I drove Dep to town in my car. Not knowing when he'd be able to return home, Brent followed me in his SUV.

Shortly after six thirty, Tom was in the kitchen preparing dough, and Jocelyn, Olivia, and I were setting up tables in the dining room. Someone knocked on our front door.

A young DCI investigator I'd never met before handed me a large carton containing our coffee and nut grinders and choppers. He pulled a receipt out of his pocket. "Sign here."

I rooted through the box, satisfied myself that the investigators had returned every appliance they'd taken, signed the receipt, and offered, "If you want to wait until we clean a coffee grinder, we can make you some coffee."

"No, thanks." As if afraid that the air in our shop might poison him, he hurried away.

We rushed around and were ready, just barely, when our first patrons arrived at seven.

The Knitpickers and retired men took up their usual tables a few minutes earlier than their usual nine o'clock. Cheryl moaned. "Two full days without your donuts and coffees! I don't know how we survived!"

Other diners told us the same thing. The police activity in our shop did not seem to have deterred customers. If anything, we had more of them than usual on a Thursday morning in late August. And many of them wanted to know why we'd been closed.

We gave them our agreed-upon response. "Nothing happened here, but the police had to make certain of it before we could open again."

Midway through the morning, Jerry Creavus came in. I asked him what I could bring him.

"Coffee, nothing fancy, just your normal one. And do you have more of your peachy sour cream donuts? I ate all of mine as soon as I got back to my office." His flash of a grin didn't look quite sincere. "But I still want more."

"We don't have any fresh fruit yet this morning, but we've just taken a batch of raised donuts containing rum-soaked raisins out of the fryer and dipped them in vanilla glaze. They're big."

He patted his stomach. "I'll limit myself to two, then, to start. You can bring them to that table over there. I'll sit with those men. They're a good bunch." He pointed at the retired men.

Across the aisle from the men, the five Knitpickers were holding their knitting still and watching Jerry as if preparing to rescue me from his speechifying.

I took him his coffee and donuts. He told the men at his table, "Law enforcement actually questioned me about Adam Nofftry, the developer who died." Jerry pointed at the donuts on his plate. "They seemed to think that something might have been wrong with the donuts I bought here. But nothing was, or I might not be here to tell you about it!" He turned to me. "Emily, see how much I trust your delicious pastries? I'm digging into more." He frowned up at me. "Did those donuts contain almonds? I didn't notice any. Maybe they were subtle?"

"We haven't put any almonds in our donuts during the past two weeks."

He tore a section off one of his raisin donuts. "I just wondered because when Adam announced he was running for mayor, I took him out for a drink. You know, a neighborly thing to do with someone you expect to work with. The beer came with a bowl of salty almonds. He didn't touch them and said he was allergic to almonds. So, I didn't think he would eat donuts from your shop if he thought they might contain nuts."

I tried to maintain a neutral expression. I wondered how many other people knew, before Adam's death, about his allergy to almonds. Could our mayor have been the only one?

He spoke again to the table of men. "The police wanted to know what I'd done with the donuts I'd bought. I ate them. Then they wanted the box they came in, of all things. I'd already thrown it in the town hall dumpster." His right hand came up to his right cheek as if he had a toothache. "Presumably, that dumpster has been hauled away."

Charlie said, "That man was kind of young to go off like that."

Jerry nodded briskly. "Exactly. And don't get me wrong. I'm sorry to see him go. I wouldn't wish an early death on anyone, let alone him. It didn't bother me at all that he was running against me. I was going to win, anyway."

Charlie's coffee mug was nearly empty. Although I hated to miss whatever Jerry was telling the others, I went to the kitchen for a fresh pot.

Jocelyn asked, "Would you like me to take that and refresh the retired men's coffees?"

"No, thanks. Jerry has interesting things to say."

"Then I'll offer coffee and tea to the Knitpickers and listen in, too."

I poured Charlie's coffee. Jerry told the men, "It's probably just as well that Adam can't build the resort he planned, at least not there. He wouldn't have had an easy time making a success of it. No one was likely to patronize a resort so far from a large airport. Duluth International is about three hours away. Not that Adam had a spark of a chance of buying that property." He looked at me and lowered his voice to a low murmur. I bent closer to hear him. "There's someone in town who wanted him to simply disappear and who has a history of poisoning people. Well, really only poisoning one person that we know of."

"Who?" I tried to keep my voice to a minimum.

"That TWIG woman, Ramona. I saw you at her meeting Monday night. Don't let her give you any food or drugs!"

Maybe he hadn't meant to sound offensive. I responded with an attempt at humor. "I'm not in the market for drugs."

"Of course you're not. That's not what I meant. Did you know she's a retired nurse?"

"No."

"She had to retire after she overdosed a patient on insulin."

I clutched the carafe more tightly. "When was this?"

"Years ago, right here in Fallingbrook. You were probably still in school. The patient died, but Ramona was never charged. It was all hush-hush. I guess that Fallingbrook Hospital didn't want anyone to know about their negligence. And the mayor's office, too, kept it quiet. That's one reason I ran for political office. I don't need the aggravation, but if I can save anyone else from a similar fate, then my sacrifices are worth it."

"That's generous."

I must have sounded like I meant it. Jerry thanked me. "I'd like to talk to Chief Westhill if I could." He stood, hitched his pants higher, and picked up his plate and mug.

"I'll tell him."

Jerry nodded toward a table for two in the corner beside

our office. "I'll wait for him back there." He carried his plate and mug toward that table.

Dep stared at him from the back of the office couch. He tapped the window with his elbow. She puffed up, hissed, and then jumped down, away from the window. She probably didn't trust him any more than I did.

I took over the frying and sent Tom to talk to our mayor.

Ten minutes later, Jerry left Deputy Donut, and Tom returned to the kitchen. "Our illustrious mayor is full of himself and full of tales. Don't believe him, Emily. For one thing, there was never a speck of evidence that Ramona Schleehart overdosed anyone with insulin or anything else. The patient's family were all up in arms about it, but the medical examiner determined that she died of natural causes. The patient did not have excessive insulin in her body. Schleehart retired from hospital nursing shortly afterward and there were rumors that she left because she felt guilty. Personally, I thought she was traumatized by the whole thing."

"Did you know her?"

"Not socially. I was the detective on the case. There were absolutely no grounds to charge her, even though the Creavus family thought we should."

"The Creavus family..."

"She was Jerry's great-aunt."

"I see."

"Exactly. Also, he's going around telling people that he would have won the mayoralty race even if Adam had lived to run against him. I don't think he's right. Jerry Creavus is not as popular as he thinks he is. Even though Adam was a newcomer, he was making a good impression on people with his promises of bringing more prosperity to Fallingbrook and the surrounding area."

"The one time I saw Adam alive, he didn't make a good

impression on me. He was blustery, pushy, and just plain mean to Izzy. No one should talk to another human the way he talked to her."

"From what I heard, he could turn on the charm."

"Lovely." I said it in my most sarcastic voice.

"Brent will know more about this than I do, but from what I can gather, Adam has owned a series of resorts. He would build one, get it going, and then sell it at a profit and start over."

"Did Jerry talk to you about our donuts?"

"He said he ate them all, threw the box in the town hall dumpster, and it was taken away. It could be true, but I noticed something about Jerry years ago. When he might not be speaking the whole truth, he tends to cover or almost cover one jaw with a hand for a second."

"I saw him doing that. I thought he had a toothache, like maybe from using his molars to bite down on peach pits and crack them open."

Tom copied my joking tone. "Could be."

I became serious again. "I wonder if he really ate a half dozen donuts. He could have scraped the icing off the peachy donuts in the box, or off any of the other frosted donuts, if he bought any. I don't remember who bought which ones, but I think they all bought some with either fudge or chocolate frosting. Jerry could have mixed almond flour and ground peach kernels into the frosting and slathered it over the donuts. Brent told me that Adam died from anaphylactic shock from eating almonds. He was allergic to them. And there were ground-up kernels from peach pits."

"Those peach kernels had to have been ground very finely for someone who avoided nuts not to notice the grit."

"True, and I just found out something possibly incriminating about Jerry Creavus. He might have been one of the few people to know, before Adam's death, that Adam was allergic to almonds." I summarized Jerry's story about taking Adam out for a beer.

"You'll tell Brent about that, won't you." It wasn't a question.

"First chance I get."

Tom pointed at the office. "Go call him now."

Brent answered, and I told him everything that Jerry had told me and Tom. I headed back toward the kitchen.

I was behind our serving counter when the front door opened and Izzy rushed inside. The baggy orange T-shirt she wore over her cutoffs was stained. Tugging at her tangled curls, Izzy strode over to me.

Chapter 18

I asked Izzy, "What's wrong?"

"Everything! Some detective, not your nice husband, and other police officers came to my house with a search warrant. They heard somehow that I had peach pits, and they wanted them! I'd already planted them in pots to try to raise seedlings, but they took most of them away. And they ransacked my kitchen, too, but whatever it was they wanted, they didn't find it. So, despite your nice husband and the interview I did with him, these other officers must want to believe that I killed Adam Nofftry somehow. With pots full of dirt and peach pits?"

"I'm sorry, Izzy, but I saw you take peach pits from our compost, and I told Brent."

Those hazel eyes looked both confused and hurt. "I thought you didn't want them."

"We didn't. We threw them out. That's not why I told Brent." I took a deep breath. "This is just between you and me, okay?"

She nodded.

I explained, "The donuts that you and I found on your property contained the ground-up insides of peach pits. As I understand it, that's not why Adam died, but someone must have added ground-up peach pit kernels to donuts from here, so the police are looking into everyone who bought that type of donuts." I hoped I wasn't telling her more than Brent wanted people to know, but I truly didn't believe she would have gone to such lengths to harm a man whose threats she believed were negligible. Or that she would purposely harm anyone, period.

"I bought some of those donuts, and my neighbors and I ate them that afternoon. And even if we hadn't, why would I tamper with them, especially adding an icky ingredient? I did take some of those peach pits apart, as an experiment. I planted most of them complete with their outer shells. But I also planted a few bare kernels in pots to see if they'd germinate faster. That detective took all of the pots containing the bare kernels away."

"They have to look into everything."

"I get that, but why me? Adam's become a worse threat to me dead than he was alive."

"They're doing their job. And although Brent doesn't tell me much, I'm sure he has other suspects, probably some who are much more likely than you."

"But Brent wasn't one of the people who searched my place."

"Did they show you a badge? Tell you where they're from?"

"I made them wait outside until my lawyers could come. The police fussed, but they showed the badge to my lawyers. Apparently, they weren't Fallingbrook police officers. They were from some agency. I forget the name of it or the initials, but it's something like the Wisconsin version of the FBI. And the detectives are called agents, like in the FBI."

"The DCI?"

"That could have been it."

"Those letters stand for the Wisconsin Division of Criminal Investigation."

"That sounds like what I remember. My lawyers agreed

that the officers were legitimate, and then my lawyers traipsed around my home after them. So did I, even though we had to squeeze past one another."

"Was the detective's name Victor Throppen?"

"I think so."

"I've met him. He'll go wherever the facts and evidence send him. He's the lead investigator on the case, but Brent will be helping him, and so will other members of the Fallingbrook Police Department, like my friend Misty and her temporary patrol partner Tyler. You said they ransacked your kitchen. Did they show you the search warrant?"

"I told them to show it to my lawyers, and they did."

"The search warrant would say what they were authorized to search for."

"I left it to my lawyers to read everything. The searchers seemed to be checking out small appliances, but my toaster didn't interest them. Then they wanted to go through things like flour and sugar, but they didn't take any of those away, either, other than a small amount of all-purpose flour. I don't bake much. Then they wanted to see my spices. I don't have many of those, either, just pepper, paprika, and cinnamon." She shrugged. "Although I want to grow greenhouse veggies and maybe fruits someday, too, I'm not exactly an adventurous cook, and until I got that money from my grandfather, I didn't splurge on things like ingredients. I still don't. His money is going to my new farm." A flicker almost like a smile crossed her face. "I don't need to cook when I have places like Deputy Donut around."

I glanced toward our display case, brimming with appetizing donuts in gorgeous colors. "What would you like today? It's on the house, since I brought law enforcement down on your head."

"Not really. Finding Adam's body was the worst thing I could do if I didn't want to be suspected of murder." She put her elbows on the counter and rested her chin in her palms. "I wish I hadn't gone up there that day. Anyway, I'm almost afraid of donuts now."

"Then how about some nice, calming chamomile tea?"

This time her smile was genuine. "Do I seem that bad?"

"No, but chamomile tea is good any time. Or maybe you'd like some of today's special coffee. It's a bold and acidic medium roast from Kenya."

"Bold and acidic. Just like me. I'd love some of that. And maybe just one donut, like, um . . ." She leaned toward our display case. "How about one of those with the mini chocolate chips all over them?"

"Those are mocha donuts with mocha frosting. They definitely go better with coffee than with any kind of tea."

"They sound delicious."

I took them to her at the counter, but she stood up. "Mind if I eat over there at the table where I usually sit?"

"Of course not, but I'll carry them."

"You don't trust me?"

"I do, but if anything's going to be dropped, we like to be the ones dropping them, if we can get to people before they start wandering around in search of better tables like Mayor Creavus does."

Izzy's laugh seemed forced, but she led me to her favorite table and sat down with her back to the wall. I wondered if she was facing the dining area to watch for Landon. However, unlike other days, she didn't stay long after she finished her coffee and donut. She didn't come back to the counter near the kitchen, but she waved and went out the front door.

I'd told her that the donut and coffee were free. She had folded bills and hidden them underneath her saucer. She'd not only paid for her snack but she'd left a big tip. No wonder she'd been in a hurry to leave before I could argue with her about accepting the cash. Sighing at her extravagance, I cleared her table. Either she was as honest as I believed, or she was a very good actor.

Tourists kept us busy until closing time. Tom, Jocelyn, Olivia, and I had almost finished tidying when Brent showed up at our locked front door.

DCI Agent Victor Throppen was with him.

Chapter 19

Both men were in suits, white shirts, and ties. Detective Throppen reintroduced himself and told us to call him Vic. "I have a few questions for all of you."

I gestured toward one of our largest tables. It had space for all six of us. "Would you like to sit?"

Jocelyn offered, "Can I bring you some coffee? And there are a few donuts left."

Vic pinched the creases of his pants and sat. "No need to go to that trouble. Join us for an informal discussion."

Brent didn't appear to expect the discussion to be informal. He removed his notebook and pen from a pocket.

Jocelyn, Olivia, and I sat up straight and folded our hands on the table like good students or interviewees. Tom amused me by slouching slightly and crossing his arms over his chest. He wasn't going to let DCI Agent Victor Throppen intimidate him.

Vic opened his notebook and smoothed the page. "When did you last see Isabella Korinth?"

I pulled my chair closer to the table. "She was in here this afternoon around two. She told me that you—I guess it was you—executed a search warrant at her place. She didn't understand why."

Vic made a note of what I'd said. "And when did you last

see this man whose name might be Landon and who might be driving a car with Minnesota plates that might or might not be a rental car?"

Jocelyn volunteered, "I don't think he's been in here since Sunday, when he bought a half dozen donuts. But Olivia, Emily, and I saw him Monday night at a meeting of the local chapter of Toward Wisconsin in Green. And then he and a woman walked to a car that was just north of here on Wisconsin Street. They both got in, and he drove south. A few minutes later, a car that could have been the same one went north past the square, but it might not have been his."

Olivia and I agreed with Jocelyn's statement.

Vic asked, "Have you seen Isabella Korinth and this Landon person together?"

I shook my head. "Not really. We saw them both on Saturday, when Adam Nofftry was telling Landon, and the rest of us, including Izzy—Isabella—to get off the property he claimed was his. But Landon and Izzy weren't together. That was the first time she'd ever seen him."

Vic took such a sudden breath that his nostrils nearly pinched shut. "Are you positive that they hadn't arranged to meet there?"

Olivia, Jocelyn, and I looked at one another, and I remembered how Landon and Izzy had appeared to be instantly attracted to each other and how Landon had seemed to find it difficult to come up with a reason for being there. Had he and Izzy known each other before? Had she, in addition to inviting us to tour the property, asked Landon to meet her there?

As always when Brent was nearby, I couldn't help looking at him. He was watching me as if following my thoughts.

It was Olivia who answered, though, seeming to choose her words carefully. "We can't be sure, but that's how it appeared. We were already there with Izzy, farther up the hill, on the lowest meadow, when we heard shouting below us and investigated. Adam and this Landon person had come onto the property without any of us noticing, and they were arguing below the trail's uppermost turn. Izzy seemed surprised that the two men were there."

Jocelyn added, "She didn't seem to know Landon's name. And he didn't use hers, either, though Adam Nofftry did, so Landon probably heard it from him. But Adam called her Isabella, and she seems to prefer Izzy, at least for people she knows. Then, on Sunday afternoon, Izzy was in here most of the afternoon. That Landon guy came in, but although Izzy watched him, and he must have seen her there"—she pointed at the table where Izzy liked to sit—"they didn't speak to each other."

Vic tapped his pen on the glass tabletop. "Could they have been trying to look like they didn't know each other?"

Tom cleared his throat. "I was at the deep fryers and didn't notice any of this."

I pictured the scene as I remembered it. "I didn't get the impression that they were pretending not to know each other. When Landon came into Deputy Donut on Sunday, Izzy stared at him until that other woman came in and called him Landon. Then Izzy stopped watching him. Later she said she was disappointed because he seemed to have a girlfriend."

Vic stared at me as if willing me to say I believed that Izzy and Landon knew each other before he showed up on the property she was buying. It was a reasonable guess, but I thought it was wrong. I gave him my other theory. "Izzy claims that a grandfather gave her a lot of money. I wonder if Landon somehow found out about it and has come to the area to find her and maybe attach some of those funds to himself."

Vic actually seemed to take my idea seriously. "That wouldn't be unusual." He wrote in his notebook, and then looked up and told us, "You can reach me through Brent. If Landon comes in again, would you let Brent know?"

We said we would.

Tom added, "But we won't try any tricks to stall him. If he leaves, we'll tell you which direction he went and leave the rest to you."

Jocelyn winked at me. Tom's hint to us wasn't subtle.

Vic muttered, "We can hope that this Landon is the one person who didn't cause all of the donuts he bought here and the box they came in to suddenly and conveniently disappear."

I leaned forward. "I know that Izzy doesn't have an alibi for the entire time that Adam might have died. She was with her neighbors for part of the time, and with me for another part of it, but there were short stretches when she was on or near that hill by herself. Do our mayor and that TWIG chairperson, Ramona Schleehart, have alibis for Sunday afternoon?"

As if annoyed at me, Vic clipped his words. "People often don't have them. People are often alone at home or in their offices. That doesn't prove anything." He closed his notebook and stood. "We'll leave you four to continue closing up shop." He nodded toward Brent, and Brent stood, too.

Jocelyn jumped out of her seat and opened the door for them.

Slipping his notebook and pen into the inner pocket of his suit jacket, Brent smiled at me. "Don't expect me early."

I smiled back. "Okay."

Dep stared at us all from the back of the office couch. Brent waved at her and followed Vic out onto the street.

Brent arrived home earlier than we'd expected, and before I began planning dinner. I told him what Tom had said about Adam's having owned a series of resorts.

Brent loosened his tie. "It's an investigator's nightmare. Adam doesn't seem to have had a recognizable brand. The names he gave the resorts are all different, and he seemed to change the name of his company whenever he started a new business venture. Frequently. And many of them were co-owned by other companies. We have forensics accountants untangling it all. They'll succeed, eventually."

"Does he have heirs, family? Like maybe Jerry Creavus, Ramona Schleehart, or a mysterious man named Landon?"

"This will sound odd. We haven't found any relatives or a will. And he doesn't have many assets, as far as we can tell. He's squandered his profits over the years, and I'm not even sure that he could have found anyone to lend him enough for the property he wanted."

"He had a nice SUV."

"Leased."

"Jerry said he was a newcomer to the area. Where did he live?"

"He was renting a modest house south of downtown Fallingbrook. He usually moves into a trailer on his recently acquired properties until an owner's suite is ready for him. Oh, and by the way, neighbors saw him at his rental home the night before he died, which fits with the medical examiner's report. He was lying dead beside that pond only a short time before you heard Izzy scream. They can't pinpoint the exact time of death like they can on TV crime shows."

"I still can't believe that Izzy could have harmed him."

"You could be right. After talking to you folks at Deputy Donut this evening, we went up to Gooseleg. Izzy's neighbors were at home. They confirmed that Izzy was with them until about a half hour or less before she called you after seeing Adam's dusty SUV. They said that since the garbage was about to be collected, she took the donut box when she left and said she would put it out by the road with the rest of the garbage that she and her landlords had already put out. They don't know if she did put it there, and of course we can't know who actually collected it."

"So, Izzy's cleared of suspicion regarding Adam's murder?"

"Not for certain. She'd have had to go home right after she left Deputy Donut, make some extra donuts, take the originals to her neighbors, sit with them for a half hour eating donuts, go back to her place, put the new donuts into the old box, speed down to her property, force Adam to eat the donuts, and hide the box with leftover donuts in it for you to find. It's possible that she did all of that in a couple of hours, but not likely. She's not a prime suspect."

"Who is?"

"We don't have one." He took off his suit jacket. "I'll change into shorts and T-shirt, and then how about if I make dinner? Something decadent like steak, french fries, and wine?"

I stood on tiptoe and kissed him. "I'd like that."

Chapter 20

When Jerry arrived in Deputy Donut the next morning, I expected him to sit with the retired men or make the rounds of the room talking to potential voters.

Instead, he took a seat by himself next to the office. Maybe, now that he was running unopposed for mayor, he was curtailing some of his campaigning.

I headed toward him. Dep sat on the back of the couch, most likely staring cross-eyed at Jerry, but when she saw me near her window, she stood and stretched. Then she leaped down to the couch cushions and probably from there to the floor beside the door, expecting me to come in and play with or cuddle her.

Undoubtedly disappointing her, I didn't go into the office. I described the day's special coffee to Jerry. "It's not one of the single-origin coffees we usually offer. Today we're making dirty chai latte."

"Dirty?"

"Not really. It's basically tea with spices, a shot of espresso, and foamed milk. To go with it today, we've made spiced-tea donuts."

" 'Try anything once,' I always say. Sure, bring me a mug of the dirty chai and a couple of those donuts."

Several minutes later, I set his mug and plate in front of him.

He waved his hand over the top of the mug and inhaled. "This smells incredible. Do you have a moment, Emily? I have an idea that will interest you." With his foot, he pushed the other chair at his table into the aisle. "Have a seat."

"Okay, unless it gets busy in here." Not entirely comfortable with him, I perched on the edge of the chair and folded my hands in my lap.

"Do you have children, Emily?"

My face heated. Where was he going with this? "No."

"What about the other women who work here?"

"They don't, either."

"Supposing that one of you did, and you wanted to continue working here while keeping close track of them. What if a day care opened right next door?" He pointed at our north wall.

"It would be convenient, but there's no outdoor space where children could play. There's a sidewalk wide enough for a patio in front, buildings on both sides, and a parking lot in back, a parking lot in a whole chain of them behind our store and other businesses."

"Part of those parking lots could be rezoned into parkland. I get complaints about people speeding through those lots as an alternative to driving on Wisconsin Street. Several of the businesses along here would like to have the chain of parking lots broken up into smaller lots divided by green spaces. What do you think of that idea, Emily?"

"I like it. The lots back there are almost never full, and if there were a day care, parents would be dropping off their kids and picking them up, so only the staff might need parking spaces for more than a few minutes at a time."

He leaned closer. "We think alike. Now, here's another idea. The day care could be directly connected to Deputy Donut if you knocked out part of a wall, and then Deputy Donut employees and maybe customers, too, could check on the children without going outside."

Considering his suggestion, I couldn't help wrinkling my forehead. Our storeroom and the stairs to the basement were along our north wall. We couldn't break through the wall where the stairs were. If we knocked out a doorway between the two buildings, we would lose space in the storeroom. "I'm not sure that would work."

"Well, think about it. Or here's another idea. At some point, you might want to expand your dining area. You can't take up space to the south, since the driveway out there provides a way to and from the parking lots. Or maybe it could be turned into a little green space, if you and Thrills and Frills no longer wanted to have a driveway between your shops. There are infinite possibilities!"

"Yes, but—"

He waggled a finger at me. "You're wondering how you could start using the space beyond your north wall. Well, I'll tell you. I own that building, and I'm thinking of selling it. I'd offer you and Tom a favorable price. I'd like to see a good, attractive business like a day care or your expanded coffee shop go in there. It's been vacant for much too long." He told me the square footage. "And I'd be giving you and Tom a deal, if you were to buy it now and save me all the bother of advertising it, et cetera, et cetera."

"Well . . ."

"Y'know, expanding your shop would bring in income that would more than pay for the additional space."

I wasn't sure he was right. "I'll discuss it with Tom and let you know. But for now, more customers have come in, so I'll need to help serve them." I jumped to my feet more eagerly than was probably polite.

"Totally understandable. You have a good business head on your shoulders." He handed me his card. "My number's on there. Call and let me know what you and Tom decide."

I left him and circulated among our customers. Predictably, so did Jerry, but while I was offering donuts, fritters, coffee, and tea, he was offering people a chance to work on his mayoralty campaign. I heard him tell the Knitpickers, "Downtown Fallingbrook could use more parkland and less parking."

Priscilla snapped, "I don't want to have to walk farther from my car than I already do."

I didn't get a chance to talk to Tom until after we'd closed and were in the kitchen together mixing up dough for the next day. Olivia and Jocelyn were tidying the dining room. I told Tom about Jerry's proposal.

"Interesting," Tom said, "and I think he has some good ideas about breaking up the parking lots. But you and I know our financial situation. We're doing fine, better all the time, but many businesses go under after they expand too fast and borrow too much."

I covered my bowl of dough. "I don't want to borrow, and I don't think there's any other way to do it. The day care idea is interesting, but someone else can take that on. I don't want to. So, should I tell Jerry that we definitely don't want to buy his building?"

Tom slid our bowls of dough into the proofing cabinet, where they'd be kept at the right temperature and humidity all night. "Right. I saw inside it a couple of years ago, and whoever buys it is going to need to do a lot of repairing, no matter what business they put in there. He hasn't been able to rent or sell it, and I'm not surprised that he's trying a hard sell to unload it."

I gazed toward our building's north wall. "Do you know what I'd like? The chef who's renting Brent's and my house is considering opening a fine dining restaurant in the area. I'd love one in downtown Fallingbrook."

Smile crinkles appeared at the corners of Tom's eyes. "That would be nice."

"I'll tell Glenn about the opportunity. During our lease negotiations, he gave me his phone number, but it's about time for me to go over there and check on things and mow the lawn."

Before I left work, I wrote a note for Glenn with Jerry's phone number and the information that Jerry wanted to sell the building next to Deputy Donut. I didn't bother with an envelope. I folded the paper in fourths and scribbled Glenn's name on it. Then I left Dep behind and walked the route I'd often taken with her on her leash. A few blocks south on Wisconsin Street, I turned west on Maple Street into a neighborhood that had been laid out in the Victorian era. The older, larger homes were closest to Wisconsin Street. Tall maples and oaks still shaded the sidewalks, and front yards displayed long-popular shrubs like mock orange, bridal veil, and forsythia.

The house we were renting to Glenn was darling, yellow brick with ivory gingerbread trim, a broad and welcoming front porch, and a gothic gable window on the second story. Someone had been deadheading the nasturtiums in the window boxes hanging from the front porch railing, and a cheerful bouquet of marigolds was on the glass-topped wicker table between two white-painted wicker chairs on the porch.

And someone had mowed the tiny square of grass in the front yard, recently, judging by the pungent fragrance. Glenn was obviously a good tenant.

Admiring the stained glass windows above the large living room window and in the top of the ornate door, I climbed up to the porch and rang the bell.

No one answered. I slipped the note for Glenn into the mailbox.

Someone unlocked the inner door, opened it a crack, and left the screen closed. "We don't want any." The voice was female, and very cold.

Chapter 21

Suddenly, I was remembering standing on this very porch on a sunny afternoon with Alec and a real estate agent. From the living room, a voice had croaked, "Go away!"

I'd taken a step backward. Alec had cupped his hand around my elbow, a light touch, communicating love and courage.

Another woman had shouted, "Just a minute!" Seconds later, a young woman wheeled an elderly, blanket-swathed woman onto the porch. The woman in the wheelchair looked half-asleep.

Alec and I had spent lots of time touring the house. When we came outside, I told the woman in the wheelchair, "We love your house."

Her answer was gracious. "That's nice, dear."

And now, here I was again on that porch, and a different woman was telling me to go away. I called through the screen, "I'm Emily Fyne, and I just came by to see if Glenn needed anything. I was going to mow the lawn, but it doesn't need it. Does Glenn want me to mow the back?"

"He looks after all of that." Her voice was still cold, and now also disdainful.

"Is he here?"

"No." The front door was closing.

"I put a note in the mailbox for him." I didn't know who

she was, and maybe Glenn hadn't told her his landlady's name. I quickly said, "I'm renting this house to Glenn."

The front door stopped closing. "Why didn't you say? He's paid his rent."

"The note is not about this property. It's just something I thought he'd like to know..." Would Glenn want me divulging details about his restaurant plans to this unknown woman? I merely added, "About restaurants."

She opened the inner door just enough to unhook the screen door. The antique hook and its eye had come with the house. We had kept them because they were vintage, and we felt they belonged. We'd seldom used them, though, and had hooked the door to the jamb only when we wanted to keep the front door open for fresh air and needed to keep the screen door from banging in the wind.

Why had this woman hooked the screen door when the (distinctly non-Victorian) keyless entry to the inner door locked itself after only a few seconds of being closed? It had been locked when I arrived—I'd heard her turn the deadbolt.

She wasn't trying to keep Glenn out, was she? If so, it wouldn't work. The code I'd programmed for him also opened the overhead garage doors and the garage's side door. He could go through one of those doors into the garage and through its rear door to the walled yard, and then he could use the same code to unlock the door from the patio into the sunroom at the back of the house.

"Restaurants?" she repeated. "Well, in that case..." She stepped out onto the porch.

I backed up, not only because she was about to barge into me. Although she wore jeans and a silk blouse instead of a skirt and matching jacket, and her dark hair was not sleeked back but fell in waves to her shoulders, I recognized her. "You came into my donut shop."

"*Your* donut shop? I guess in a tiny town like this it's easy to own half the town. Anyway, I don't do donuts." She pulled the note out of the mailbox.

"Co-own," I clarified. "I co-own this house and Deputy Donut."

The haughty mouth twitched with something like difficult-to-contain amusement.

Trying not to show my annoyance, I told her, "You came into our shop and spoke to one of our customers. You called him Landon."

"Did I?"

Afraid she was going to disappear into the house before I could grill her about the mysterious Landon, I quickly made up a story. "That man might have left something behind in our shop. Do you know his last name?"

"No. Maybe it's Landon. Did you say he left something behind?" Her eyes were hard. She could probably tell I was lying.

"A key, like a house key. We noticed it shortly after he left, and we asked other customers. It wasn't theirs, so we figured it might be his. Do you know how to get in touch with him?"

"I barely know him, so, no. I must have met him at a party or something."

"I think the car he's driving has Minnesota plates."

"That's probably where I met him, at a party."

An interesting conversation, I thought, *with both of us politely spewing lies*. I knew better than to ask her about the donuts Landon had bought. She would undoubtedly pretend she hadn't noticed them and hadn't discussed them with him. Also, if anyone was going to question her about Landon's donuts, it would have to be Brent or Vic. I wasn't about to let her know that Landon's donuts might be important in a murder investigation.

I heard the familiar slam and bounce of the sunroom's screen door. A man called, "Hope?" I hadn't talked with Glenn much, but it sounded like his voice.

The woman half turned toward the living room. "I'm in the front. With your landlady." She made me sound about as old as the house. "Glenn's back," she told me unnecessarily. She must have realized that I would know he'd been on the property all along. He couldn't have returned without our seeing him unless he had scaled one of the high walls that surrounded the house's rear garden. Hope added, "He must have been outside."

Glenn came through the living room and joined us on the porch. "Hi, Emily. What's up?"

"I came to mow the lawn, but it's already been done. You don't have to mow or weed or do any of those things."

"I enjoy it. I just did the back, too." I realized that the smell of freshly mown grass was also coming from the grass-stained hems of his jeans. He added, "It's not like you have great, sweeping grounds."

"Thank you for doing it. I brought you some information I thought you'd like."

Hope leaned back against Glenn and handed him the note over her shoulder. She hadn't unfolded it. While he read it, she flashed a look at me. Triumphant? Wanting to show me that she'd never had the intention of destroying the note if, after she read it, she decided he shouldn't have it?

Her eyes were hazel like Izzy's. "Hope," I repeated. "Do you know Izzy Korinth?"

"Who?"

Glenn folded the note and shoved it into his jeans pocket and put an arm around Hope's waist. "Your cousin."

The corners of her mouth turned up in something that was definitely not a smile. "Izzy? I don't know anyone with that name."

I doubted that, but I explained, "Her full name's Isabella."

"Oh, her. I haven't seen her in years, but I think she lives around here somewhere. Do you know her?"

"Yes."

Hope snuggled into Glenn's embrace. "Great! That's partly why I'm here. When I found out that Glenn was coming out here, I decided to take my vacation with him and see if I could reconnect with her. Do you know how to contact her?"

I didn't quite trust her sudden transformation into a friendly person excited to see a long-lost cousin. I had Izzy's phone number, but I wasn't going to give it to anyone without her permission. I told Hope, "Izzy often comes into Deputy Donut. The next time I see her, shall I tell her to come over here to meet you?"

Hope pinched her lips together. "I might not be here."

Glenn suggested, "Why don't you give Emily your phone number, and she can pass it on to your cousin?"

Hope's resistant expression didn't change. "I suppose that makes sense." She rattled off her number.

I entered it into my phone. "I'll tell her."

Hope reached back for the screen door. "I look forward to catching up with her." She would have been as convincing if she'd said she couldn't wait to be bitten by a rattlesnake. "Thanks for stopping by, Emma."

"Emily," Glenn corrected her.

My smile was about as sincere as Hope's words. "You're welcome. As always, let me know if you need anything or have any questions." I trotted down the porch steps and strode to the sidewalk. Behind me, I heard the screen door bang against the jamb, heard the hook that I had almost never used squeak into place, and then I heard the front door close. Whoever shut it didn't wait for the deadbolt to automatically engage. They turned it immediately, causing it to make the mechanical growl it would have made by itself.

They had to know that I had my own code and could unlock the door whenever I wanted or needed to. Maybe that's why they were hooking the screen. "Not that I would barge in," I muttered, "without giving them notice, or if they asked me to go in and fix something. And besides, I could go in through the garage, and unless they've installed one, the screen door in back doesn't have a hook or a lock."

I headed back toward Deputy Donut and the small, fuzzy cat who was probably already feeling abandoned.

I took her home and made a pasta salad with more green beans and tomatoes from our garden, and a tangy dressing. I covered the bowl and put it into the fridge.

By nine, I was hungry and about to eat without Brent, but I heard his step on the porch and ran to greet him. Dep galloped beside me. Brent swept us into his arms and buried his face in my hair. "You're so good to come home to."

Eventually, we remembered that we hadn't eaten dinner. I added chunks of Wisconsin gouda and freshly grated parmesan to the salad and took it out to the catio. Sitting across from Brent, I told him about Jerry's offer to sell the building on the north side of Deputy Donut.

His face neutral, Brent listened carefully. "Have you and Tom made a decision?" He gave no hint of his opinion.

"We decided we didn't want to take it on. We like things the way they are."

"You two are good at knowing what you want."

"But I have occasionally been slow to express it."

A smile lit those gray eyes. He murmured, "Me, too, but we did finally come to our senses."

Maybe it was a good thing that there was a table between us, or we might not have finished our dinner. I cooled the temperature. "But I figured out who should buy that building—our tenant Glenn. I would love to have a great restaurant next door to Deputy Donut. I took a note about the offer to our house on Maple Street, and you'll never guess who opened the door."

"From the way you asked, I'd say it wasn't Glenn."

"It was the woman who got into the mysterious Landon's car on Monday night after the TWIG meeting."

Brent tilted his head in a question.

"She's also the woman who called him Landon in Deputy Donut. Izzy said at the time that the woman reminded her of her cousin Hope, and Glenn called the woman Hope. Both women have hazel eyes and similar petite builds, but their personalities seem to be total opposites. I asked Hope if she knew Izzy, and after she determined that I was talking about Isabella, Hope claimed she came to Fallingbrook to join Glenn, but also to search for her long-lost cousin."

"I detect some skepticism, Em."

"She walked right past Izzy in Deputy Donut, but maybe she was distracted by seeing a man she knew. Maybe I just didn't like Hope, based on the rude comment she made about donuts. Nearly everyone in our shop could have heard her."

He grinned. "She probably didn't convert any of them into donut-detesters. Didn't you say she walked out of Deputy Donut with Landon?"

"Yes. This evening, I told her he'd left a key in Deputy Donut, which isn't true, and asked her if she knew how to get in touch with him. She said she barely knew him and wasn't sure if Landon was his first or last name. But on Monday evening, she got into his car. You see why I'm skeptical of anything she says."

"And when she called him by name in Deputy Donut, didn't you tell me that he had just bought donuts?"

"Yes." I raised a finger in the air. "I carefully did not ask her about what he did with those donuts. I didn't want to edge into your territory."

He reached across the table and covered my hand with his. "Thank you."

"What if, despite Hope's apparent dislike of donuts, she got Landon to give her the entire box? If there's one person in town who might be good at replicating other people's recipes, it could be Glenn. I know. I'm reaching."

"It's as good a theory as any." He always kept his police notebook nearby. He wrote in it, and then we finished our dinner.

I purposely didn't tell him one thing about my day—Jerry's suggestion that with three women working at Deputy Donut, opening an adjoining day care might be a good idea. Brent wanted children as much as I did, and I didn't want to force him to pretend he wasn't sad because I had not yet become pregnant. We had discussed adoption, and possibly adopting older children, since we were getting older ourselves, but even if we decided to adopt, I might still need tests and surgery.

Chapter 22

The next day was Saturday, and all of us were working. Midway through the morning, Tom was frying donuts, and Olivia was near him in the kitchen, arranging her decorated donuts on trays. Jocelyn and I had served everyone in our dining room. Jocelyn started making a pot of coffee, and I cleaned the serving counter next to our display case.

Izzy bounded into Deputy Donut and came to me. "Guess what!" She included Olivia and Jocelyn in her glance.

Olivia quickly slid a tray into the display case, and Jocelyn flipped the coffeemaker's switch to 'on.' Jocelyn and Olivia joined me at the service counter. We all asked Izzy, "What?"

Izzy did a little dance. "The woman I thought was my cousin Hope really is my cousin. She lives in New York, but she came up here to try to find me. As she said, we don't have many family members, and it's a shame to lose track of the ones we do have." Looking barely older than a child in her red T-shirt, denim cutoffs, and sandals, she scooted onto a stool.

I had not yet given Izzy Hope's phone number. I asked, "How did she locate you?"

"Looked me up online. Isn't it exciting?" Apparently Izzy had forgiven me for telling Brent about her taking peach pits from our compost.

Jocelyn agreed with her. "That is exciting."

Olivia folded her arms. "I don't like how just anyone can look us up online and contact us."

Izzy wriggled on the stool. "But she's my cousin! Don't you think it's exciting, Emily?"

"I was excited to meet you again after all those years." I thought, but didn't say, that it was odd that Hope had been in town for several days before she supposedly looked Izzy up, and even odder, considering that when I'd left Hope and Glenn the evening before, Hope had expected me to give her phone number to Izzy.

Maybe Glenn, who seemed more interested in Hope's cousin than Hope did, encouraged Hope to find Izzy. And why would that be? Did Glenn and Hope know about the money that Hope and Izzy's grandfather had sent Izzy? Were they and Landon all interested in relieving Izzy of some of that money? Hope's story that she barely knew Landon had to be a lie. I'd seen her get into his car and ride away with him, toward, as it turned out, the house Hope's boyfriend was renting.

I asked Izzy, "Didn't you say that your and Hope's fathers stopped talking to each other?"

Izzy flipped her hand back as if batting a fly off her shoulder. "That's that generation. Ours can do what we want. And here's the great part—she invited me to dinner at the house she's renting."

I gave the counter another wipe. "Guess who she's renting it from."

Izzy clutched at the throat of her T-shirt. "Mr. Mystery? Landon?"

"No, Brent and me. At least her boyfriend, Glenn, is renting it from us."

Izzy's hazel eyes became wider, and her mouth drooped. "Is Glenn Mr. Mystery? Is his name Glenn Landon, and Hope's his girlfriend?"

I patted the counter beside her hand. "Don't worry. Glenn

and Landon are two different people. And you're probably in for a treat if Glenn does the cooking. He's a chef."

Jocelyn elbowed Olivia. "The chef isn't single, after all."

Olivia glanced out toward the sunny street. "I thought he was too old, anyway."

Jocelyn's eyes glinted. "And then someone younger and handsomer came along."

Olivia blushed. "Stop it."

But Jocelyn didn't stop. "And he blushes whenever he sees you."

Olivia returned to the marble island in the center of the kitchen. Still baiting Olivia, Jocelyn headed for the coffee carafe she'd turned on. The coffee was almost ready.

Izzy gazed toward the tempting donuts in our display case. "Her boyfriend is a chef? That sounds wonderful. They must know hardly anyone around here. Wouldn't it be wonderful if they invited Landon, too?"

"Not," I said dryly, "if he's a murderer."

"He isn't. He can't be. I won't let him." She turned her innocent gaze on me. "Why would you suspect him?"

"Because he was there the day before Adam died, and he was arguing with Adam."

"Adam was doing the arguing. That was just how he was. Landon and I defended ourselves. Verbally. That doesn't mean that either of us set out to murder Adam." She spun her stool toward Dep, watching us through the office window, and then spun back to me. "Oh! I might have figured something out. The police seem to think that the donuts I bought had something to do with Adam's death. And peach pits were somehow involved. And Landon bought donuts that day, too, and that's why you suspect him." Her smile wavered. "And you don't suspect me because you know I would never hurt anyone. Never."

"I believe you, but Hope is unlikely to invite Landon to

dinner. I asked her about him. She said he was only an acquaintance."

"At least he's not her boyfriend." Izzy raised her hands in the air and snapped her fingers. "I have a chance!" Sliding forward on the stool, she risked falling off it. "What's your special coffee today, and what donuts do you recommend to go with it?"

"Today we have a single-origin coffee from Guatemala. It's a dark roast with hints of caramel, brown sugar, and citrus."

"Is it bold enough for me?"

"Is anything?"

"Maybe mysterious men with brooding eyes."

"I'm going to ignore that. How about a fudge donut with caramel drizzled over the fudge frosting?"

"Sounds good." She turned the stool until it faced our south wall. "How about if I sit at my regular table? It's free at the moment."

"Be my guest."

"It's just that"—she gave me her most impish look—"you'll have to carry it farther, at your advanced age."

"I think I can manage."

I took the plate and mug to her at her favorite table. She was staring toward a painting on the wall between the dining area and the hallway to the restrooms. "That little waterfall could almost be one of the ones on my property."

"It's pretty, isn't it? The artwork on our walls is for sale through The Craft Croft, the artists' co-op down the street."

"I've heard of it. Emily, I was just thinking. You have a reputation."

"Uh-oh." I thought I knew what was coming.

"A good one. My lawyers said that you've helped solve murders in the past."

"I didn't do much. I was in the right place—though some might say it was the wrong place—at the right time, and even before I married Brent, I could tell him things I happened to find out, like from listening to conversations in here."

"But Landon and I might be suspected of murder, and that just isn't fair. We're not murderers."

I didn't think Brent would want me to tell Izzy that, as far as he was concerned, she wasn't a prime suspect, so I didn't, and I also didn't confirm that, as far as I knew, both Brent and Vic still suspected Landon. I asked, "Do you have any idea who might have wanted Adam dead?"

"Ramona Schleehart, the TWIG lady, for sure. Even though Adam wasn't going to be able to buy the place I'm buying, he would have probably opened a resort in the area sooner or later, and he would have had to cut down trees. And then there's Fallingbrook's mayor, Jerry Creavus. He's a phony. He's been pretending he likes my idea for greenhouses, but I think that was just because he didn't want Adam to succeed at anything. Adam was running against Jerry Creavus for mayor. And now he isn't. He can't because he's dead. So, I'm betting one of them did him in, and it might not have had anything to do with donuts. So, what if you and I put our heads together to try to figure out which one of them—or both—killed Adam?"

"Welllll . . ."

"Your husband probably has to work late. Come up to my place after work, and we can order a pizza or something while we figure things out."

"With your aerial photos and your paper cutouts resembling greenhouses?"

"I'll make other cutouts. One for Mayor Creavus and some for Ramona and her followers."

"That sounds like fun. Is it okay if I bring my cat, or should I take her home first? Our place is on the way to Gooseleg."

Izzy clapped her hands and sent a warm smile toward our office. Dep was still sitting on the back of the couch, but she had turned around, probably to continue watching us. With her eyes half closed, the little cat looked about to fall asleep. "Bring her! She's darling."

"And the dinner with Hope isn't tonight?"

"That's tomorrow. My place is just west of Gooseleg. You can get there by going straight up County Road C and taking the turnoff to Gooseleg and driving through Gooseleg and out the other side, but I'm sure you'd prefer the scenic route, which just happens to go past where I'm going to build my greenhouses."

I made a face that I hoped looked serious and earnest. "I'm sure that's the best route."

She giggled. "Follow County Road H until it ends at Pioneer Trail. Turn right and keep going, over the Gooseleg River. I don't know what poor goose they named the river and the town after. I've never seen a goose with legs as crooked as the bend in that river."

I laughed. "Neither have I. People always wonder that. Maybe it wasn't a poor goose, maybe the river and town were named by someone who had never seen a goose."

"So, I guess you know that there's a second bridge that goes over the railway tracks?"

"I've been up there."

"The driveway to my place is after the second bridge, the first turn on the left. My neighbors use the same driveway. After it divides, the right branch goes to my neighbors' house, which is closer to the road. The left branch goes farther back and ends at my place."

"That sounds easy enough. I can be there a little after six."

"Great!" As always, Izzy seemed more excited than other people would be in the same situation. "And for sure, bring your darling cat!"

Chapter 23

After work, I put Dep and a small box of donuts into my car. I was sure that Izzy wouldn't mind if I came to dinner in my Deputy Donut shorts and shirt. Besides, by not going home to change first, I would have time to take Izzy's preferred "scenic route." I drove up County Road C and turned left on H.

Between grasses the color of straw, the farm track leading to the creek looked undisturbed, as if no one had driven along it recently or had collected an autoinjector that might or might not have had anything to do with Adam's death.

Without Izzy waiting on the side of the road, I couldn't tell for sure where her property was. Coming from the east, no one would be able to see the break in the nearly solid line of pines where the trail led up to the meadows. There was no police tape, and I might not have been certain where Izzy's future property was if it hadn't been for the small green and white sign stuck haphazardly into the ground among weeds on the land sloping upward beyond the ditch. I slowed. SAVE OUR TREES, the sign said, above the acronym TWIG. I crept a little farther, stopped, and craned my neck so I could see back over my right shoulder. I could just barely make out the trail winding upward between pines.

I continued slowly along the road. It curved toward the right and started downhill. A miniature cascade of water tumbled from the woods above the road and ran into the ditch. It must have been almost below the dammed-up pond where Izzy had come upon Adam's body. I caught a glimpse of a break in the pines—another former driveway, possibly also from early settler days? County Road H continued downward, and I realized that it skirted the hill where Izzy's property was near the top. Evergreens lined both sides of the road, occasionally blocking the sun's rays. A blue jay darted between treetops.

At the end of H, I turned right, onto Pioneer Trail. It took me gradually into the Gooseleg River valley. Crossing the bridge over the river, I caught glimpses of rapids, like froths of lace decorating the water's velvety teal surface. The railroad tracks mostly followed the river, but the elbow in the river was sharp, and the tracks made a wide, gentle curve around it. The farthest part of the arc looked about a half mile inland from the river. My tires rumbling over expansion joints, I crossed the second bridge. That bridge sloped down onto level land, and I turned left onto the driveway leading to Izzy's place.

Branches arched over the driveway, and the nearly weedless grass on both sides had been recently mown. Everything seemed green and tranquil. I took the narrower left branch of the driveway. No one had cut the weeds close to this section. Butterflies flitted among the white and lavender asters and the deep yellow goldenrod that took advantage of sunlight filtering through the leafy canopy.

The driveway led into a clearing surrounded by tall trees. At the far side of the clearing, a bright red caboose sat on a set of railroad tracks. Tubs of flowers lined the edge of a deck along the length of the caboose. To the left, green beans twined up poles, tomatoes ripened, and the rounded sides of butternut and pattypan squash showed above floppy leaves. Near the other end of the caboose, a small greenhouse, plastic tarps draped over a framework of two-by-fours, held pots containing plants that I couldn't identify through the semi-translucent plastic.

Izzy's car was parked in the shade of a massive oak.

Grinning and waving, Izzy stood up from a chair beside an umbrella table on the deck. She ran down the steps and called out, "Park anywhere!" She was still wearing the outfit she'd had on in Deputy Donut, a red T-shirt, cutoffs, and sandals.

I pulled in beside her car, attached Dep's leash to her harness, and let her walk, stopping to investigate bugs and random blades of grass, across the lawn. Izzy bent, cooed to Dep, and petted her.

I gazed around the serene oasis. "Wow, Izzy, you do go for the unusual, don't you? This place is charming, and right out of a storybook."

She straightened and beamed. "Isn't it wonderful? I'm only renting, but I hope to stay here for a long time. I love it."

I handed her the box of donuts. "I didn't want to go home for wine."

"Yum. I like these better, and I'm not even going to share them with you. I'll have them for breakfast in the morning. Come on up, and I'll show you around."

To my left, unseen vehicles rattled over the nearest bridge. I couldn't hear the river or anything on the bridge crossing it. Behind me and to the right, I heard the *da-bop, da-bop, da-bop* of a tennis game, shouts of jubilation when someone must have scored a point, and excited woofs from what sounded like an enormous dog. "My neighbors," Izzy explained. "They're very nice. They don't bother me, and the tennis and swimming pool noises are happy ones. And the dog is a lovable galumph who can flatten tomato plants in a second."

Judging by the voices, the teenaged boys she'd mentioned were probably the ones playing tennis. "Are those the neighbors who helped eat your donuts?" The woods hid the house from me, and the tennis court couldn't have been very close to Izzy's charming caboose and yard.

"Yes. They own this place, and they let me have a garden and erect my pet greenhouse."

I grasped Dep's leash more firmly. "Pets?"

"I don't have animals, but that greenhouse is like a pet for the bigger ones I plan."

"Were you doing all of this gardening before your grandfather sent you money?"

"That's how I knew what I wanted to do with it."

Walking to the deck took time. Again Dep attempted to sniff out beetles or other crawly things.

Izzy led me along the deck past the umbrella table, which was set for two, to the steel porch at the east end of the caboose. "Would you and Dep like a tour of my tiny house?"

"I'd love one. I'll carry Dep to keep her out of trouble."

Izzy scratched Dep's chin. "You wouldn't cause trouble, would you, sweetie?" Dep purred. Izzy opened the door into a minuscule but perfect kitchen. The caboose was about nine feet wide inside, with no hallways. We went from the kitchen to a combination office and living room with a two-seater sofa, a table big enough for two place settings and for working at the laptop computer on it, a comfy-looking desk chair, and a second chair. Izzy explained, "In case two of us need to eat indoors." I could see her imagining Landon folding himself into the small space. Bookcases hung on the walls between the caboose's original windows. The books I noticed were mostly about nature and gardening.

Beyond a pocket door, Izzy's bedroom featured a bunk bed, the kind with a double bed at the bottom and a single bed on top. "My landlords set this up so that a family could stay here. The loveseat in the living room can be opened into a small bed, too. And look at this. It's probably original to the caboose. Maybe they kept food in it?" A full-length metal cabinet served as her closet. She opened a door beyond the bed. "And here's the bathroom." It was big enough for a toilet, sink, shower, small linen closet, and a stacked washer and dryer. She opened the caboose's back door to another steel porch, again part of the original caboose. "And if I get muddy in the garden, I can come in this way and wash up in the bathroom. And look at this!" She closed the back door and slid an enormous bolt into an equally huge steel loop. "Originally, the caboose's door bolts would have been on the outside. They moved them inside. I can lock the place from outside or inside, but if I want to feel doubly secure, I can throw these bolts."

Everything in the tiny home was beautifully designed and finished. "I see why you love it here."

"Not just the caboose, which I adore, but also the setting. The beauty is relaxing, I can think and make plans without people bothering me. If I want company, I can visit my neighbors, go into town, or come down to Fallingbrook. And it doesn't take long for the police to search a tiny home and be confident that they didn't miss even a crumb."

Still carrying Dep, I followed Izzy back to the kitchen. "I hope that never happens again."

"How likely would that be? Is it okay if we eat outside?"

"That would be great."

Izzy opened the oven door. "The pizza came shortly before you arrived. I stuck it into the oven, which isn't turned on but has good insulation, to keep it warm."

"I'll take Dep outside and come back to help carry things." Out on the deck, I looped Dep's leash around a leg of the umbrella table. Izzy put the pizza box and a pie server on the table, and then I followed her back to the kitchen.

She took a bowl out of the fridge. "I'm not much of a cook, but the salad is fresh from my garden, picked today.

What would you like to drink?" She listed options, including a hoppy, sparkling, non-alcoholic drink from a local craft brewery.

Knowing how delicious the beer-like beverage was, I chose that, and she handed me two cans of it.

We took them and the salad to the table.

Sliding gooey, cheese-covered slices onto our plates, Izzy apologized. "You'd have made it yourself, from scratch."

"Not like this." I pointed at the charred blisters on the crust. "I don't have a wood-fired oven. I'd order this, too, if I lived near Gooseleg."

The boys must have ended their tennis game and taken the dog inside. The traffic on the railway bridge, what little there had been, diminished, and now the loudest sounds were cicadas singing in trees and crows shouting dares at one another. Dep's leash, still looped around the table leg, was long enough to allow her to jump into my lap. She curled into a ball and purred.

Izzy and I demolished the pizza and salad, and then Izzy brought out bowls of fresh raspberries and cream for dessert. "The raspberry canes are on the far side of the garden."

I tasted the berries. "Sweet, tart, and scrumptious. What a great place you have!" I glanced in the direction of the train tracks and river, but all I could see were trees. "I haven't heard a train. Do they go by often?"

"That line is hardly used anymore. The most likely time to hear one is around two in the morning. I love the sound of it, so I don't mind, even when it makes that haunting wail for the crossing way up the river. It echoes from hill to hill."

We cleared our dishes, took them inside, and washed and put them away, and then Izzy offered, "Would you like to see the few planted peach pits that the police didn't take away?"

"Sure."

She ushered Dep and me into the greenhouse, which had

barely enough room for two humans to turn from one set of shelves to the ones across from them. Dep stuck her head underneath a bottom shelf. Izzy picked up a pot, dug into it with a teaspoon-sized trowel, and popped out a peach stone, its indentations clogged with dirt. "See? None of them had sprouted, and the shells weren't even cracked. However, they took all of the kernels I'd painstakingly removed from their shells. Luckily, they left me a few of these." She pushed the stone into the soil, tamped it down, and set the pot on the shelf. "I would never grind up the inner part of a peach pit. I want to grow trees, not destroy their seeds. That makes no sense."

"Where did you put the shells that you took off the kernels?"

She pointed toward the woods behind the caboose. "I carried them down a path back there and buried them. Don't look so horrified! I told the pointy-nosed detective where I'd put them, and we all, including my lawyers, tramped back there, and the detective's people dug them up, along with some of the other things I'd composted there recently, like corn cobs that take a long time to decompose. I have a compost bin for things that disintegrate quickly, like the peach skins I got from behind your shop." She fanned her face. "You're turning red. Sorry it's so warm in here."

I looked down at my cat, luxuriously rolling around. "I think Dep likes it."

"I dried catnip in here last summer. Let's go back to the deck. I'll bring out my laptop, and we can develop a plan for figuring out who might have ground up some peach seeds and put them into donuts that he or she fed Adam. Plus, I suspect from the disappointment on that pointy-nosed detective's face when he couldn't find any almonds in my kitchen that someone might have added almonds to the donuts. Though, why they would, I don't know. Those donuts were delicious. Oh, and I guess there was a spice the investigators were searching for, too, as if the donuts we found on my property had a spice in them that you didn't put in your donuts?" Although she posed it as a question, I didn't answer, and she made another hint. "Whatever it was, they didn't find it here."

"Hmm." I still didn't let on that I believed they'd been looking for cardamom.

Walking across the lawn toward the deck, she repeated that Adam had had no hope of preventing the sale of the property to her. "And even if he could have, like if he could have successfully pressured the current owner to back out of the contract, I could have found another property that I'd like almost as much or maybe even better. All I'd have lost is time."

I didn't point out that, if what she'd told me before was true about her grandfather expecting her to show him in a year that she'd begun a viable business, losing time could have been crucial.

She brought out her laptop plus a pitcher of ice water with lemon slices in it. She went back for glasses and then poured the drinks.

She pulled a couple of pieces of paper from her pocket. With a sly look at me from beneath her eyelashes, she set a couple of cutouts on the table. One was a tall man with the initial J on his T-shirt. The other was a short woman wearing a green T-shirt emblazoned with TWIG.

I burst out laughing. We sat down in front of the laptop. After making certain that both of us could read the screen, Izzy started a spreadsheet with columns for Jerry Creavus and Ramona Schleehart.

I asked, "Should we have a column for the mysterious Landon?"

Izzy made a face but gave him one, too. Then, with her hands in fists, she straightened her arms above her keyboard.

"I'm not making a column for myself or for you folks at Deputy Donut. That would be ridiculous. We need to focus on these three people, well, really, on Jerry and Ramona."

Izzy typed Jerry's name into a search engine. He belonged to every service club in Fallingbrook and had been mayor for several years. He owned a small and fairly primitive hunting camp on a wooded acreage that he sometimes rented to outsiders. I considered telling Izzy that Jerry also owned the vacant building next to Deputy Donut, but I decided that the information probably wasn't helpful.

On the spreadsheet, Izzy typed a comment under Jerry's name. "Potential competition in renting out vacation cabins." She looked up at me. "Maybe Jerry was hoping that Adam would buy his property. But Jerry could have offered it to Adam. Maybe he did, and Adam turned it down. That could have made Jerry mad."

Dep leaped into my lap. I stroked her. "Mad enough to kill?"

Izzy added that idea to Jerry's column. "Who knows? But Jerry must want to stay on as mayor, and Adam posed a threat to him that way. I don't know what other income Jerry has besides what he gets as mayor. Legitimate income, that is." She made a note in Jerry's column about Jerry not wanting Adam to become mayor.

She moved the cursor to Ramona's column and typed in Ramona's fear that Adam might one day cut down trees to build a resort. Izzy opened the search engine again. "Let's see what Ramona has been up to."

I didn't tell Izzy about Jerry's allegations against Ramona, and there was nothing online about Ramona's having been suspected of giving someone an insulin overdose. We found that she'd always participated in causes related to the environment, and ever since she retired from nursing, she'd been even more active in her environmental work.

I knew that Jerry was single. It appeared that Ramona was, too.

Izzy made the two paper dolls dance along the edge of the table. "Maybe it's time for a little matchmaking, even if she is almost twenty years older than he is. Maybe having a younger boyfriend would improve her outlook on life. I don't understand why she has to be so grumpy all the time. Is that any way to get people to join your cause? But maybe she's friendlier when she's talking to people in her organizations."

"She isn't, at least not much." I told Izzy about the TWIG meeting on Monday evening.

Izzy made the TWIG paper doll take a bow. "I wish I'd known about it. I'd have come, too."

Reluctantly, it seemed, she typed the name Landon into the search engine. That brought up thousands of entries. Adding Duluth didn't lower the number much. She joked, "See, there's nothing nefarious about him." She plunked an elbow on the table and rested her chin in her palm. "Our spreadsheet isn't helping a lot."

Again, I couldn't tell Izzy that I'd surmised from Vic that neither Jerry nor Ramona had alibis for the time that Adam probably died. Our "joint" effort at sleuthing was mostly Izzy coming up with the ideas and adding them to her spreadsheet. She pointed at the column she'd set up for Landon. "What if he gave the donuts he bought to someone else, someone we don't know about, who was Adam's sworn enemy?"

"Like your cousin Hope? He offered to share them with her."

"But then she said something rude about your donuts." Izzy turned to me, excited. "So, she could have done something to those donuts and fed them to Adam!" Izzy slumped in her chair. "How can I say that about my own cousin? For one thing, why would she do that?"

"Could Hope be jealous because your grandfather contacted you after a long time and sent you money?"

"I suppose it's possible, but Hope might not know that he

gave me money or even that he's in touch with me again. I'm glad that he is. Maybe he's forgiven my father for refusing to work for him."

"But if Hope did know that your grandfather is no longer estranged from you, and she's jealous about it, she has a reason to harm someone—anyone—on your property. She might expect you to be blamed, and your grandfather might never speak to you again."

"That sounds like a roundabout way to sabotage someone."

"It does. I'm just thinking outside the boxes on our spreadsheet. And finding a way to show that your Landon is innocent."

"That's a plus, I guess. I wonder if Hope still works for our grandfather." Izzy searched for the name "Hope Korinth" and showed me the results. "Just as I suspected, she's still at one of his companies. But look at this—she's now Executive Director of Marketing in one division of one of the companies. Whoop-de-do. And she told me her boyfriend's last name. It starts with an S."

"Sitherby."

"That's it." She typed it into the search engine. "He's worked his way up as a chef. It looks like he owned a restaurant called Hot Pepper in upstate New York. It doesn't say if he still owns it, but it looks like he has since worked in at least one other restaurant, Purple Pepper."

"He said he wanted to name the restaurant he's planning something like Sweet Pepper."

"I'll add him and Hope to my spreadsheet, but I don't have much to say about them. She might have killed Adam because she's jealous of me, or Glenn might have killed Adam because he . . . because he wants to do a favor for his girlfriend?" And then she made the same suggestion I'd made to Brent, though it had seemed far-fetched at the time. "A chef would be able to copy other people's donuts without needing the recipe, right?"

"Probably."

After Izzy finished adding those clues to cells in her spreadsheet, I asked, "Can you search for Hot Pepper and Purple Pepper restaurants?"

She did and sagged back in her chair. "Purple Pepper might still be open. I can't tell. Reviews are mediocre and none are recent. Hot Pepper closed over five years ago. But it had great reviews."

"You'll have a fantastic meal tomorrow."

"You and your husband could sort of drop in on landlordly business right before dinner. I bet they'd ask you to stay."

"That's a great, if devious, idea. Don't you think that a chef will have everything planned down to the last bite? He won't have extra servings for drop-ins."

"Restaurants do."

"True, and with luck, Brent will have finished the investigation by then." I patted the kitty nestled in my lap and thought, *If so, we'll probably want a nice, quiet evening at home together.* I said aloud, "Speaking of which, I should get going in case he finishes whatever he's doing earlier than most evenings lately." I plucked Dep off my lap. Still hugging her, I unfastened her leash from the table leg.

Izzy walked us to my car and helped insert my recalcitrant kitty into her carrier. Dep did not approve.

I started down the tree-shadowed driveway and glanced into the rearview mirror. Looking small and alone back there in her cutoffs, T-shirt, and sandals, Izzy waved. The driveway curved slightly toward her neighbors' place, and I could no longer see her.

I remembered the little girl telling me a tearful goodbye that day, years ago, at Fallingbrook Falls. "I'll come back someday, okay, Emily?"

And she had, finally, but it would never be the same.

Because of the overhanging trees, it was already dusk on that driveway, including the wider section. I turned on my headlights. At Pioneer Trail, I stopped. I was about to turn right, toward the bridges, and go back the way I'd come, past the property where Adam had died.

I checked to my left for approaching vehicles.

There were none, but a car with its bright red taillights shining was on the right shoulder about fifty feet away. I couldn't see the car well, but it was a dark color, and the lit plate on the back had those greenish swaths across the top and bottom, like it could have been from Minnesota.

Chapter 24

The car's brake lights flashed on and then off. Someone was in the driver's seat.

That person could have noticed my headlights and my white car nosing out toward the road. I shifted into reverse and eased away until my car was, just barely, hidden by trees.

I'd possibly called attention to myself with the maneuver. I turned off the engine to extinguish the lights. The sudden lack of glow at the end of the driveway was probably obvious, too, if the person in the car was paying attention to what was going on behind him.

I flicked off the interior lights, opened the door, and left it gaping. Listening for sounds of the dark car turning and rushing toward me, I ran on tiptoe almost to the road and peeked around a tree trunk. I hoped that none of my shirt, even whiter than my car, showed.

The dark car edged out onto the road, allowing me to see more of it from the side. It definitely resembled the car Landon had been driving. And from what little I could see of the silhouette of the driver's head, I thought the driver was a man, possibly Landon. If there were passengers, I couldn't see them.

Ready to pivot and run to my car if the other one turned

toward me, I watched until he started driving east, away from me.

I ran back to my car, slammed myself inside, and started the engine. With only my daytime running lights on, I drove to Pioneer Trail and stopped.

The dark car was gaining speed toward Gooseleg. To my right, a black pickup truck came down off the bridge. I waited for it to pass and then swung into the lane behind it. I stayed below the speed limit, and the distance between us increased. As soon as the two vehicles were far enough ahead, I turned on my headlights and accelerated to approximately the speed the pickup was going. I kept up that pace until, ahead of me, the sedan and pickup entered downtown Gooseleg and slowed down. I braked, too.

Gooseleg was smaller than Fallingbrook. Focusing on the dark sedan in front of the pickup truck, I caught glimpses of some of the town's businesses. A pub's patio was crowded, with candles already lit on tables. A laughing couple carried flat white boxes out of Izzy's favorite pizza shop. I passed a barbershop, a library, and a tiny museum, all of them dark and closed for the evening.

On the other side of Gooseleg's business section, homes on large lots lined the road. The dark sedan turned right, but because of the pickup truck and a bright yellow convertible that had slipped in between me and the pickup, I couldn't see the dark sedan's entire side or the license plate. The car was gray, shiny, and new. I couldn't rule out that it was the one I'd seen Landon driving.

I slowed and put on my right turn signal.

A sign at the intersection warned that the road was a dead end.

I didn't turn. I wasn't about to drive into a trap, and if Landon had not already recognized my car, I wasn't about to put myself into a spot where he might get a better look at it and at me.

My heart beat hard, and my shoulders tensed. Why had the man, whoever he was, been near Izzy's driveway? And why, more than a week ago, had Landon been walking on the property she was buying? What was his connection with Izzy's cousin, and why had Hope said she barely knew him?

Izzy might have a black belt in karate, but was she safe from the man she called Mr. Mystery, the man she wanted to know better? Was Hope safe from him?

I had my car phone Izzy. I told her what I'd seen and added, "This might be a good time for you to bolt yourself inside."

She promised that she would.

Biting my lip, I drove on. Now that I was on the east side of Gooseleg, I was on the shorter route home, and there was no point in driving past the hillside where Adam had died. It was nearly dark, and I wasn't likely to see more than TWIG's crookedly placed sign.

I passed scrubby fields and wooded hillsides. Ponds were almost as dark and calm as polished onyx. No vehicles were ahead of or behind me, and when I stopped at County Road C, none were coming in either direction. Dep moaned, but softly. I turned south, toward home. The moon was a white crescent high in the pale indigo and still starless sky.

I had the road to myself, so when I saw an intersection ahead, I slowed. The road leading off to the right was County Road J. I turned and pulled onto J's shoulder. According to my car's navigation system, J curved west and then south, skirting Chicory Lake, and ending a mile or so beyond the state forest boundary without intersecting with H or going close to Izzy's property. Before County Road J dead-ended, a minor road or track led south from it. I enlarged the map. It didn't show that track meeting the one that ran north from H, but they could have connected, if only as a path tramped out by deer and other animals. The stream didn't appear to be much farther from J than it was from H.

Stars began to show in the deepening blue sky. Brent wouldn't be home for hours. I drove along J for several miles until I reached the track that might lead down to the valley where Dep and I had found the autoinjector. I turned left and let my headlights illuminate this dirt road.

It appeared to be a former driveway, packed earth, but navigable, with flattish ground farther down a slight slope near a huddle of shrubs. I should be able to turn the car around down there. "Though," I told my cat, rustling in her carrier on the seat behind me, "we can back out if we have to."

"Merrowl."

The shrubs were farther away and taller than I'd thought—lilacs, leggy and not blooming at this time of year, but recognizable by the way their heart-shaped leaves angled downward. Years ago, someone must have planted them on three sides of what was now a weed-strewn yard surrounding the remains of a foundation. A heap of stones might have once formed a chimney. An old-fashioned water pump was missing the end of its handle. I shut off my car's engine, headlights, and interior lights, got out, and stood beside my open driver's door. Silent and listening, I waited for my eyes to adjust to the near darkness.

A bullfrog croaked in a pond that had to be nearby. Dep had been silent for a few seconds, but now she responded with a croak of her own. I smiled.

Not using my phone's light, and feeling with the toes of my sneakers for tripping hazards, I stepped carefully down the stony, rutted track. Beyond the lilacs, the former driveway curved and then headed south, down the hill toward the creek. It was a trail fit only for ATVs and hikers. In daylight, I might have tried taking Dep for a walk down it.

With my light still off, I started back toward my car and my cat.

I almost missed the soft clank in the woods to my left, on the other side of an overgrown pasture. I quickly turned my head. Had I seen a light move, or had that been only a trick of my imagination? I picked my way to the car and locked myself inside with Dep. With my headlights on, I bumped my way to County Road J, and then I drove toward County Road C, probably more quickly than I needed to.

Who had been back there in the woods? Was Landon camping? The day we'd first encountered him, had he turned north on that dirt road to go all the way up to the woods back there, risking at least the undercarriage of his rental car? And what about this evening? Unless there was a shortcut from Gooseleg to County Road J that I hadn't seen on my map, he couldn't have beaten me to that forlorn former farm and the woods beside it.

I was almost at the intersection of J and C when a dark sedan sped south on C.

Landon?

I told myself that I couldn't possibly be seeing Landon everywhere, and too much time had elapsed since the car had turned onto that dead-end road in Gooseleg for its driver to have successfully followed me down C, where no one had been behind me. Besides, there had to be hundreds or thousands of late-model dark sedans in northern Wisconsin.

I took my time turning onto County Road C, and by the time I did, the sedan's taillights were far ahead. I opened my window and enjoyed the warm, fresh night air. Dep must have approved. She barely made a noise. I drove at the speed limit. The car ahead disappeared around a curve, and again Dep and I had the road, and the night, to ourselves.

The road swooped downward through the northern part of the Chicory Lake State Forest, crossed the bridge over the western end of Chicory Lake, passed Brent's and my nearest neighbor, a lakeside canoe and horse and carriage rental place, and then rose up the hill. Near the top, our driveway was on the left.

I turned onto it. Behind me, Dep announced that we were nearly home.

Solar-powered lights lined the driveway, and other lights came on as we approached the chalet. Brent's SUV wasn't there.

Hugging Dep close, I carried her into the house. She purred.

We were still up when Brent came home. I gave him a big hug and asked, "Have you eaten?"

"We didn't take time for more than a few snacks. Vic wants to wrap up the investigation quickly."

Tutting, I grabbed garden scissors. "Change into something comfy, and I'll be right back." I went out to our vegetable garden. What would Izzy think of my harvesting a tomato, a cucumber, and a red pepper in the dark? Probably that it was entirely normal.

In the kitchen, I cut up the veggies for a salad for Brent and arranged julienned ham, roast beef, Wisconsin Swiss cheese, and a handful of pepitas on the veggies. I drizzled Italian dressing over it all. Brent came back into the kitchen in shorts and a T-shirt. He ruffled my hair and gave me a kiss. "That's exactly what I wanted, but didn't know I wanted."

"Wine?"

"A little."

"How about a very dry red?"

"Perfect."

I got out a glass for each of us. He opened the wine, and we went out to the catio. Dep came, too.

Brent looked tense. While he ate, I stood behind him and massaged his shoulders. "Mmm," he said. "I don't know how I survived police work before we were married."

I kissed the back of his neck and then sat beside him. I told him about visiting Izzy. Although Vic had searched her place,

Brent hadn't heard that she lived in a caboose. "It's wonderful," I said. "So very Izzy. When I left, though, I spotted a car that might have been the one Landon's driving. But maybe you'll tell me that you were with him somewhere else around eight this evening."

"We haven't located him. Where did you last see him?"

I described the dead-end street in Gooseleg. "But then, later, I saw a car that could have been his, speeding southward on County Road C near County Road J."

Naturally, he picked up on my use of the word "later." "What were you doing in the meantime?"

I took out my phone and showed him a map. "I was looking for a connection between H and J that goes down into that valley where Dep and I found the autoinjector. A trail might go all the way through there, but it's not navigable with a car. Not with mine at night, anyway."

"Not with yours at any time. The trail, such as it is, does go all the way through. Forensics hasn't linked that autoinjector to anyone, and they might not."

"I didn't stick around. I thought someone might have been camping in the woods west of that abandoned home site."

"It's a common occurrence there, not something to worry about."

"I wasn't planning to go back, anyway."

"Just as well."

"Did you talk to Izzy's cousin yet and worm any information out of her about who Landon is?"

"She told me the same thing she told you—she doesn't know him well."

"Which I strongly doubt. And what did she say about the donuts he bought?"

"She walked less than a block with him and doesn't know what he did with them."

"I hope you find him soon."

"We will. And in case you're wondering, Hope and Glenn were together Sunday afternoon and evening. Hope raved about the dinner he spent the day making."

"Hope invited Izzy to dinner at their place tomorrow evening, so she'll also get a taste of Glenn's expert cooking. Izzy and I looked him up this evening. He managed a restaurant in upstate New York. And Hope works in New York City. Maybe she met him through his restaurant or her job."

"Who needs a chef when they have an Emily?"

I leaned against him. "Or a Brent, who is every bit as good a cook as anyone out there."

Chapter 25

The next afternoon at Deputy Donut, I was behind the serving counter when Hope came in. The lime-sherbet tint of her linen sundress looked like it could lower the temperature outside by several degrees. The dress and her sandals were simple yet elegant, and I suspected they'd come from chic and expensive New York boutiques. And her expression was at least as cool as the color of the dress.

She came straight to the serving counter. "Emma." Her voice was low and controlled.

I didn't correct her. Instead, I offered, "Would you like a coffee? Tea?"

"I can't stay. The smell of frying and sugar makes me bilious. I understand that you and my cousin Isabella are friends?" She made it into a question.

"Yes."

"Glenn and I have invited her to dinner tonight. Glenn is the most marvelous chef. Would you like to join us?"

It might be a chance to learn more about the mysterious Landon. Plus, who could pass up a meal prepared by a chef? And I wanted to see how the ever-bubbly Izzy would interact with her iceberg of a cousin. Maybe Hope would thaw a little. "I'd love to come."

"Drinks at seven, then. You know where to find us." Her

mouth formed something like a smile. It looked almost painful.

She hadn't mentioned Brent. I wondered if she had connected her landlord Brent Fyne with the Detective Fyne who had talked to her the day before. Maybe she had, and she had purposely not included him. Even the most law-abiding people were sometimes intimidated by detectives and other police officers. Or maybe she understood that Brent would probably have to work late and wouldn't be able to attend.

Her posture perfect and her walk graceful, Hope glided to our front door. A man at a nearby table jumped up and opened it for her.

Olivia joined me at the service counter. "That was the woman who knew Mr. Mystery, right? How does she get men to rush to her aid like that?"

"Walk like a princess," Jocelyn said, demonstrating.

Olivia and I laughed.

"Confidence," I suggested. "Believing she's the most important person in the room." I stood straighter. "I should try it."

"Me, too." Olivia raised her chin, lowered her shoulders, and glided back into the kitchen.

Jocelyn followed her. "That's it, Olivia! Keep doing that."

Olivia turned back to us. "I don't want to look fake."

"You don't," I said. "You look regal."

Jocelyn squinted up at Olivia's face. "Or you would if you weren't wearing your Deputy Donut hat. No offense, Emily."

I shrugged. "Tom and I designed them together."

Standing at the deep fryers, Tom grinned and took a bow. "It's hard to believe that woman is Izzy's cousin. Why was she here? She didn't buy anything, did she, Emily?"

"No. The smells of frying and sugar make her bilious. As Izzy told us yesterday, Hope and Izzy are cousins, and Hope invited Izzy to dinner tonight. Hope came in just now to invite me, too."

Olivia folded her arms. "Good. I'm not sure Izzy should be alone with her cousin. What if Izzy starts acting like her? You can immediately tell her to stop."

Jocelyn warned, "Don't expect fried foods or sweets."

Olivia added, "Take Brent with you."

"He wasn't invited. Anyway, he probably has to work tonight. And Hope implied that Glenn, the chef, will be doing the cooking. Maybe he's not averse to sugar."

Jocelyn glanced at Olivia. "Such a pity that the chef has a girlfriend."

Olivia blushed. "I don't care."

Jocelyn started toward customers in the dining room. "Of course not, when a certain cute guy in a uniform is single."

Olivia raised her chin. She was obviously trying hard not to smile. I looked past her and winked at Tom.

Olivia wasn't looking at him, so she missed the almost fatherly smile he aimed at her. He glanced beyond me, and his smile became strained. He cocked his head toward the front door.

I turned around. Striding inside with his own form of confidence, Mayor Jerry Creavus approached a table of diners. He shook hands all around and then started toward us.

Olivia stooped to whisper in my ear, "It's time to practice your own swagger, Emily."

I hoped that Jerry Creavus thought my wide smile was meant for him.

He came to the serving counter. "Can I talk to Tom?"

I looked over my shoulder. Tom was concentrating on the fryer in front of him, turning donuts. I met Jerry's gaze. "Sure, if you don't mind waiting a few minutes. Timing is crucial with frying donuts." I could have gone back into the kitchen and taken over for Tom, but maybe I was too busy practicing my swagger. "What can I get you while you wait?"

"I'm not sure it will wait. You and Tom are partners, right? Business partners, that is."

Pretending I hadn't heard that hint of innuendo about me and the man I thought of as a second father, I kept a straight face. "We own this place fifty-fifty."

"Then I'd better discuss this with you. You told a chef about my plans of selling the building next door to you, right?"

"Yes. Glenn Sitherby."

"Glenn is very interested in the property, so I thought I should give you and Tom, who are long-term residents of Fallingbrook, a chance to buy it before a newcomer does."

I thought uncharitably, *A newcomer probably won't be qualified to vote in the mayoralty election.*

Jerry beamed down at me. "So, here's what I thought I'd do. I can lower the price for you and Tom if you act quickly and pay cash."

I flattened my palms against the cool marble counter. "That would be impossible. And besides, I would love having a restaurant like the one Glenn's planning in downtown Fallingbrook. I would eat there, for one thing, and it would attract others, including tourists."

"It could be unfair competition for you."

Maybe I shouldn't be interpreting so many of Jerry's comments as insults. . . . I raised my chin in an attempt at looking regal. "We're not open at the dinner hour, and we serve different sorts of meals than he would serve."

"Okay, I get that. Listen, do you know how to get in touch with that young woman planning a greenhouse business?"

"She comes in here from time to time."

He set one of his business cards on the counter. "I want to talk to her about her plans. So, the next time you see her, can you give her my card? She can meet me in my office some evening."

An evening meeting? Just the two of them? Trying not to make a face, I put the card in my apron pocket. I would suggest to Izzy that if she wanted to attend the meeting, she should take at least one of her lawyer friends with her.

Jerry swept his fingers across the counter like someone who had just accomplished an important goal. "Let me talk to Tom."

"Okay." Head high, I glided, princess-style, around the half-height wall into the kitchen. At the fryers, I told Tom, "I'll take over so you can go talk to Jerry." With my back to Jerry, I scrunched my face into an expression that I hoped served as a warning that Jerry was being irritating.

I could tell that Tom wanted to laugh, but he managed to give me a neutral look before, smiling toward Jerry, he headed off to the serving counter.

I lifted a basket of donuts out of the hot oil and hooked the basket over the side of the fryer to allow the tiny bit of oil clinging to the donuts to drip back into the fryer. We always used fresh oil, and we kept it at a temperature that cooked the donuts without soaking into them. To me, it all smelled delicious. Hope didn't know what she was missing. I lowered more donuts into the oil.

Tom returned to the fryers. Over the half wall, I could see Jerry strutting through our dining room. He greeted more of our customers and then left without buying anything.

I handed Tom the wooden rod we used for turning donuts. "I gather you told him the same thing I did."

"I told him we're not interested."

"I told him we couldn't."

"Same thing. I also said I couldn't make decisions without discussing them with you."

"Thank you. I didn't mention that. I think he took it for granted that you were the primary decision-maker. At first, he asked to talk to you, not to me."

"Too bad he's now running unopposed for mayor. Maybe a woman should run against him."

"Not me. How about Cindy?"

Tom's wife, in addition to being Alec's mother and my

mother-in-law, was a high school art teacher. I couldn't imagine her wanting to embroil herself in politics."

Tom laughed. "She'd hate that."

I heaved a dramatic sigh. "I know. I wonder why Jerry's so suddenly interested in selling. And quickly. For cash, if he can."

"He bought some of those donuts the day that Adam Nofftry died, didn't he? The donuts that Brent and the other officers found so interesting?"

"Yes."

Tom made a guess like Izzy's. "So, if Jerry is short on funds, maybe he needs to be mayor for the salary. And from what I hear, Adam was making inroads on Jerry's popularity. Which gives Jerry a motive to kill Adam." Tom seldom indulged in speculation about police cases. He was relaxing after his days as detective and police chief.

"And maybe Jerry wants to sell his assets quickly for cash so he can disappear into a new life to avoid being arrested. Oh, and he wants to arrange a meeting with Izzy, some evening in his office."

Tom's eyebrows lowered. He hadn't completely relaxed his retired police officer personality. I took advantage of it to ask for advice. "I told Brent about Jerry's offer yesterday. Do you think I should call him about Jerry's apparent desperation today and his slightly questionable offer to meet with Izzy?"

"What do you think?"

"I think you know I would call Brent no matter what you said."

"You were also sure I'd say you should call him now."

Laughing, I glided, Hope-style, toward the office.

Visiting Dep in the office was fun, if not always calming. I shut myself in and sat on the couch. Where was Dep?

I looked up. Her tail was hanging out the end of a tunnel high up on one of her catwalks. The tail swished back and forth, a sign that mischief was brewing in the little cat's brain. I touched Brent's number on my phone.

He answered, "Hi, Em, what's up?"

A rubber squeaky mouse crashed down onto my lap from Dep's catwalk. Managing not to gasp too audibly, I told Brent about Jerry's latest offer. "Tom and I aren't going for it." I explained why Tom and I thought that Jerry's need for cash could point to a motive for killing Adam and could also point to Jerry's possible guilt and desire to quickly flee from Fallingbrook. I added, "As you know, Jerry is the one person I've heard of who knew before Adam died that Adam was allergic to almonds. Or have you cleared Jerry as a possible murderer?"

"We haven't."

Dep ran down one of her kitty ramps and stood on her hind legs on the floor, batting with one velvety front paw at the rubber mouse on my knee. I said to Brent, "I guess you might have spoken to other people who knew about Adam's allergies."

"No one has come right out and said that, but maybe no one would, at this point, if they've heard about the questions Vic and I have been asking."

"Jerry also asked me to give Izzy his card. He wants her to call him so he can arrange a meeting with her in his office to discuss her plans. I worry about what he's up to."

"It should be okay if she doesn't go alone."

"That's what I thought. I was already worried that Landon was going to try to scam her out of her windfall, and Jerry obviously knows she has money. Maybe this is another way he's hoping to have enough cash to escape arrest, or something."

"Could be."

"I have other news. Izzy's cousin Hope came in this afternoon and invited me to join her and Izzy for dinner tonight at our Maple Street house. Glenn's preparing it, and he's a chef, so I'm looking forward to it. Hope didn't specifically invite you, but she also didn't specifically not invite you."

"I do have to work. What will you do with Dep?"

"I'm invited for drinks at seven, so I'll take her home and change out of my Deputy Donut shorts. Hope tends to dress up."

"Better you than me. If you're not home by nine, don't worry. I probably will be and can console Dep for being abandoned for over two hours."

Promising to see each other later, we disconnected.

Chapter 26

Dep unsheathed her claws and plucked the rubber mouse off my lap. She shook her paw, and the toy flew across the office. Her feet sliding every which way, she chased it.

I called Glenn and apologized for interrupting his meal preparations.

"Everything's under control. I look forward to showing you the world-class cuisine I'll feature in my restaurant."

I told him about Jerry's latest offer. "He said you were interested in the building, so I thought you should know how low he's willing to go for cash."

There was a pause. "I toured the place with him yesterday, and quite frankly, Emily, the inside of that building has been neglected for years and needs a lot of work. I'd rather build new on a larger lot with gardens and dedicated parking. Besides, Jerry told me that you were interested in the building. I wasn't about to buy it if you wanted it."

"Tom and I don't want to buy it, no matter what shape it's in. We can't expand right now."

"I guess when I turned Jerry down, I was a little too tactful."

"It's more like he's playing us against each other."

Glenn sighed. "I'm afraid you might be right. But I guess his high-pressure sales pitch isn't working with either of us."

Over the phone, I recognized the beeping of the timer in

my former kitchen. I laughed. "I'd better let you go. See you at seven."

We disconnected. I wondered how long Glenn had been searching for the perfect place to open a restaurant. How could he afford to spend time without producing revenue?

I returned to Deputy Donut's kitchen. Tom and Jocelyn were mixing dough for the next day, and Olivia was rearranging the donuts in the display case, consolidating them and removing the trays she'd emptied.

Jocelyn looked toward the front door. "Olivia, you should go wait on them. Walk like a princess."

Olivia asked, "Who?" She looked toward the front door and blushed. "Oh, them."

Misty had come in with her husband Scott, and Tyler was with them. Scott was in the dark blue pants and shirt he wore when on duty in the fire station. Misty and Tyler must have still been enjoying their days off. Misty was wearing gray capris and a red blouse, and Tyler was in navy shorts and a white polo shirt that showed off his muscles. Misty and Scott waved at me. Tyler blushed.

I told Olivia, "I'll go with you."

Actually, I led the way, so I couldn't tell if Olivia was practicing the walk that Hope had inspired in us. I glided, chin up, to the table where Misty, Scott, and Tyler sat. "What can we get for you three? Misty and Tyler, you don't look like you're here on business."

Misty's smile was huge. Either she was laughing at the way we were walking, or she was telling me she was trying to give Tyler and Olivia a chance to get to know each other better. "We thought that Scott doesn't take enough breaks, so we brought him here. What's your special coffee today?"

"It's Monsoon Malabar from India. It's been processed to resemble coffee beans that fermented in the dark and damp lower decks of ships long ago. It sounds iffy, but it's nicely mellow, a tiny bit earthy, and very good."

Misty elbowed Scott. "Do you get anything that good in the fire hall?"

"Of course we do. We buy our beans from Emily and Tom, and they taught us how to make decent coffee. I'd like to try anything with the name 'monsoon' in it."

Tyler didn't take his eyes off Olivia. "I'd like to, too."

I suggested, "And how about some of the donuts we only started making today—almond donuts with cardamom?"

I thought Misty was going to choke, but she managed to order one.

"We didn't put peaches in these," I deadpanned.

Tyler told Olivia, "I'd like two of them."

Scott smiled. I suspected he was a co-conspirator in Misty's matchmaking. "Can you bring me two of them, too?"

Olivia and I returned to the kitchen, and then Jocelyn and I held back and watched Olivia head toward Misty, Scott, and Tyler with the tray of plates. Jocelyn elbowed me, "Olivia's doing it, walking like she's the most important person in the room."

I grinned. "I guess Tyler already thought that." We took the coffee and mugs to Scott, Misty, and Tyler.

Scott's break ended shortly before we closed for the day. Misty and Scott started toward the door, but Tyler lingered at the table while Olivia cleared it. I couldn't hear what Tyler said to Olivia, but they both smiled. And blushed.

All of us were in a cheerful mood when we tidied and locked up, but Olivia had a special glow. I was careful not to ask, and, I noticed, so were Jocelyn and Tom. Jocelyn, however, would probably quiz Olivia about it while walking her bike beside Olivia. Having strolled down Wisconsin Street after work with them often when I lived in the Maple Street house, I knew that they would walk together until Jocelyn turned off Wisconsin and rode the rest of the way to her parents' home, and then Olivia would stay on Wisconsin for another few blocks to her apartment.

I drove Dep to our home on Chicory Lake. I'd barely gotten inside and fed Dep when Izzy called. "Hope told me she invited you, too, Emily! This is going to be great. Want me to pick you up and take you home?"

"It would be fun to ride together, but I have to work early in the morning."

"We wouldn't have to stay late. Hope and I might run out of things to say to each other by seven fifteen."

"Or you might want to talk all night. I'll drive myself, and you can be free to leave at seven fifteen in the evening or seven fifteen in the morning, when I'll already be at work."

"I can't imagine that happening, but, okay, I'll go straight there. I don't know what to wear. What's the house you're renting to them like?"

I laughed. "Why?"

"So I won't clash."

"Did I clash with your home last night?"

"No. But the décor is neutral. What if your house is red inside, and I wore purple?"

"Good guess. The house is originally Victorian, but updated. The living room is white and decorated in jewel tones, mostly deep red and cobalt blue, to go with the stained-glass windows. The dining room also has stained-glass windows high up on both sides of the fireplace, but the dining room's decor is mostly white with chrome and glass. It gets its natural light mostly through the living room and kitchen. If you wear muted orange, you might fit in with the kitchen with its terra-cotta tile floor, pine cabinets, and granite countertops. The granite is mostly gray but has hints of orange. Does that help?"

"Well, what are you going to wear?"

"I hadn't thought of matching the house, but whenever I've seen Hope, she's been dressed up, even when I dropped in at the house. That time, she had on an expensive-looking silk blouse with designer jeans. You saw her in Deputy Donut in her business suit. Today she had on a gorgeous sundress. I don't have any as expensive as that one, but I was thinking of a sundress and sandals, with a sweater in case we eat out on the patio. If you want to match the outdoors, consider that the wall around the yard is, like the house's exterior, yellow brick, aged to a tannish hue. And the grass is green, and the bark on trees and shrubs is . . ."

Izzy was laughing. "Okay, stop. I get it. But really, what are you going to wear?"

"I hadn't decided, but after this discussion, I think I should wear my emerald-green dress."

"Ooooh, that will go so well with your dark hair. Your deep blue eyes will really pop." She gasped. "I didn't mean that literally. Sorry, Emily."

I controlled my laughter. "It's okay."

"Maybe I'll wear the black dress I wore when your husband interrogated me. Is he coming tonight?"

"No, so you don't have to try to match his dark gray suit and navy-striped tie."

"I guess he has to work."

"I guess he wasn't invited."

"What? I thought Hope would be a stickler for etiquette and invite a couple if there is a couple. Maybe she's changed over the years. See you tonight." She disconnected.

I went up to our spacious bedroom suite in the loft, showered, and put on the green dress and a chunky green and black handmade necklace from The Craft Croft. Despite Dep's rubbing against my ankles, I slipped my feet into a pair of shiny black sandals. "Good thing I won't be walking much," I told my purring kitty. "These are definitely not as comfy as the shoes I wear in Deputy Donut."

"Meow."

Downstairs again, I opened the fridge. Suspecting that I would never be able to choose a wine that would appeal to a chef, I selected a chilled bottle of one of Brent's and my favorite pinot grigios. I put it into a sheer purple drawstring bag.

I carried the bag along with a sweater and a tiny purse containing my phone and driver's license, but not much else, toward the front door. With only one eye open, Dep was lying on a couch. I told her, "Brent will probably be back before I am." She opened her other eye, yawned, stretched, closed both eyes, and curled into a ball, apparently content to snooze in a cozy spot until we returned.

Driving south, I wondered if Glenn and Hope might serve dinner outside on the patio. It should be another perfect evening—warm but not hot. The slight breezes would probably end when the sun went down.

Izzy's car was already parked near the Maple Street house. No cars were in the driveway, but maybe Glenn or Hope had a car in the garage. Not wanting to block it in, I parked on the street behind Izzy's car.

The front door was ajar, and the screen was closed. I rang the bell. Hope opened the screen door. She hadn't hooked it, this time. "Emma. Come in." Her black raw silk tunic was almost hidden under thick ropes of gleaming gold chains. Her capris matched the tunic. The clear band over the forefoot of her stiletto-heeled sandals made all but the soles and heels of her shoes seem almost invisible. I slipped out of my uncomfortable sandals and left them underneath the table beside the door. I laid my purse on the table and handed Hope the wine.

She pinched the bag's ruffled top between one thumb and forefinger as if she didn't want too much of her hand to come into contact with it. "You didn't have to do that." She backed up and waved at the ruby-red velvet couch, the matching armchair, and the cobalt-blue wing chair, all of which I'd inherited from my grandmother and had had reupholstered. And thoroughly cleaned after we moved Dep out. "Have a seat." She strode toward the kitchen. The pulled-back bun on the back of her head looked tight and painful.

With her knees together, her black linen dress pressed, and her curls combed and mostly tamed, Izzy perched on the edge of one of the couch cushions. As if she couldn't help adding touches of whimsy to her life, she wore silver ballet slippers with large silver pom-poms resembling chrysanthemums on the toes.

During the years before Brent and I had begun cuddling on the couch together with Dep, Brent had nearly always chosen the wing chair. Even though he wasn't invited to this particular event, I avoided the wing chair and sat on the other end of the couch from Izzy. The room was the way Brent and I had arranged it, except we'd taken our personal belongings and artwork to the chalet. The clear glass shelves beside the windows where I'd kept vases echoing the colors in the stained-glass panel above the window were still empty, as was the glass-doored case beside the stairs, except for something—a book?—on the lower shelf. If, like Brent and me, Glenn and Hope kept books and magazines on tables near the couch and chairs, they had, as we usually did, tidied them away when company was expected.

Behind me and beyond the dining room, dishes, pots, and pans clattered in the kitchen that Alec and I had designed and that Brent and I had also shared and enjoyed. I heard Glenn's and Hope's voices but couldn't make out more than the occasional word.

It was both familiar and distressingly otherworldly, my house, but not mine. Did I really want to keep renting it to strangers? Maybe I shouldn't have accepted the dinner invitation.

I told myself to relax and enjoy the evening. The meal would be exceptional, no doubt, and part of the reason I was here was to support Izzy, who was meeting her estranged cousin for the first time in years.

What, if anything, had been said before I arrived that made Izzy sit stiffly as if she were missing her tiny home and deck?

Actually, I would have rather been there, too. Without the icy cousin and the chef who was too busy—quite understandably—to greet his guests.

I turned toward Izzy. We exhausted almost every possible detail about the drive down County Road C. Finally, Glenn came in with a tray of tall, frosty glasses tinkling with ice cubes. Each drink was garnished with a sprig of lavender and thin slices of lemon. Glenn set the tray on the coffee table. "French lemonade," he announced, waiter-like. "With freshly squeezed lemons, sparkling water, and lavender syrup. Help yourselves." He was wearing a chef's hat and a chef's apron over a pressed white dress shirt and jeans that looked at least as expensive as the ones Hope had worn the previous time I'd visited this house.

Hope followed Glenn with cocktail napkins. "And no alcohol."

I scooted forward and picked up a glass. "It's just as well, since we both drove."

Izzy chose a glass.

Leaving the third glass on the tray, Glenn and Hope headed toward the kitchen. I wondered what her stiletto heels were doing to our wide-plank pine floors, the house's original subflooring, which had been covered by carpeting in Victorian times, and was now protected only by area rugs. I could almost hear the antique wood splinter with each step she took. I hoped that the kitchen floor's tiles held up to those heels.

Izzy pointed at the lone glass on the tray on the coffee table and held up one finger, then cocked her head back toward the kitchen, held up two fingers, and wrinkled her forehead in puzzlement.

I whispered, "Maybe they share?"

She covered her mouth for a second to hide a giggle, then suggested, "They ran out of lavender syrup?"

Did I somehow miss that Brent was supposed to come? My face heated. I sipped at the drink and said loudly enough that someone listening from the kitchen might hear me, "Delicious!"

Glenn had appeared silently at my elbow. With a courtly bow, he handed me a small plate with three canapés on it. "Glad you like it." He described the three canapés. "This one's a mushroom tartlet. That one's smoked trout and mascarpone on a toasted slice of baguette, and the third one is fresh fig slices with honeyed goat's cheese on French spiced bread."

He gave Izzy an identical plate and explained each delicacy again. It was no wonder that I hadn't heard him coming. His leather shoes apparently had very soft soles, as if they had been made for someone whose work required him to stand for hours at a time.

I asked, "Did you bake the baguette and the spiced bread yourselves?"

Hope handed me a tiny fork. "Glenn did. I don't do kitchens except to help carry things if I have to, like tonight. Glenn gets up early to bake, and he's been working all day on this." It was the most congenial remark I'd ever heard her make. She walked to the window and looked out for a second as if she were watching for someone. Again wondering if I'd been supposed to pass the invitation along to Brent, I felt myself blush even more. Without another word and with her heels beating against the floor, Hope followed Glenn to the kitchen.

Izzy tasted her lemonade and said quietly, "Fancier than what I served."

I murmured, "But not as much fun."

She threw me a conspiratorial smile, glanced over her

shoulder toward the kitchen, and sighed. It was going to be a long evening.

One feature of our old-fashioned wooden porch was that, unless one set one's feet down carefully, footsteps resounded over the hollow space underneath.

Someone had come up onto the porch. Not a woman in heels, and not, I thought, Brent.

The doorbell rang. Izzy jumped and turned toward the door.

From the kitchen, Hope called in a cheerful voice, "Come in!" Although remote, it seemed warmer than the welcome I'd received.

A man stepped into the living room.

Landon, aka Mr. Mystery.

Chapter 27

Landon, or whatever his name really was, returned my gaze and nodded. A flush mottled his cheeks.

Izzy's fork slid off her plate and landed on the rug.

Landon glanced her way. The color drained from his face. He took a step backward and placed his hand on the screen door as if he were about to open it and run away.

Izzy made no attempt to pick up her fork. Her mouth hung open.

Hope's heels pounded into the soft wood floor of the dining room, and then the living room, until my inauthentic Persian rug absorbed some of the force of her footsteps. "Landon! So glad you could make it."

He stammered out, "I . . . um . . . here." He shoved a bouquet of showy dahlias at her.

She kept them from falling onto the floor. "Sweet. Is that what made you late, stopping at a farm stand?"

He defended himself. "Sorry. I thought you said seven thirty. For drinks." His voice was as deep as I remembered but somehow less calming.

Hope trilled a brittle laugh. "And you're fashionably late even for that. Come in and meet my cousin Izzy and our landlady Emma."

Izzy corrected her. "Emily."

"Emily? My bad." She turned toward the dining room and gestured to Glenn, who must have come in silently again. "And this is my almost-fiancé Glenn. Everybody, this is Landon Bafter, someone I met in New York."

We greeted each other in various ways, all of them awkward. Landon sounded as stiff as Izzy looked.

Hope, however, seemed totally comfortable and, I thought, in control. She waved toward the armchair and wing chair. "Have a seat, Landon. Your French lemonade with lavender is there on the coffee table. If the ice melted too much while waiting for you to arrive, I'll get you a new one." Maybe Hope couldn't help her snide and hurtful remarks.

Landon seemed to almost stumble over his feet on his way to the armchair across from me. "This is fine." I wondered if he chose that chair because it was farther from Izzy. His face still red, he picked up his French lemonade. The frost on the glass had become water droplets that ran down the glass and, as I knew from my own drink, made the glass slippery. Where were the coasters I'd kept on the coffee and end tables?

Behind me, Glenn said, "I'll get the rest of the appetizers." He picked up the tray the drinks had been on and returned to the kitchen. Hope clopped behind him.

Izzy bent down and retrieved her fork.

I set my plate on the coffee table in front of me. Grasping my slippery glass tightly, I went to the glass-doored bookcase beside the stairs and peeked in. What I thought might have been a book on the bottom shelf was actually a neat stack of my coasters. Knowing I was probably being too pushy, I distributed more of the coasters than we probably needed on the tables. Finally, I found something to say. "We three meet again." How inane.

I sat down and put my glass on the coaster nearest me on the coffee table.

Landon cleared his throat. "Yes." He spoke as if he could barely force the word out.

I badly needed to tell Brent where Landon was, but I'd left my phone in my purse on the table near the door. Rushing to get it and then sending Brent a message would be even ruder than helping myself to coasters. Also, if Landon guessed what I was doing, he might bolt. Trying not to squirm, I asked him, "What brings you to northern Wisconsin?"

"Work." He must have remembered the first story he'd told us. "First to Duluth, and then here, and then, um, I go back to New York."

Izzy didn't say a thing, so I continued my questions. "What kind of work?"

"Law."

"Law enforcement?"

"No. I'm a lawyer. Corporate law. Nothing interesting."

Or nothing he wanted to disclose.

Izzy sat uncharacteristically still and mute.

Glenn and Hope returned. This time the tray held two more glasses of lavender-infused lemonade and three plates of the canapés. They gave Landon a plate, and then Glenn sat in the wing chair.

Holding her plate, Hope eased down onto the couch between Izzy and me. "Well, isn't this cozy?" she cooed. "Just us girls." She picked up a coaster and then glanced toward my glass on its coaster. "Quaint, like visiting a grandmother."

I felt like a fifth, and entirely unnecessary, wheel. Also, I missed Dep. Usually, when I'd sat in this spot, Dep had been on my lap or on the cushion beside me. Also, I could imagine Brent sitting here and hiding his amusement to share with me later. Strengthened by picturing my comforting kitty and empathetic husband, I bit into the mushroom tartlet. "Delicious, Glenn." Maybe I was necessary at this party, after all, if the only other person who was going to say anything was Hope, who had little to offer besides poorly veiled criticism.

I tried to start a conversation. "So, we know that Glenn's a chef, and an excellent one, Landon's a lawyer, I make and sell donuts and coffee, and Izzy is a budding entrepreneur. What do you do, Hope?"

"Oh, executive things in New York, like everyone else there."

I looked at her left hand. No ring. "And Glenn's your almost-fiancé?"

"He's popped the question, but I'm waiting for the right time to give him my answer."

Izzy finally found her voice. "It sounds like we know what your answer is going to be."

Glenn grinned, nodded, and gazed admiringly at the smoked trout canapé in his hand. "It seems I need to hire a photographer to document the occasion the next time I ask her."

Hope added, "And invite our guest list." She turned toward Izzy. "Isabella, what have you been up to since your snot-nosed brat days?"

"Wiping my nose, apparently." *Good for you, Izzy*, I thought. His face neutral except for that betraying blush, Landon stared intently at Izzy. She went on, "School, a degree in biology, and now I'm looking into raising crops in greenhouses."

Hope made an obvious shudder. "Aren't you going to give that up now?"

Izzy looked honestly perplexed. "Why?"

"It's morbid. Didn't a man die where you're planning to put your greenhouses? Or did I misunderstand what people are saying? Aren't you afraid the place will be haunted, and all of your vegetables will shrivel on the vine?"

"No."

There was another pause in the conversation. Silence would have been preferable to the chewing and swallowing of people who apparently had nothing they wanted to say.

Hope gathered our empty plates. "I believe that Glenn is ready to serve the soup course now."

I stood. "I'll just make a quick trip to the bathroom."

Hope raised her eyebrows. "I'd have thought you'd have, oh, never mind. You live somewhere way out in the boonies, don't you? Don't worry. The soup is supposed to be cold. We won't serve yours until you're back. I guess you know your way." There was that icy laugh again.

"Yes, thank you." Walking around the back of the couch, I could see into the dining room. The table was tastefully and beautifully set—with my dishes, cutlery, and starched white linen place mats and napkins—for five people, which confirmed that Hope had expected Landon, and no one else. Not Brent.

I grabbed my purse from the table beside the door and ran upstairs.

Chapter 28

I shut myself into the bathroom and sent a text to Brent, telling him that Landon was in our Maple Street home and had claimed to be a corporate lawyer in New York. I gave Brent Landon's last name and said that we were about to start the soup course, and there would probably be several more after that.

Brent texted back immediately. He asked me to let him know when the party was breaking up.

I was halfway down the stairs when I heard Hope call to Glenn, "You can serve Emma's soup. I hear her clomping down now." My bare feet were hardly making a sound on the runner on the wooden stairs.

I trotted the rest of the way down to the first floor. Trying to look like I didn't want to waste time finding somewhere to put my purse, which still contained my phone, I hurried into the dining room. "Sorry for holding everyone up."

Glenn was setting a clear glass bowl of white soup onto the clear glass plate at one of the two place settings in front of empty chairs. "Here you go, Emily." He had removed the hat and apron, but I was amused to see that he still wore a scabbard for one of a chef's most prized implements—his chef's knife. This scabbard was made of black silicone. No knife handle stuck out of the top of it, and its decorative circular cutouts confirmed that it was empty. Glenn must have felt secure in a kitchen where only his almost-fiancée was helping him, and he didn't have to protect the precious knife from someone who might use it for prying the lid off a jar. I nearly groaned at the thought.

Hope's hand hovered over her soup spoon.

The round, glass-topped table could accommodate six people. Izzy was between Hope and Landon, who sat next to the chair that had to be Glenn's. Trying not to be obvious about keeping my purse with me as if I feared I was in a den of robbers, I slipped into the chair next to Hope and put the purse on my lap.

Glenn went around the table and poured an inch of white wine into our glasses. "Sauvignon blanc," he told us.

He sat in the other vacant chair. A bowl of soup was already at his place. He announced, "This is chilled cucumber soup with dill and fennel. I know that not everyone loves cumin, but I hope that the other flavors balance the pinch of it I put into the soup."

Hope lifted her spoon. "We can begin."

I tasted the creamy soup. "It's wonderful, Glenn."

Everyone else agreed, even Landon, who had barely said a word in my hearing.

I sipped the wine. "Mmm. Perfect."

Hope turned to Izzy. "How did you and Emily meet?" She'd finally caught on to my name. "It was a long time ago, wasn't it?"

Izzy put her spoon down. "My parents took me to a campground to visit friends whose campsite was across the road from where Emily and her parents were camping."

Hope shuddered. "Camping." She glanced around the room. "This is roughing it enough for me. Not your house, Emily. It's furnished with everything a vacationing couple could want, if they're into vintage grandmother, but Fallingbrook isn't exactly New York where, of course, most of us live in apartments."

Izzy defended my parents' campground. "That wasn't a roughing-it campground. Most of the people there had RVs and trailers that were probably bigger than the average New York apartment, and it seemed to me then, when I was small, that the sites were big. Are they really, Emily? And surrounded by woods and trees so that everyone has plenty of their own space?"

"My parents still spend most of their summers there. The sites are large and wooded. And there are shared areas, too, like ballfields, a recreation hall, and even a little chapel."

Izzy became more like her usual animated self. "But the great part about where Emily's parents stay is next to it—the river and the waterfall and all the trails through the woods around that waterfall. It was magic!" Landon glanced up from his soup bowl at Izzy, then at Hope, then back at his spoon. Izzy seemed to be ignoring him. She went on, "I was only there for one day, which I spent with Emily, who was a teen and, I guess, was charged with keeping me from falling off boulders or into the river."

"I did it because I wanted to. We had fun that day." I turned toward Hope. "Izzy was a wonderful companion. She still is."

Hope sipped from her spoon and didn't respond.

Izzy finished her soup. "After that day, I decided to spend as much of my life outdoors as possible, preferably in this area. And I've worked toward that goal ever since."

Hope laid down her spoon. "Intriguing. Glenn, shall we pick up the bowls and wineglasses?"

He pushed back his chair and stood. "Let's."

I asked, "Can I help?"

Hope's sniff of a laugh sounded derogatory. "Tonight you're a guest in this house, not the hostess. You three should stay put. What's next, Glenn?"

"The fish course."

Glenn and Hope carried dirty dishes into the kitchen.

Izzy asked me, "Didn't you and your friends have names for the trails around the falls?"

She and I discussed the trails and the routes we'd taken. Landon might as well not have been there. Finally, I asked him, "Have you visited Fallingbrook Falls yet, Landon? It's one of our biggest tourist attractions."

He fiddled with his fish fork. "No, but it sounds like I should."

"Definitely," Izzy told him.

He glanced at her, and I understood the term "smoldering eyes."

Glenn and Hope returned with plates of food. Glenn gave me mine. "Yellow perch brought in today from Lake Superior, lightly fried in browned butter on a bed of pureed baby potatoes." Mashed potatoes, in other words. "And surrounded by tender-crisp baby peas."

He gave us fresh wineglasses. "We're drinking pinot gris with our fish." He gave me a slightly embarrassed look. "It's the same grape variety as the pinot grigio you brought, Emily, but this is French wine, not Italian."

The fish was light and flaky, done just right, the potatoes were silky and redolent of browned butter, and the peas were perfectly, and barely, cooked. I told Glenn how much I liked the dish. "And the wine you paired with it."

Eating, we barely spoke to one another, which was fine with me. I simply savored the food. After I finished, I felt like I'd eaten a complete meal, but Glenn stated that after a palate-cleansing break, we'd have our main course.

He and Hope brought everyone a minuscule bowl of tangy lemon sorbet. We ate it with the demitasse spoons they'd set at our places. Glenn returned to the kitchen. Smelling veggies roasting and beef being seared, I realized that I probably could eat more. The serving sizes had been reasonable, and he gave us lots of time between courses.

He brought us red wineglasses and poured a little Syrah into each one. The hilt of a chef's knife, one that I recognized as top-of-the-line and ridiculously expensive, now protruded from the scabbard.

He returned to the kitchen and came back with sizzling cast-iron dishes that fit into specially made wooden platters. "American Wagyu beef," he announced, "with fresh green beans from Emily's garden in back, and cherry tomatoes, also from her garden, halved and roasted with onions, plus shiitake mushrooms sauteed in butter and flavored with Syrah."

Izzy asked, "Wog-you beef?"

Glenn set her platter in front of her. "It originally comes from Japanese breeds of cows. Some have been brought here and bred with American cattle. They produce marbled and extremely tender beef. Because of the amount of fat, we serve it in small pieces."

Also because of the expense, I thought, but I said with enthusiasm, "A real treat." I had never been willing to spend so much on a cut of beef.

Glenn gave me my plate. "The best way to cook it is to sear it, and then if more doneness is required, finish it in a hot oven. To me, it should be eaten rare, so that's how I've prepared it, cooked only on the stovetop."

After everyone had their plate of beef and vegetables, Hope lifted her fork, and we all started eating. We barely needed our steak knives to cut the beef. I commented, "It's like cutting through butter, and it nearly melts in the mouth, too. And I love the Syrah with it." Knowing I'd be driving home, I was glad he was giving us little more than tastes of the wines.

"Glad you like it, Emily. I can tell from your kitchen that you're a professional. I'm glad you only cook donuts, though. It will be less competition for me if I open up near you."

"I hope you do. Everything has been superb. I'm sorry you're not buying Jerry Creavus's building, but I understand."

"There are other options nearby."

Hope lifted a mushroom on her fork. "Near Manhattan would be better."

Glenn looked at her. "Owning a restaurant does not necessarily mean living near it. I plan to open several restaurants. We could live anywhere." I couldn't read his expression.

She tapped her bare left ring finger. "New York, preferably."

Was she refusing to become engaged to him if he wanted to live too far from New York City to suit her?

I loved northern Wisconsin, but if Brent wanted to move somewhere else, I wouldn't hesitate. I would go with him. Home was with Brent.

Hope obviously didn't feel as strongly about Glenn, so maybe it was just as well that she had not yet said yes to his marriage proposal.

And possibly, after some of Hope's caustic and condescending comments to Izzy, Landon, and me that evening, Glenn wouldn't pop the question again. But he hadn't seemed to notice her rudeness. Maybe, for him, her other qualities outshone it.

Very likely, I was extra prickly and sensitive due to having to act like a guest in the house where I still felt like I should be running things and making decisions.

And where, as host, I had always tried to be polite to my guests. I hope I'd succeeded.

However, I was entirely capable of unkind thoughts. With a wealthy grandfather and a father who worked for that wealthy grandfather, Hope might have enough money to help her husband build a chain of restaurants. Maybe she didn't want to. That could explain her reluctance to let Glenn put a ring on her finger.

We didn't talk much as we ate, and it seemed that only Izzy and I were willing to keep the conversation going with our praise of northern Wisconsin.

Hope's usually pinched smile had more than a touch of smugness about it. Was she, like me, a matchmaker? But her smug smile couldn't be because she was succeeding. Landon and Izzy were almost totally ignoring each other. Then again, maybe their avoidance of more than a glance in each other's direction proved that they were interested in each other. I was sure that Izzy had a crush on Landon, but despite the smoldering eyes, I couldn't tell what he thought. He appeared to wish he was anywhere but in a cute Victorian cottage on Maple Street in Fallingbrook, Wisconsin. And eyes might smolder from an entire range of emotions.

Maybe love. Maybe hate . . .

And maybe, considering that he could be a murderer, I should hope that he would soon be far from Izzy.

Why had Hope invited both Izzy and Landon? Did she think that Glenn was jealous of Landon or hope that Glenn might become jealous enough to host the proposal party of Hope's dreams?

And where did I fit in, other than as someone who would likely appreciate Glenn's skill? Maybe insulting me was another way of jabbing, figuratively, at Izzy and Landon. And why did she criticize and insult us? Was it only her personality?

Maybe I understood why Hope's and Izzy's fathers had stopped communicating with each other.

No one left even a speck of beef or veggies on their plates. Glenn and Hope cleared the dishes and then brought us salads of baby greens in a light walnut oil dressing topped by a sprinkling of lightly toasted walnut pieces. Glenn paired it with merlot. Landon, Izzy, and I requested only a taste. I joked, "Aside from not wanting to drink and drive, I don't want alcohol on my breath when I go home to my detective husband."

Landon raised his head quickly and stared at me with those intense eyes. "You're married to a detective?"

"Yes. He works here in Fallingbrook." I didn't add, *And he intends to find you and talk to you as soon as you leave here tonight.*

Izzy praised the salad. "Crisp baby greens in August! Hard to find, but you did it." I could tell by her smile that she was picturing the greens she would produce in her greenhouses.

Glenn carried away our salad plates. Hope asked, "Who wants coffee or tea with dessert?"

Izzy said, "I'd like coffee."

Landon waved his hand dismissively. "Nothing for me."

I'd left enough good, freshly roasted coffee beans in the kitchen for Glenn and, as it turned out, for Hope, too, that I knew I would probably get a good cup of coffee, so I asked for some, too.

Hope heaved a gigantic sigh. "Glenn and I aren't much of coffee drinkers. How do you make it, Emily?"

I stood and put my purse on my chair. "I'd be happy to do it." I remembered Glenn thanking me for the coffee and tea and other groceries I'd left in the kitchen for him, and I also remembered that in Deputy Donut, he'd drunk tea.

Hope glanced toward the kitchen. I could hear Glenn out there puttering with plates. "Okay," Hope said, "if you don't mind."

"Not at all. Do you want tea? I can heat the water while the coffee drips through the coffeemaker."

"Would you? I'll just stay here and catch up with Izzy and Landon."

Like you haven't been doing much of, all evening. But I only said, "I'll be glad to make the tea. That's another thing I can do besides donuts and coffee."

Izzy piped up, "Which you're very good at!"

"Thanks, Izzy." Still barefoot, I padded toward the kitchen.

I carefully didn't say that I would prefer to make the coffee than to drink some made by a non–coffee drinker. Though, to be fair, Glenn probably knew how to properly brew coffee.

Behind me, Hope called out, "Glenn, Emily has kindly agreed to make the coffee that she and Izzy want. And our tea."

Glenn didn't respond, and when I arrived in the kitchen, I understood why. Standing at the island, he was obviously concentrating on arranging a plate of pastel French macarons, lime green, baby pink, and the palest of yellows. They were beautiful with their meringue-like outer layers and their fillings in colors perfectly matching the meringues.

I pointed. "Did you make those macarons, too, Glenn?"

"Of course."

"This is a real feast. I can hardly wait for you to open your restaurant." I started heating the kettle and removed the bag of coffee beans from the shelf where I'd put it before Glenn and Hope moved in. The bag was still sealed. I was selfishly glad. The beans would be fresh.

I opened the cupboard where I kept the coffee grinder.

It wasn't there.

Chapter 29

I quickly shut the cabinet where the coffee grinder should have been. Barely thinking, I opened the cupboard below the coffeemaker. That was silly—Alec and I had placed upright separators in that cabinet to hold baking trays and cooling racks, and the coffee grinder wouldn't have fit.

From the island behind me, Glenn asked, "Can I help you find something?" He sounded amused.

I closed that door quickly, too, and turned around. "Glenn, what flavors are those macarons?"

"Green tea, raspberry, and lemon."

I tried to look like I was thinking about macaron flavors, and not about my missing coffee grinder. "Tea might go better with them than coffee. Your wine pairings were perfect. What do you think about green tea with the macarons?"

"That would be best, but I didn't want to be bossy about it. I know how you die-hard coffee drinkers insist on coffee with anything."

I didn't point out that the French probably drank coffee with macarons. I put the sealed bag of coffee back into the cupboard and took out a package of green tea. It had been opened, but there were plenty of leaves in the bag. The water in the kettle was beginning to hiss and rumble. I went into the dining room. Since all three of its occupants were silent, I didn't have to wait for a break in the conversation. Landon turned to look at me as if he hoped I could normalize the strained gathering, which was seeming more and more impossible. *Who had moved my coffee grinder, and why?* Izzy gazed toward her hands, which were folded on the table, and Hope reached across my placemat and straightened my teaspoon.

Telling myself that non–coffee drinkers might put a coffee grinder somewhere that was not in their way, I pasted on a cheerful smile. "Izzy, Glenn and I have made an executive decision. Tea goes better than coffee with the luscious dessert that Glenn made, so you and I are having green tea, okay?"

Izzy looked up into my face for a second. I didn't change my phony smile. "Sure," she said, "if that's what you two experts think."

I gave her a quick wink that Hope couldn't have seen.

Landon might have, however. His eyebrows lowered slightly over those burning eyes.

I asked him, "Do you want to change your mind?"

"No—"

Removing her hand from the few pieces of cutlery left at my place, Hope interrupted Landon. "With lemon and sugar, Emily. Lemons are in the fridge. Be sure to slice them thinly. One of your own knives should be sharp enough." She managed to put doubt into her voice. "And remove the seeds. Your sugar bowl is with the cups and saucers. Glenn will bring them in."

The kettle was close to boiling, which meant that at any second, the water would be too hot to properly brew green tea. I hurried into the kitchen, removed the kettle from the heat, warmed the teapot with some of the water, poured that out, spooned tea leaves into the pot, and poured in the almost boiling water. While the tea steeped and Glenn carried the tray of teacups, saucers, and the sugar bowl into the dining room and then made a second trip into the kitchen for the plate of macarons, I mechanically prepared the lemon slices. *What had happened to my coffee grinder, and where was it?* In case it had been put to a nefarious use, I was not about to ask.

But maybe it hadn't been.

I took the teapot, tea strainer, and a plate containing the lemon slices and tiny tongs into the dining room.

Hope told me, "You've done all of the work, so you may have the honor of pouring the tea."

"Thank you." I wasn't sure if I sounded gracious or sarcastic.

Hope handed the full teacups on their saucers to everyone, and Glenn urged us to try all three flavors of macarons.

Izzy bit into a lemon macaron. "Oooh, I love this! Why is the name so similar to macaroons? What's the difference besides these French ones have fillings? Oops. I made them sound like teeth."

No one laughed.

Ordinarily, I might have, but I sat tensely, waiting for Glenn's response. Would he admit that macarons contained almond flour while macaroons were made with coconut? And if he did admit it, would it be because he didn't know about the almond flour in the donuts that killed Adam Nofftry? Or would it be because he himself had put the almond flour in those donuts, and he wanted to look innocent? As far as I knew, only a few of us had heard about the additions to those donuts or their frosting.

If I remembered correctly, one of the few things I'd left in the freezer in this house was a bag of almond flour. And there had definitely been cardamom among the spices when Glenn moved in.

Glenn's answer wasn't helpful. "Macarons and macaroons

both contain egg whites and sugar, and like all reputable chefs, I tweak recipes to improve them and make them my own, and of course I don't give away trade secrets."

Hope and Izzy both said, "Of course not."

My purse, with my phone inside it, was again on my lap. I felt my phone give that slight vibration that meant I'd received a text. No one else seemed to notice the tiny sound it made, and while I desperately wanted to text Brent, I didn't want any of these people, one or more of whom might have been a murderer, to guess that I was in contact with a detective.

What had Landon done with the donuts he'd bought? Although Hope had said she barely knew him, that had obviously been a lie. Had Landon spent part of the previous Sunday afternoon in the kitchen here? Had Hope or Glenn known what he was doing?

He could have been using my coffee grinder to grind the kernels from peach pits, and then he might have realized that the kernels had damaged the grinder. He could have discarded it. The trash should have been picked up on Maple Street at least once since then.

And then I thought of something else. When I'd peeked for a moment in the lower cabinet that housed the baking trays and cooling racks, I'd seen something that had not been there the last time I looked. I had a couple of pans that were specifically designed for baking circular cake-like pastries and calling them baked donuts, similar to but smaller than the baking pans we'd used in Deputy Donut to make our peachy sour cream donuts. Because I seldom used those pans, I stored them in the basement, not in that kitchen cupboard where I'd just seen them.

Adulterating the frosting had seemed simpler than replicating our donuts from scratch, but Vic Throppen had implied that the donuts themselves had contained ingredients that we hadn't used in ours.

Izzy had gone up to Gooseleg and shared donuts with her neighbors on Sunday afternoon. She could not have had time to be in this kitchen grinding the insides of peach pits and mixing them into donuts. I still ruled her out of harming Adam.

Hope claimed that Glenn did all of the cooking, and he was certainly clever enough to taste a donut and copy it, with a few additions, like substituting almond flour for some of the wheat flour, and seasoning with cardamom in an attempt to disguise the slightly bitter ground-up peach pits. But how could he, Landon, or Hope have known about Adam's almond allergy?

Why would any of them have tried to harm Adam?

I didn't know of a connection between Adam and Hope or Glenn.

Landon had at least one reason to be angry at Adam, but being yelled at hardly seemed like a motive for murder.

However, the afternoon that Landon and Izzy had first encountered each other, Landon had looked at Izzy like she was the sun, the moon, the stars, plus a few waterfalls and rivers, all combined. Could Landon's eyes be smoldering not only with adoration but also with an obsession to protect Izzy? Not that he'd been great protection. Thanks to him, or whoever had given Adam donuts laced with almond flour, she was possibly in danger of losing her freedom.

Not if I could help it.

How quickly could I leave this difficult dinner party without making it obvious that I might be running to my detective husband?

I tasted the raspberry macaron. Perfect. It would be a pity not to stay and savor the macarons, and although the tea was cooling in the thin china cups, it was still too hot to drink.

Hope must have thought so, too. Without taking a sip of

tea, she set down her cup and leaned toward Landon, more or less across the table from her. "Landon, are you in this area to spy on both Isabella and me for the old man, or just on me?"

Landon blushed. "I'm not spying on anyone."

Izzy had been about to bite into her green tea macaron. It slipped from her fingers and landed on her plate.

With her forefinger and thumb, Hope spun a lemon macaron on her plate. "Don't be ridiculous. The old man gave Isabella and me both money, and we're to report to him in a year about how we spent it. But I know the old man. Mere reporting wouldn't be enough. He would want someone else, like an untested new lawyer, to make certain that we weren't spending the money in ways he wouldn't approve of."

Landon set a half-eaten yellow macaron on his plate. "No. Mr. Korinth knows you, Hope, or at least he knows the side you choose to show him."

Hope's icy demeanor cracked slightly, and she displayed some heat. "What's that supposed to mean?"

Landon didn't take the bait. "He knows about your plans to start a restaurant chain with one of the country's best chefs. He approves. But how could he have sent me here to spy on you? You told him you're doing a staycation in the city."

Izzy said in a small voice, "Are you saying that you work for my, I mean Hope's and my grandfather, Landon?"

"Yes, but—"

Hope interrupted him. "And the old man, our grandfather, is in the process of adjusting his will. My father should be the one inheriting the most, and then me, because we have always cooperated with the old man, unlike Isabella and her father."

Glenn held up one hand and spoke loudly. "Wait. What are you saying? That you and your cousin are heiresses?"

Hope's hazel eyes flashed flames at him. "Well, I won't be

one if Landon and Isabella gang up and cut me out of the will. Not that it can be possible." She poked an index finger toward Izzy. "You and your ridiculous farmer-girl schemes shouldn't have a chance. If Landon were any kind of a man, he would tell the old man that."

Anger welled inside me.

I must not have been the only one. His face burning, Landon pushed his chair back. "I don't know what you're talking about, and I have very little influence with Mr. Korinth."

Hope picked up her teacup by its dainty handle and swirled the tea. The lemon slice threatened to slosh out. "You mean you haven't been chasing after Isabella to learn more about her?"

Landon's face became an even brighter red. "I have not."

"You're going to tell the old man that Isabella should be his sole heir, but you weren't going to tell Isabella you knew about her prospects until you safely had a ring on her finger."

Izzy flung her chair back so hard that I thought it might tip over. "Tell me the truth, Landon Bafter. Have you been spying on me? And you dropped in at my place last night, not because you were interested in me and tracked me down on your own like you implied, but because my grandfather told you to come see me, and he also told you where I live? You were spying?"

Landon must have gone back to her place after I stopped following him in Gooseleg.

Izzy turned to Hope and spat, "It was only one innocent conversation out on my deck, not a date." She brushed the back of one hand across her eyes, ran into the living room, and grabbed her purse off the couch.

Landon leaped to his feet. "Izzy, you don't understand." The linen napkin that had been on his lap floated to the floor.

Izzy pushed the screen door open. "I understand perfectly." She might have sounded as icy and sarcastic as her cousin if her voice hadn't caught on something like a sob. She fled out onto the porch.

The screen door banged against the jamb.

Landon picked up the napkin, flung it onto the back of the couch, and strode out onto the porch. "Izzy, wait!" I heard his footsteps on the wooden steps. He was running. "I told Mr. Korinth . . ."

I didn't hear the rest.

A car door slammed.

Chapter 30

Her smile even more smug than before, Hope pulled a raspberry macaron apart and snapped the top meringue in half. "That's the way the cookie crumbles. My cousin hasn't outgrown her snot-nosed brat stage. So much for a nice, civilized dinner party."

Hope had planned this all along. That was why she had invited Izzy and Landon to dinner. And now I knew why I'd been included. Hope had wanted to humiliate Izzy in front of Izzy's Fallingbrook friend.

In that moment, I didn't care if Hope was one of Izzy's few relatives. I had to get out of the house—my house—before I let Hope see how much I disliked her.

She rose gracefully and picked up Izzy's and Landon's dishes.

Clutching my ridiculously small purse, I stood, too, and placed my napkin beside my plate and my uneaten green tea macaron. "Thank you for the delicious dinner. I should go, too. It must be after ten, and I have to be at work at six thirty in the morning."

Glenn picked up his and my plates. "I'm glad you enjoyed it."

It was all I could do not to dash outside like the other two had. I managed sincere-sounding praise. "I can hardly wait for you to open your restaurant." At the door, I slipped my feet into my sandals, and then I went out, shutting the door carefully behind me. I maintained a sedate pace until I reached my car. Izzy's car was gone, and I didn't see Landon anywhere, either. I flung myself into my driver's seat. Planning to turn around, I pulled into the driveway I was renting to Glenn.

My headlights shined on a slim leather portfolio in the grass next to the left side of the driveway.

Landon had arrived late. In his hurry, either then or when he left only moments ago, had he accidentally pushed the portfolio out of the car he was driving?

I eased forward until my door was next to the portfolio. I glanced toward the house. I didn't see anyone on the front porch or looking out windows. I opened my car door, stepped out, grabbed the portfolio, and threw it onto the passenger seat. I quietly backed out of the driveway and onto Maple Street. Still seething at the way Hope had treated Izzy, I drove at the speed limit for a couple of blocks toward Wisconsin Street, and then I pushed harder on the gas.

Where was Izzy? Was Landon chasing her to her tiny home in that almost isolated clearing? And then . . . what?

Maybe he wasn't going to harm Izzy. Maybe he was driving to Duluth to catch the next flight to New York.

I didn't see either of their cars. Remembering my promise to let Brent know when the party was breaking up, I swerved into the parking lots behind the buildings on Deputy Donut's side of the street. I stopped and texted Brent that Landon might be following Izzy, possibly to her place outside Gooseleg. I gave Brent directions to Izzy's caboose. I took a deep breath and added that Hope and Glenn might have been involved in Adam's death, and that Landon could have given them the peachy donuts, and the box they'd come in, that he bought at Deputy Donut. Or Landon might have used their kitchen to create similar donuts.

I didn't wait for a reply. I bumped north through the parking lots as far as Deputy Donut, drove down our driveway, and turned north on Wisconsin Street.

Passing the square on my right, I spotted Olivia and Jocelyn strolling south, laughing and talking. I pulled off the road into the parking lane, opened the passenger window, and called to them. They ran to the side of the car.

Bracing myself with my left hand on the steering wheel, I leaned toward the window. "Landon might be following Izzy to Gooseleg, and I'm afraid of what he might do. Want to come with me to make sure she gets home safely and locks him out of her house? It might take a while, but I'll bring you back to Fallingbrook."

My two assistants didn't hesitate. Olivia climbed into the rear, and Jocelyn picked up the portfolio and sat in the passenger seat. With my foot on the brake, I waited while they fumbled with seat belts.

A late-model dark sedan sped north past us, and I caught only a glimpse of the driver. Glenn? Last I knew, he was cleaning up after the dinner party.

Another dark sedan, possibly a navy one, followed the car that I thought Glenn was driving. The license plate was JC MAYOR.

Jocelyn pointed. "There goes Jerry Creavus! Or that must be his car, anyway."

As far as I knew, Jerry had not arranged a meeting with Izzy some evening in his office. Had he decided that chasing after her in her car would work as well for whatever he had planned for the so-called meeting? Had someone alerted him to where she might be driving? I asked, "Seat belts latched?"

"Almost," Olivia answered. I heard the click, and then she said. "Go, Emily!"

I couldn't. Another car was coming up fast behind us. The car passed, and I groaned. "That was Landon, Mr. Mystery."

Jocelyn settled the portfolio on her thighs. "What's going on, Emily?"

Pulling into the road and starting north behind Landon, I summarized the dinner party, including Hope's rudeness, Landon's apparent job of spying on Izzy and his probable interest in her money, and my surmises about my coffee grinder going missing and the donut baking pan showing up in the kitchen.

Ahead of us, Landon was driving fast. His taillights diminished to two red blurs in the misty darkness. I couldn't see either Jerry Creavus's or Glenn's cars.

Jocelyn looked over her shoulder and teased Olivia, "Maybe we should call your new friend."

"It was only a walk," Olivia said. "And you were with us most of the time."

"I just happened along, and you both invited me to go with you." Jocelyn was bouncing on her seat almost as much as Izzy would have, at least before the dinner with her cousin. Jocelyn crowed, "Olivia was with Tyler Tainwright, that yummy policeman. You didn't see him, Emily, because he had already left us to get ready for his next shift, patrolling with Misty."

I realized then that Olivia was wearing her chestnut hair down, with soft waves settling on her shoulders, and her jeans were topped with a frilly, untucked blouse, mostly white with pink roses scattered over it, and I thought I remembered seeing sandals on her feet. She definitely looked dressed for a date. I met her gaze in the rearview mirror. "I hope it's just the first of many walks with him. And maybe some Poohsticks. But I don't think you need to call him yet about people possibly following Izzy, Olivia."

"I wasn't going to." Olivia could sound very prim, but I heard the undercurrent of excitement in her voice.

Jocelyn turned toward me, "Poohsticks? I read *Winnie-*

the-Pooh, but why would Olivia be playing Poohsticks with Tyler?"

I explained, and Jocelyn clapped her hands. "He's perfect for you, Olivia."

Olivia merely said, "Pooh!"

Jocelyn laughed. Unlike Olivia, Jocelyn didn't appear to have dressed for a date. She wore black jeans, a black, long-sleeved shirt, and a black ball cap. Her sneakers were red.

Wisconsin Street became County Road C. Houses were farther apart, and the road was mostly bordered by forest.

Jocelyn complained, "There's no moon."

Olivia corrected her. "It's only a quarter moon tonight. We'd see it in the southwest if it weren't for the trees, but it's setting. It'll disappear in about forty-five minutes."

Jocelyn was silent for a second, and then she asked, "Were you and Tyler moongazing before I caught up with you tonight, Olivia?"

"Sort of. He keeps track of things like that when he's on the night shift."

Barely able to make out Landon's taillights ahead of us, I stepped harder on the gas. "I've already told Brent that Landon might be heading north toward Gooseleg, maybe going to Izzy's cute tiny home, so Brent might arrive there before we do. I wonder why Landon let Izzy get ten minutes ahead of him. But he doesn't need to follow her home." I explained why Landon knew where she lived, and asked, "Can one of you text Brent?" It wasn't the first time I'd been glad that we had one another's emergency contacts in our phones.

Jocelyn pulled her phone out of her pocket. "I will."

"Please tell him that Glenn and Jerry might also be following Izzy, and that we're not doing anything besides trying to see where Landon goes. But we won't follow him all the way to Duluth."

Jocelyn worked on her phone and then pocketed it again. "Brent wasn't able to leave right away and he's still at the police station. What's this thing that was on your passenger seat when I got in?"

"I found that in the yard after I left that horridly tense dinner party. I guess Landon dropped it in his hurry to chase after Izzy. Then, maybe he went back for it, but I'd already picked it up."

Jocelyn laughed. "Good for you. So, I can look inside?"

I grinned. "I would if I weren't driving."

Chapter 31

Jocelyn shined her phone's light into the portfolio's interior, pulled out a messy sheaf of papers, laid the portfolio flat on her lap, and used it as a desk as she looked through the pages. She was quiet for a long time.

Olivia asked, "What is it, Jocelyn?"

"I don't think these documents are Landon's. They all seem to be about Glenn Sitherby."

I guessed, "Maybe Landon lied about not spying on Hope. Maybe he was collecting information about both her and Glenn."

Jocelyn picked up a page. "Here's a letter to Glenn from ten years ago, offering Glenn a position as manager of a restaurant."

I asked, "What's the company name? Is it anything to do with Adam Nofftry?"

"Not obviously. The company is Wilson Family."

Olivia groaned. "That's a huge conglomerate owning everything from rail lines to greeting cards. Who signed the letter?"

"Ted Wilson. Do we know a Ted Wilson?"

Olivia and I said that we didn't.

Jocelyn turned the letter over. "Someone wrote on the back, a column for pros and a column for cons." She was silent for a few seconds. "One of the cons is that Glenn would have to sell something called Hot Pepper, both words capitalized."

I told Jocelyn and Olivia, "Izzy and I searched him on the Internet. Hot Pepper was a popular, successful restaurant. It closed about five years ago." I took my right hand off the wheel to point toward the documents on Jocelyn's lap. "Can you tell if those are originals or copies?"

Jocelyn rustled through papers. "I can't tell. Copies can be really good. Oh, here's an employment contract with Wilson Family. An unusual stipulation, that Glenn appears to have signed, is that the restaurant Glenn manages, Purple Pepper, will never serve almonds or almond products."

Olivia breathed, "Wow! When did Glenn sign that?"

Jocelyn turned the page over. "Ten years ago. And the other person who signed it was this Ted Wilson, whoever that is." Still using her phone's light, she scanned more pages. She pulled one out, put it on top, and slapped the entire set of papers onto the portfolio. "Here it is, a possible link to lots of things. A termination letter. From two years ago. Glenn was fired from Purple Pepper for cause, but it doesn't say what the cause was. And Ted Wilson signed that letter, too. But someone scrawled across the bottom of the letter, 'Who snitched? He wasn't there, so he couldn't have been affected.' " Jocelyn raised her head. "To me, the writing looks like the writing of the pros and cons of accepting the job as manager of Purple Pepper."

"For cause," Olivia repeated. "Like maybe serving almonds although he agreed not to. Or am I jumping to conclusions?"

Still watching the taillights far ahead, I said, "Maybe, but I want to jump to that one, too."

Jocelyn flipped to another page. "Me, too. A non-competition agreement is stapled to the termination letter. Glenn promised not to open a new restaurant in the next ten years—ten years!—within fifty miles of any of the restaurants owned by Wilson Family. And here's a handwritten note stuck to the non-competition agreement. Same writing as before, I'm guessing. And it's a huge clue about who owned this restaurant." Jocelyn cleared her voice and read aloud in a stern and booming voice, " 'It doesn't say I can't open a restaurant within fifty miles of land he's contemplating buying.' Again, that sounds like Glenn could have been referring to Adam Nofftry."

I agreed. "And I bet that Brent and Vic have been plowing through Adam's business records and trying to find something like this. They probably know about the Wilson Family connection, but drilling down through all of the correspondence of all of the conglomerate's subsidiaries could take months. Someone in the DCI is probably working on that. Meanwhile, either Landon collected these documents, or these are Glenn's records. If Glenn wrote that comment about snitching, and if the person who wasn't there and therefore supposedly was not affected was Adam Nofftry, there's a possible motive for Glenn to have killed Adam—revenge for being fired after Glenn sold his own successful restaurant to manage one of Adam's. And it sounds like whoever bought Glenn's Hot Pepper restaurant ended up closing it. That might have made Glenn angrier about all of it."

Jocelyn straightened the sheaf of papers. "Fired two years ago. How has he been making a living since then?"

"A girlfriend," I guessed. "Probably Izzy's cousin Hope. Tonight she claimed that she would accept Glenn's proposal of marriage if he threw the right sort of party for her."

Olivia made a disgusted sound. "I would never do that."

I told her, "You're a better catch than Hope."

Olivia breathed out a loud and phony sigh. "Not financially."

I stated firmly, "In every other way. And Tyler's a better catch than a chef who would date a bully like Hope."

Jocelyn added, "He is."

Olivia sighed. "Would you two stop? It was only a walk. One." Again, I heard a smile in her voice.

"And it was only a quarter moon," I joked. "When's the next full moon?"

Olivia laughed. "I don't know."

I predicted, "Tyler will. And he'll ask you out to gaze at it." Then I reminded myself what dating—or marrying—a police officer was like. "If he's not working."

Jocelyn tapped at the portfolio. The leather made a hollow sound. "Back to important business. If our theories are correct, Glenn had to know there was a reason why he wasn't allowed to serve almonds or almond products in the restaurant he managed. And even if he didn't know for sure that Adam was allergic to them, he could have guessed. Then Glenn bided his time until he could feed almonds to Adam."

Olivia asked, "But how? Force him to eat donuts containing almonds? Adam must have known not to accept food from someone who held a grudge against him and who also knew or might have guessed that Adam was allergic to almonds."

I told them, "Adam didn't seem to have one of those autoinjector thingies with him. Maybe he thought he did and took a risk."

Olivia sat back. "People do things like that."

I hazarded another guess. "Or Glenn took it from him." I told them about finding an autoinjector in a creek several miles from the murder site.

Jocelyn turned another page and held up a finger. "Wow, here's something I didn't expect to find, a marriage certificate. Glenn and Izzy's cousin Hope are married. To each other."

I couldn't help turning my head sharply toward her. "When did that happen, Jocelyn?"

"Two months ago." She paged through more documents. "And they lost no time signing wills and making each other their beneficiaries. Here are the wills."

I said dryly, "That would have been about the time that Izzy and Hope's grandfather gave Izzy funds to invest. According to Hope, the grandfather gave money to both Izzy and Hope, and the grandfather will judge how well they use it before he decides how much each of them should inherit. This evening Glenn acted like he didn't know that Hope was a potential heir. Hope didn't dispute that. She said that she wouldn't be one if Landon convinced the grandfather to choose Izzy. I'm sure Glenn knew that Hope could inherit a lot, if only from her father, who also works for the grandfather."

Jocelyn snorted. "Of course he did. Does Glenn have an alibi for last Sunday?"

I bit my lips and then tried to relax my too-grim expression. "Not a great one. Hope and Glenn said they were together in my house on Maple Street during that afternoon and evening. Maybe I can check that."

Jocelyn asked, "How? Do you have spy cameras in and on the house?"

"Nothing so fancy. Brent and I installed keyless entry locks on our doors. We can program different codes for different people. Glenn and Hope have only one code that they must be sharing. I'm going to pull off onto the shoulder. My phone will tell me when they unlocked the front door last Sunday." I quickly checked the lock's audit trail. "Aha. Someone unlocked the house from the outside shortly after Landon and Hope left Deputy Donut with Landon's box of donuts. A couple of hours later, the door was unlocked from the inside and locked itself. And then someone came in about an hour after Izzy found Adam's body." I put my phone away and pulled out onto the highway. "It's not conclusive, and I probably didn't need to risk losing track of Landon by checking.

Brent has probably already done that and discovered that Glenn's and Hope's alibis could be false."

Jocelyn pointed ahead. "I've been watching, and I think Landon's way up there, turning onto County Road H."

I told my car to phone Izzy.

She answered.

I quickly told her, "Izzy, I'm afraid that three men in three cars might be following you—Glenn, the mayor, and Landon."

"I saw them. I might have lost the first two, but one car is coming up fast behind me. I'm driving as fast as I dare."

I asked, "Could it be Landon?

"Maybe." Her voice was small. Of course she was remembering the disappointing ending to the dinner party and Landon's betrayal.

"We're not too far behind him."

"Thank you. Oh! What does he think he's—" From the speaker in my car, we heard a horn blaring and tires squealing. Izzy screamed, her voice high with terror. A series of thumps and bangs ended in sudden silence, as if Izzy's phone had been turned off.

Or had been smashed.

Chapter 32

All three of us in my car gasped and called Izzy's name. My natural reflex was to hit the brakes even though no obvious danger was directly ahead of us. I fought the impulse and floored the gas pedal.

Jocelyn shoved the portfolio and papers off her lap onto the floor near her feet. "I'm calling emergency."

Olivia shouted, almost calmly. "I already am. You help Emily watch the road." In a businesslike voice, she said, "A car crash. Probably on County Road H not too far west of County Road C."

We were quickly approaching the intersection with H, and I had to slow down. A vehicle hurtled south on C toward us.

"Go!" Jocelyn whispered.

I couldn't risk it. I had to slam on the brakes and wait long seconds. A heavy truck roared past, and then I turned, my tires squealing, onto H.

Woods crowded the road. We climbed a hill, rounded a curve and then another one.

The woods receded, and I drove between abandoned fields pocked with boulders and scraggly cedars. Far ahead, red lights flashed.

Several yards beyond the dirt lane that Landon had swerved onto after we first encountered him, a dark sedan was parked crookedly, its front angled slightly toward the ditch and its hazard lights blinking, on the road's shoulder. The part of the car we could see appeared undamaged. With a hint of optimism, Jocelyn asked, "Is that Izzy's car?"

I slowed. "It looks too big." Frightened, my movements robotlike, I pulled onto the shoulder several car lengths behind the dark sedan. My headlights lit its rear license plate. Probably Minnesota. And the car was gray. "I'm sure it's Landon's." My voice sounded dead. We had allowed Landon to get far enough ahead of us to—what?

Beside me, Jocelyn peered out her side window. "A car's in the ditch. It's right side up, but dented and smashed, like it rolled. I think it's Izzy's. A man is prowling around it with a flashlight."

She reached for her door.

I cautioned, "Don't open it."

Jocelyn put her hands in her lap. "I won't. He's coming this way. Are all the doors and windows locked?"

"Yes," I said.

Olivia was relaying everything to the emergency dispatcher.

His hair unkempt and his eyes wild, Landon arrived at the top of the embankment. He shouted something about Izzy and 911 and then took off running toward his rental car. He leaped into it and sped west.

All three of us unlocked our doors and clambered out. Olivia continued telling the 911 operator what we were doing. Shouting Izzy's name, Jocelyn and I used our phones' lights to help all of us negotiate the steep slope. Weirdly distorted shadows gyrated as we slipped and slid among dusty grasses and wildflowers, many of them bent and broken. The straps of my sandals bit into my feet. Grit lodged between my toes.

Izzy didn't answer. Her driver's door was open. Her windshield had become a zillion sparkling crystals that had flung themselves all over the ground and the car, as if trying to echo the stars in the cloudless, moonless sky above us. A front airbag had inflated but now hung from the steering wheel like an unwanted rag, and another airbag, also deflated, dangled from the inside of the driver's door. No one was in any of the seats.

A silver ballet flat sporting a jaunty pom-pom that resembled a multi-petaled flower lay on the ground near that open door.

I told the others, "When Izzy ran away from Hope's dinner party, she was wearing two shoes like that. Where's the other one, and where's she?" I raised my voice. "Izzy!"

No answer.

Jocelyn aimed her phone's light on the side of the driver's seat. "There's blood, and the seat belt's broken, but it's a straight cut, as if someone slashed it with a machete." The lid of the trunk was bashed in and open enough for us to peek inside. Empty, except for a half dozen plant pots.

I checked the slope between us and the road. A bumper, an entire fender, and bits of metal, plastic, and glass were scattered among weeds and loose gravel. We walked around the car in ever-widening circles. Olivia said it for all of us and to the dispatcher, "She does not seem to be near her car."

Jocelyn shined her light into the weedy field stretching north from the road. "I didn't understand what Landon yelled at us, but was it something like 'kidnap'?"

I gazed up toward the road. Moths fluttered through the beam of my headlights. "He might have. Was he rushing off to search for her, or was she in his car, and he was rushing off to take her somewhere? A hospital, maybe. Or a place where no one would find her? Maybe we should have followed him."

Jocelyn waved her light past Izzy's wrecked car and shined it on the dirt lane. "If you two want to try to find him, I'll stay here and search in case she's lying injured nearby." She must have seen the look on my face. She attempted to reassure me. "I'll be safe. I'll hide in the bushes if I hear anyone coming either on the road or up that farm lane." She patted the front pocket of her black jeans. "And I have my phone."

I asked Olivia, "What do you think?"

"We should probably try to find out where he went so we can tell"—she held up her phone—"them."

I agreed. Avoiding the debris from Izzy's car, Olivia and I scrambled up the bank to my car.

We shut ourselves inside. Olivia told the dispatcher that Jocelyn was staying behind. "And Emily and I are following the suspected kidnapper in Emily's car." Holding the phone away from her face, Olivia asked me, "How long will it take help to get here?"

I eased off the shoulder onto the road. "They'll come fast, so maybe fifteen minutes since you first called. They could be at the crash scene in about ten minutes. But Brent is probably already on his way and could be there sooner." I sped up.

Olivia told the dispatcher that Detective Fyne might be nearby. I had my car phone Brent. He answered from inside his car. I described Izzy's crash and added, "We're not sure what Landon had to do with it and what he yelled at us through our closed windows, but he might have said that Izzy was kidnapped. He's ahead of us now, speeding west on H."

"I'm on C, close to H." Brent sounded reassuringly calm. "I'll go directly to the crash site and help Jocelyn search for Izzy while we wait for more officers, an ambulance, and firefighters. Meanwhile, do not approach Landon, and if you spot him or his car, let us know, and then you go back to pick up Jocelyn."

"I see something like a red flashing glow ahead."

"It could be first responders from Gooseleg."

"Or it could be Landon's hazard lights again. As soon as I figure out where he's going—maybe it's to the caboose—I'll let you know. If he's trying to rush her to a hospital, he's going the wrong way." Gooseleg didn't have a hospital. The nearest one was in Fallingbrook. Landon could drive to that one by continuing west on H and then turning left at the end of H, but it would take longer.

Brent reminded me, "Stay out of danger, Em."

"I will. And Olivia's with me. She has 911 on the line."

"I'm turning onto H now."

"Okay, I'll let you know what we find, if anything."

Treed on both sides, the road climbed. The night was lit only by stars, our headlights, and that flashing, pinkish glow ahead. A forested hill rose to our right. Ahead, the flashing lights appeared to be stationary and in or beside the right lane.

Although figuring out if Landon was holding Izzy captive was urgent, I slowed, prepared to respond if the vehicle with the flashing lights tried to force us off the road. We wouldn't be any help to Izzy if my car, with Olivia and me strapped inside, ended up rolling down the hill and into trees across the road from the property Izzy was buying.

I recognized Landon's car, even though the flashing hazard lights made me want to close my eyes. With its headlights off, the sedan was, I thought, parked close to the former driveway leading up to the meadow where Izzy had found Adam's body.

Beside me, Olivia said into her phone, "The car that fled the crash scene shortly after we arrived there is parked farther west on County Road H." Olivia sounded the same way I felt—dry-mouthed and not quite able to swallow.

Telling myself to be calm and rational, I turned on my own four-way flashers and parked behind Landon's car. If he was in it, I couldn't see him.

Olivia told the dispatcher where we were, and I updated Brent. We both got the same answer. *Stay in your car with the doors locked and stay on the line.*

Olivia and I looked at each other. Brent could reach this

spot soon if we needed him, and other officers had to be on the way. We shook our heads and obeyed only the last part of our orders. Holding our phones, we quietly stepped out of the car. In case we needed to rush back for shelter, I turned off the interior lights, and we didn't quite shut the doors.

Landon hadn't quite closed his driver's door, either. We quickly checked the sedan's seats and popped the trunk open. Izzy wasn't in his car.

With our phones' lights showing the way, we ran down into the ditch, jumped over the trickle of water, and dashed up the slope past TWIG's sign, now bent almost to the ground.

We'd barely started up the trail into the canyon of fragrant, softly whispering pines when a man on the hill above us shouted "Izzy!" His voice was deep and musical. Landon.

However, I thought I detected a note of panic similar to mine. Despite everything he'd done in the past half hour, I wanted to believe that he wouldn't harm Izzy.

I didn't dare.

Running as quietly as we could in darkness lit only by our phones, which we shielded partially with our hands, Olivia and I rounded the bend near the cave-like niche where I'd found the box with donuts in it.

And then we were on the meadow. We heard nothing more from Landon.

Olivia and I turned off our phones' lights. The hillside was huge. We didn't dare yell and let Landon know where we were. We stood still, listened, and let our eyes adjust to the darkness.

Olivia pointed toward the pond where Izzy had found Adam's body and whispered, "Someone's over there with a light." A glimmer showed between cattails shifting in slight breezes.

Again, we turned on our phones' lights, but we covered most of them with our fingers and shined thin beams ahead of us. Taking long strides, we ran through the meadow. I hoped that Olivia's sandals weren't hurting her feet. I tried to steady and quiet my breathing. We slowed as we approached the glow near the hillside's lowest pond.

Beckoning to Olivia to follow me, I shielded my phone's light against my chest and tiptoed around the rock where I'd made Izzy sit when she'd appeared about to faint. I peeked around the stand of cattails.

Silhouetted by the light from his phone, Landon knelt over Izzy's prone body. She was lying almost exactly where she'd found Adam's body. Her feet were bare, and the elegantly simple black linen dress she'd chosen for Hope's dinner party was sopping and mud-covered.

Landon's hands were on Izzy's shoulders, close to her neck.

He bent closer.

Chapter 33

Screaming, "Get away from her," I whipped out my phone and shined it on Landon. Olivia also caught him in the glare of her phone's light.

I was dimly aware of a car moving quickly below us on the highway. Brent?

Landon raised his head. Barely glancing toward us, he lifted one hand in a gesture that could have meant we should go away or that we should come closer. "Help," he gasped, and lowered his face to Izzy's.

I barged past reedy cattail stems to him. "What are you doing?"

He raised his head again. His previously smoldering eyes were bleak. "Mouth-to-mouth." He pinched Izzy's nostrils together and breathed into her mouth.

Olivia pushed through the rushes to stand beside me. "Why?"

He raised his head. "She's not breathing."

Without caring about my own once-lovely dress, I landed on the damp ground almost as quickly as my heart seemed to plummet. *Izzy, the spunky little girl, racing up and down rocky trails with me, searching for hidden treasure...* I scrambled up onto my knees close to Izzy and Landon and plunked my phone next to my foot. I took a deep breath, trying to center myself and find the inner stillness I knew I needed if I was to help my young friend. "Was her head in the water?"

Landon answered between rescue breaths, "Under it."

No, oh, no, no, no. Despite my fears about Izzy, my voice wavered only slightly, "I have first aid training. Did you clear her airways? Roll her onto her side to empty water from her mouth and nose?"

Every question I asked him required time for him to inhale and then blow the air into Izzy's mouth. "Yes."

"Do you want me to take over?"

"Not yet."

"Did you call for help?"

"No time."

Behind me, I heard Olivia tell the dispatcher where we had found Izzy.

I pushed Izzy's wet curls from her forehead. As if he had waded into the pond to pull Izzy out, Landon was as wet and muddy as she was. "Breathe, Izzy." I was barely aware I was speaking.

I heard Brent's voice from my nearly forgotten phone. "Em? Where are you?"

I shouted toward the phone, "At the pond where Adam's body was. Landon's trying to resuscitate Izzy. Her head was under the water." My voice broke.

Brent spoke in the even tones he probably used in any crisis. "I'm almost there. Jocelyn's okay. Other officers and firefighters arrived and an ambulance is on its way. I'll have it sent to where you are, instead."

"Okay. They should park in front of the car in front of mine. I left my flashers on. Landon's are on, too."

"I'll give them your license number. See you soon."

In case Landon didn't know who Brent was and also, in case Landon would act frightened or run away after he heard that a detective was on his way, I told him, "The man on the other end of the line is my husband Brent, Fallingbrook's detective."

Landon raised his head, glanced only briefly at my face, and took a deep breath. "Good." He blew into Izzy's mouth again. In that brief look, I'd seen pain and fear in Landon's eyes, the kind of pain and fear one felt for a person one cared deeply about.

I again offered to take over the resuscitation. Landon shook his head. In case he hadn't overheard, I said, "Brent's sending the ambulance here." Landon gave me a thumbs-up and concentrated on Izzy.

Olivia said into her phone, "Detective Fyne is nearby, and we're on the line with him." She disconnected and told me, "I'm calling Jocelyn." Seconds later, she said quietly into her phone, "We found her." Jocelyn must have asked if Izzy was okay. "We hope so." Olivia had probably tried to sound upbeat. She didn't quite succeed.

I asked Landon, "How did Izzy get here?"

"A man took her."

"Out of her car?"

"Yes."

"Who?"

I had to wait for him to take another breath. "Don't know. Tall man."

"Could it have been Glenn?"

Landon shrugged. "Could've."

"Mayor Creavus?"

"Don't know him."

"Did you see the tall man's vehicle?"

"Yes."

"Van, sedan, pickup, SUV?"

"Sedan."

Landon's splintered description of a tall man driving a sedan could have applied to Jerry, to Glenn, or even to Landon himself.

However, as far as I could tell, Landon was trying to save Izzy's life, not kill her. But what had he done before Olivia and I arrived? I asked him, "How did Izzy get this far from her car?"

"In his car." He breathed into Izzy's mouth and took a breath of his own. "Must've carried her up here." He said it so fast that it sounded almost like one long word.

"Did you see his license number?"

"Too far away."

"Was his car at the base of the trail when you parked?"

"He had just pulled away." He tried again to get Izzy breathing on her own, and then added, "I guessed he'd dropped her off there." A few seconds later, he added, "So I parked." More seconds passed before he could tell us, "Called her name, searched the trail, ran up here."

"Did you see him up here?"

"No. Kept calling her." Another set of breaths, and he continued his disjointed story. "Heard a splash. Found her."

I guessed, "So, she wasn't underwater long."

"Hope not."

"Where did the tall man go? Did he pass you running down the trail while you were running up?"

"No." He nodded toward the trees on the west side of the pond. "Something . . . over there."

"On the neighboring property? Could he have parked down there, around a curve from where we parked? When I drove past here yesterday, I noticed a waterfall down there that probably came from this pond, and then, not much farther along the road, there was another possible trail up the hill between trees."

Olivia looked toward the dark and silent woods. "I heard a car race away after we got up here, but I couldn't tell which way it was going."

At the time, I'd wondered if it had been Brent, but if it had, he'd have been with us by now. "I heard it, too."

Landon resurfaced. "The important thing is for Izzy to breathe." He sounded almost desperate. He gulped in air and put his mouth over Izzy's again.

"Emily!" It was Brent, calling from the far side of the meadow.

Hoping he'd see my phone's beam, I pointed it upward and waved it. "We're beside the pond!"

Izzy made a burbling noise. The fingers of the hand closest to me curled downward into the mud. She opened her eyes.

Landon rocked back on his heels and let out a huge sigh.

I congratulated him. "You did it."

"Did what?"

"Saved her."

"We don't know how long she was unconscious. She couldn't have been underwater for long, but . . ."

Olivia phoned Jocelyn again. "Izzy's going to be okay."

Izzy squinted up toward Landon's face. "Hope!"

"I am," he said.

Shining a light in front of him, Brent rustled through the cattails. He was still in his suit and tie. I stood and slipped my hand into his free one. Mud in my sandals did not make my feet feel less bruised and blistered.

Izzy struggled in the oozy mud. "Help me sit up, please, Landon."

Tenderly, Landon raised her upper body until she sat in the mud beside him. He supported her with one arm around her back. She leaned her head on his shoulder.

Brent asked gently, "What happened?"

Izzy answered, "Someone ran me off the road? And then, I don't know."

Brent continued in his kind tones, "Can you tell me who ran you off the road?"

"Could have been Fallingbrook's mayor. Or maybe I dreamed he was carrying me, jostling me. Someone tall. My head hurts."

Olivia told her, "Stay still. An ambulance is on the way."

"Hope!" Izzy nearly shouted it.

"We don't have to hope," Olivia told her gently. "We know."

Izzy's hands fretted at the sides of her head. "I can't think."

Landon closed the small, restless hands inside one of his larger ones. "We'll get you to the hospital. And I'm sorry. I would have been right behind you, but I had to find an open gas station and fill up."

Brent squeezed my shoulder. "Can you and Olivia go down to the road and direct the EMTs here? We'll get your and Jocelyn's statements later."

I stood on tiptoes and brushed my lips across his cheek. "Sure." I whispered in his ear, "I don't think Landon hurt her." I said more loudly, "See you at home, later."

I bent over and squeezed Izzy's shoulder. "You're going to be okay." I asked Landon, "Look after her, okay?"

"I won't leave her side." His voice, still deep, had become nearly toneless. He thinned his lips in one firm, determined line.

Brent tapped the screen of his phone. "It's late, but I'll try to get her lawyer friends to meet her at the hospital."

Landon repeated, "I'll stay with her."

Passing Brent, I patted the sleeve of his jacket.

Olivia and I quickly followed the light from our phones through the dark meadow.

Sirens sounded in the distance.

Chapter 34

Olivia and I hurried down the trail and jumped over the water in the ditch.

An ambulance sped toward us. Olivia and I waved our phone's lights in arcs above our heads.

The two EMTs wasted no time getting out. They each grabbed a case of equipment.

I pointed. "The victim's up there. We were sent to lead you to her. She's conscious, but she wasn't when she was thrown into the pond. She nearly drowned, and she may have a concussion. Her car crashed a couple of miles back."

The driver asked, "How'd she get from that crash to up there?"

"Apparently, she was driven and then carried."

"Can we take a wheeled stretcher, or would the kind we have to carry be better?"

I frowned. "I'm afraid that the kind you carry is a safer bet. She probably weighs only around a hundred pounds, and Brent Fyne and the man who revived Izzy will likely want to help carry her." I pointed at Olivia. "And we can, too."

The EMTs unlatched a rigid orange stretcher from one of the ambulance's interior walls. Wearing lights on their foreheads and carrying the stretcher and cases of gear, they followed Olivia and me up the hill and across the rocky meadow.

Brent backed away from Izzy, who still sat, barefoot and in her ruined linen dress, in the mud, protected in Landon's embrace. The EMTs rushed to her.

Brent told Olivia and me, "I have one more job for you two tonight in addition to picking up Jocelyn and then all of you going home. Vic's on his way. Can you help him find this place? I'm not sure I made it clear which pond."

I agreed. "Unless we'll be needed to help carry the stretcher."

"You won't be."

Olivia and I crossed the meadow again. She muttered, "We're going to know this place better than Izzy does."

Down at the road, I summarized some of what we'd learned. "Landon saw a car pull away from near here. He ran up this trail calling for Izzy. In the meadow, he heard a splash. He didn't see the tall man. That man must have done what we guessed earlier. He ran down through the woods on the far side of the pond."

Olivia pointed west. "Could the tall man have parked a little farther down the road? Like he stopped here, planning to drop Izzy off, but he saw Landon's headlights in his rear-view mirror, so he drove on?"

"And Landon thought the man had brought Izzy to this spot, so Landon parked here. But the tall man could have taken Izzy farther west, but only around that curve, to a spot below the pond. He could have parked there and carried her up an ATV trail to the pond while Landon was parking and running up the path we all knew about. Shall we go see what's beyond that curve? If we hear a car that could be Vic's, we can run back."

"Let's do it."

Shining our lights on the gravel verge, careful to walk on the pavement where we wouldn't disturb evidence, and listening for Vic, we walked around the curve. Beyond the narrow cascade of water below the pond, the road started downhill. I showed Olivia the break between trees.

She aimed her light at their trunks and the spaces between them. "That definitely looks like the remains of a road or driveway that might have once led to a homestead."

It slanted up through the woods on the west side of the pond. I guessed aloud, "It could be a shorter route to that pond. Oops, maybe that vehicle coming from the east is Vic."

We turned to go, and my phone's light glinted off something that didn't belong on that grassy slope, something sparkly and silver.

It was a cute ballet flat with a chrysanthemum-like pom-pom on the toe. Olivia sucked in a gasp of a breath. "Izzy's other shoe."

Leaving it where we'd found it, we loped back to the cars. My sandals rubbed at newly formed blisters.

Vic parked an unmarked cruiser and got out. Shining a powerful flashlight at the ground in front of him, he asked, "How's the young lady who was in the crash? I left there as soon as a team of DCI investigators arrived." Like Brent, Vic was dressed in a suit, white shirt, and tie.

I told him, "She's lucky to be alive. From what we can piece together, someone ran her off the road, slashed her seat belt, removed her, unconscious or semiconscious, from her car, and drove her to a spot a little west of here." Olivia and I shined our lights toward the curve in the road and explained our theory about where the tall man parked and how he took Izzy to the pond and then fled. I added, "When Landon was in the meadow up there, he heard a splash. She would have drowned if he hadn't come along. He knows rescue breathing."

Vic asked me, "Why is everyone going up this trail if there's another one that could be shorter?"

"We didn't know about that one. Olivia and I wondered,

so we just walked down there. And we saw something there that you should see."

He gave me a curt nod. "Let's have a look."

We all walked, only now I was limping, around the curve. I shined my light on the gravel. "I can't say for sure where he parked." I moved the beam to the silver ballet flat. "See? Izzy was wearing a pair like this at a dinner party we both attended this evening."

Vic aimed his light at the shoe. "It looks like the mate to the shoe at the crash scene." He waved his arm toward the pines above us. "We'll investigate this possible access to that pond, too. Misty and Tyler are on their way from the crash. I'll radio them to photograph the shoe and its surroundings and collect the shoe as evidence."

We started back toward the cars, and I thought Olivia took a quick skip at the thought that Tyler might be near us soon.

However, when we reached the lineup of cars and the ambulance, Vic dismissed us. "There's no need for you two to stick around in the woods in the dark." He glanced up toward the rustling pines. "No telling who might be around. Collect that other young lady from the crash scene, and then you can all go home. We'll get your statements in the morning after we investigate here. I don't need guides the rest of the way."

Even in the dim light, he must have noticed my stiffening at his hint that a murderer might be nearby. He explained simply and without emotion, "I'm armed." Flashlight on, he jumped the ditch and started up the hill.

Chapter 35

For a few seconds after Vic disappeared on that narrow driveway through the dark forest, I heard his dress shoes on the rocky ground, and then all was silent, and though I strained my eyes, I couldn't make out the slightest glint from his extra-bright flashlight.

Above us, the sky was black velvet sequined in stars, no clouds, and no moon. Olivia and I started toward my car. I asked her, "Can you tell if it's warm or not? I think it's cold for the middle of the night in August, or at least colder than predicted, but maybe it's just my own shock and adrenaline."

"I'm not sure."

"Poor Izzy and Landon. They're soaked."

"And muddy. The EMTs will warm Izzy up. I know Landon said he wouldn't leave her side, but will the EMTs even let him into the ambulance?"

I guessed, "Vic and Brent probably won't let him ride with Izzy. He's not exactly cleared yet. He was acting like he really cared about her, but it could be an act."

"Do you think it was an act?"

"No, but that could partly be because I don't want Izzy to be hurt."

"I thought his concern was genuine." Olivia gurgled a

sound between a sigh and a laugh. "Landon might have to drive to the hospital. He'll get that rental car all muddy."

"More likely he'll end up riding with Brent, Vic, or Misty and Tyler. His rental car will need to be checked for signs of colliding with Izzy's car or that she was inside it."

"Is Brent driving his own car, or the department's?"

We had just walked past it. "His own."

"You got a little muddy, too."

"This dress is washable. I hope I can get the mud out. It's probably already dried." I brushed one hand across the back of the skirt.

"You're limping."

"I thought I was only going out to dinner, not running around in the wilderness. These sandals are giving me blisters."

"You have a first aid kit in your car, don't you?"

"Yes, but Jocelyn's waiting . . ."

"Vic said investigators are at the crash scene. She'll be safe for a few minutes longer while we bandage your blisters."

I laughed, but it wasn't a real laugh. How long would it be before either of us felt like truly laughing or smiling again? "I can do it."

"Do you need me to drive?"

"Thanks. I think I'll be fine, but I'll let you know if I change my mind. And I have a sweater in the back, too."

Slipping the sweater on and covering the blisters with cushioning bandages took only a few minutes. I would be home soon and could clean the grit out of any open sores. Wincing at the thought, I started the car.

Olivia buckled herself into the seat beside me, and I made a U-turn and headed east. Halfway to Izzy's car, a cruiser, its strobes flashing but its siren silent, sped west past us.

Olivia exclaimed, "That's them! Tyler and Misty."

"Too bad we didn't happen to be at the same place at the same time."

"He's working." If I'd had any doubts, which I didn't, about Olivia understanding duty and appreciating a man who served others because he wanted to, those doubts would have been dispelled by her simple acceptance of what Tyler needed to do that night.

"I know the feeling, but at least I got to spend a few minutes with Brent."

"And anyway, it's not like we're dating."

Yet, I thought, but didn't say. Ahead, a fire truck was parked on the other side of the road. I braked. The fire truck's flashing lights were so bright that I could barely see the DCI forensics van behind it.

I parked on the right shoulder. Olivia and I clambered out and ran across the road. The bandages helped my feet feel better, sort of.

Jocelyn stood beside the truck with Scott. Even in the strobe-lit night, my bedraggled state must have been obvious. Jocelyn demanded, "What happened to you, Emily? Mud wrestling?"

"Almost. You should see the other guy. And Izzy."

Scott asked, "Will she be okay? Her car's totaled." The fire truck blocked our view of Izzy's crumpled car.

I looked up at Misty's handsome, and very concerned, husband. "That wasn't all. She might have been concussed in the crash, and then someone pulled her out of the car and tried to drown her. A visitor to this area saved her life."

Scott whistled and looked west over my head. "I think the ambulance is coming back with her now."

Olivia asked, "Why are you firefighters still here?"

"In case her car has a hot spot and sets the dried grasses on fire, but the car and debris should be picked up soon, and then we'll head back into Fallingbrook. Unless we get a call sooner."

Lights flashing and siren blaring, the ambulance sped by. It turned off its siren after it passed us and presumably had the road ahead to itself. We hadn't been able to see the driver, let alone anyone else inside it.

Jocelyn, Olivia, and I said goodbye to Scott and walked to my car. Olivia waved Jocelyn toward the front passenger seat. "I'll sit in back again and try to be comforted by Dep's carrier, even though she's not in it."

At County Road C, Olivia asked if we needed to detour to Brent's and my chalet to make sure Dep was okay. "Or bring her along to Fallingbrook, since she's so fond of riding in cars."

I choked back a laugh. "She's probably sound asleep and not missing us at all. And especially not missing a road trip. Though, believe it or not, she seems to be mellowing about them, especially when you're back there with her, Olivia."

Driving south toward Fallingbrook, I couldn't quite fend off my mental replaying of the night's terrors. Where was Izzy's attacker, and was he the one who had attacked Adam? Was he planning to target other people?

Who was he?

Glenn? Jerry Creavus? It was possible that Landon had attacked Izzy and had only started trying to revive her when I screamed at him.

I didn't want to believe he'd merely been putting on an act. When he followed Izzy out of the dinner party, everything about him, his facial expressions, his body language, and even his voice, usually low and calm but suddenly higher and almost frantic, had made him appear anguished. I'd been sure that he cared about her and wanted to make things right between them.

A bright light streaked across the sky. Jocelyn exclaimed, "A meteor!"

Falling star, I thought. Was Landon a bright light who had saved Izzy, or a man who needed to fall out of her life?

The road became Wisconsin Street. I slowed. We passed the

village square and Deputy Donut. We were almost at Olivia's apartment when I again mentally replayed the scene of Izzy's regaining consciousness in the flashlit darkness amid whispering cattails. I spoke over my shoulder to Olivia. "Remember Izzy shouting 'hope'? I thought she was telling us to hope, which would be like her, but could she have meant her cousin?"

"Could be."

I continued thinking aloud. "Hope was mean to Izzy at the dinner party, but what if something happened during or after Izzy's injuries that caused her to worry about Hope?"

Olivia leaned closer to the front seats. "Like maybe someone has a grudge against their grandfather or someone else in their family, and that person ran Izzy off the road, and Izzy was afraid he would do something to Hope, too?"

I asked, "Would you two like to come with me to surreptitiously check on the house where Glenn and Hope are staying?"

Naturally, they said they wanted to go with me. Jocelyn added, "We don't have to open Deputy Donut until seven. We've got almost six hours. Tons of time!"

I turned into the quaint neighborhood of Victorian homes and drove slowly. A half block from the house where Izzy, Landon, and I had endured a strained dinner party, I could see the rear of a dark sedan near the street end of the driveway. That car hadn't been there when I'd turned around in the driveway a few eons, it seemed, ago. I veered to the curb, doused the headlights, rolled the windows down, and turned off the engine.

Tense in the seat beside me, Jocelyn said, "That could be the car that passed us when you stopped to pick us up at the village square this evening. I don't think it can be Landon's, but I suppose it could be the one with the mayor's vanity plate."

As if my engine were still running, I tightened my hands on the steering wheel. "Another one similar to Landon's passed us, ahead of Jerry's car. I thought it might have been Glenn, driving north instead of cleaning up after his dinner party. Maybe he left Hope behind to do that, or he came right back, and now Glenn and Hope are innocently tucked in bed, and Izzy didn't need to worry about her cousin. Let's just watch for a few minutes and not interfere."

The other two agreed, but Jocelyn undid her seat belt. "I'll just go a little closer and reconnoiter through that bridal veil bush."

I warned quietly, "We're underneath a streetlight."

"I'm wearing black."

Olivia pointed out, "Your shoes are red."

Jocelyn took off her ball cap and undid her ponytail. "Red looks almost black in the dark."

Olivia retorted, "Reflective stripes don't."

"That bush droops down to the sidewalk." Jocelyn bent her head forward until her hair hung over her face. She plopped the hat onto her head and then turned toward me, peering between strands of long black hair. "And no one will see my face."

I said dryly, "Or notice anything odd about you."

"All of me will be behind that bush." She quietly opened her door. The interior lights were still off. She slipped out. She allowed the door to close most of the way but not latch.

In the too-bright street, Olivia and I silently watched the back of the car we thought was Glenn's while also keeping an eye on Jocelyn, who, at least from the back, was camouflaged by the motley, moving shadows of maple leaves on branches between her and the streetlight.

As far as I could tell, no one else was around, at least not on the street or sidewalks. Rolling my shoulders in a mostly unsuccessful attempt to loosen tense muscles, I told myself that I should take my two assistants home so that we'd all get some sleep. Hope was probably fine.

And then I heard it, the slow creak of the antique hinges on the screen door that I'd lovingly restored years ago.

Seconds later, an engine started and the dark sedan backed out of the driveway.

Jocelyn eased farther into the dangling branches of the bridal veil.

I scooted down in my seat and ducked my head.

Behind me, Olivia murmured. "He's going the other way."

The taillights disappeared, and Jocelyn dived into the passenger seat. "He was carrying a small suitcase, and he seemed to be in a hurry."

Olivia asked, "Was it Glenn or Mayor Creavus?"

Jocelyn pushed her hair out of her face. "I'm not positive, but I don't think it was Jerry. Or his license plate."

I demanded, "Was he alone?"

Jocelyn buckled her seat belt. "No one else got into the car before he drove away, but that doesn't prove he doesn't have someone tied up in the back or the trunk."

Olivia said in a fake-serious voice, "You're such a ray of sunshine, Jocelyn."

"I know! Also, I couldn't see any lights at your house, Emily. Don't you have a motion detector on your porch light?"

"Yes."

Jocelyn put her hair into a ponytail and pulled it through the back of her ball cap again. "I don't think the porch light came on when he left, and he wasn't using a flashlight, not that he'd need one with all of these streetlights."

I peered toward the now-empty driveway. "Did either of you notice any damage to his car? I was hiding my face in case he came this way."

Olivia said, "I barely peeked over the back of your seats."

Jocelyn pointed toward where we'd last seen the car. "I don't think his right headlight was on."

Behind us, Olivia crowed, "Great detective work, Jocelyn!"

"Yeah," I agreed, "as long as he didn't notice the amateur detective hiding behind her hair in the bushes."

"He didn't look this way at all, so he didn't recognize your glaring white car, either."

I gave her a high five and then called Brent and told him where we were and what we'd seen, including a possibly non-functioning right headlight. I added, "I'm worried about Izzy's cousin Hope, like maybe she's been immobilized in the back or the trunk of his car. We found out on the way here that she's married to Glenn, and they've already signed wills making each other their beneficiaries. At the dinner party, he pretended to be surprised that she might be an heir, but I guess that she's bankrolling him and his new venture, and that her resources are the reason he can delay finding the perfect spot to open his restaurant. If so, he has to know she's wealthy and potentially wealthier."

Beside me, Jocelyn shuffled her feet and wiggled.

Brent told me, "Izzy's at the hospital and her condition is stable. She's safe. Misty and Tyler dropped Landon off at our headquarters so we can question him. They're on their way to talk to Jerry Creavus, but I'll redirect them to Maple Street. Stay where you are and tell them what you told me, okay?"

"Sure."

"Vic and I are still at Izzy's pond. See you later at home." We disconnected.

Jocelyn turned around in her seat and asked Olivia, "Do you have that portfolio and Glenn's documents back there?"

I peeked back at Olivia. The only thing in the seat with Olivia was Dep's carrier. Olivia lifted it and felt underneath where it had been. "They're not back here. I never saw or touched them. Where were they?"

Jocelyn patted her sneakers against the mat in front of her seat. "Here, on the floor. They aren't here now."

I turned on the interior lights, and we searched. I got out and opened the back hatch. I slipped into the driver's seat again and shut the door. The lights dimmed. "They're gone," I said.

Chapter 36

The lights inside the car dimmed completely, but the street was never completely dark. I could see my bewilderment mirrored on the others' faces. How had we lost the portfolio and the documents inside it?

Olivia was the first to come up with an answer. "After we arrived at Izzy's property, we left the car unlocked and the doors unlatched so we could quickly get inside. Someone must have taken the portfolio and the papers."

Jocelyn waved an imaginary wand. "And who would want them?"

Her question was obviously rhetorical, but Olivia and I both answered, "Glenn."

I added, "Which puts him at the scene around the time that someone dumped Izzy into a pond."

Olivia told Jocelyn, "A car accelerated past when we were up at the pond, but we didn't know which way it went. Do you remember seeing Glenn drive past after Emily and I left you near Izzy's wrecked car?"

"I was listening and planning to duck out of sight if any vehicles came near. None came from the west, where you were, and then I stopped worrying about it after Brent arrived."

Olivia and I told Jocelyn about seeing Izzy's second shoe almost directly below the pond where Landon found Izzy and our theory about where her attacker parked. I added, "And after he ran back down to his car, he drove or walked to my car, took his portfolio and papers, and then accelerated west in his car. Does that agree with what you heard and saw, Olivia?"

"Yes, except for why he would bother carting her away from the accident? Why not be content with forcing her off the road?"

My mouth was dry with horror. "He discovered that she survived the wreck, though she was probably unconscious, and he needed to make certain she would die. If it hadn't been for Landon, she probably would have."

Olivia leaned forward and put her hands between our headrests. "Glenn didn't have to pass the crash scene to come back here, right? He could have gotten back to Fallingbrook by heading west on County Road H, couldn't he?"

"Yes," I said, "and driving south on Pioneer Trail. It would probably take less than ten minutes longer."

I called Brent and told him quickly about someone taking documents from my car, and why we thought it was Glenn. I added, "If he's the one who did it, he was at or near Izzy's property shortly after she was dumped into the pond."

He thanked me. "I'll put out a BOLO for him. Point Misty and Tyler in the direction he was heading, then you can go home."

I told Jocelyn and Olivia that Brent was having officers be on the lookout for Glenn.

A marked police cruiser slid into place beside my car. Tyler opened the passenger window. Misty was driving.

I opened my window all the way and told Tyler and Misty, "Glenn pulled out of the driveway five minutes ago. He took a small suitcase and appeared to be alone. And Jocelyn noticed that his right headlight wasn't working."

Tyler peered past me at Jocelyn. "Visibly broken?"

Her mouth twitched in a rueful smile. "I couldn't tell."

I pointed ahead of us. "He went west."

Misty called across Tyler, "Thanks, Emily." She sped away.

I told my passengers, "I don't like Hope, but Glenn stands to inherit if she dies. I'm going to stroll over to my house and ring the doorbell. If I wake her up and she yells at me, fine. If you like, I can take you two home first."

Jocelyn reached for her door handle. "I'm coming with you."

Olivia opened her door. "Me, too."

I wasn't surprised.

We closed our doors as quietly as we could, and I locked the car. Without speaking, we walked the half block to the house that Alec and I had bought when we were first married. Everything seemed dark inside, and our arrival on the porch didn't set off the light's motion detector. I squinted up at the fluted glass fixture.

The bulb was missing.

I took a deep breath and rang the doorbell. I knew from experience that it could awaken a sleeper. We waited silently. I tried again. No one came. Maybe Hope slept more soundly than I had. Or maybe she had been with Glenn in his car. I whispered, though if the bell hadn't awakened Hope, I probably could have shouted, "Let's check the garage. If there's a car there, it probably means that Hope has her own and either hasn't gone anywhere, or she left with Glenn." I frowned. An empty garage would prove nothing.

We walked quietly down the porch steps and across the lawn to the driveway. If Hope looked out the bathroom window, she'd see three people silhouetted against the garage's tan siding. Maybe she would call the police or come out to confront us, and we could stop worrying about her.

We peeked through the window in the garage's side door.

An unfamiliar, small, and new-looking car was parked inside the garage.

Olivia breathed, "Uh-oh. Maybe we'd better look into that car."

Jocelyn asked, "Does your rental agreement allow you to go in, Emily?"

"Brent and I can go through the garage to mow the lawn and do other work behind the house." Surrounded by its high yellow brick wall, the yard was inaccessible except through the house or the garage. I entered the code on the door's lock. If the bathroom window was open and everything else was quiet, the beeps could be heard inside the house, but no one came outside or yelled at us. I ushered Jocelyn and Olivia into the garage and locked the door behind us.

Jocelyn glanced back at the door. "Doesn't Glenn have a code to open the garage, too?"

I clenched and unclenched my hands. "That will slow him down if he does come back."

Olivia added, "And we'll listen for those beeps."

We left the overhead door closed and used our phones' lights to examine the car. No one was in the seats. Knowing we risked getting in trouble with the police for touching anything, we tried the trunk. It opened. No one was in it. We tried not to slam it. A sticker from a rental company was near the rear plate. It was from Minnesota, which wasn't surprising. Hope and Landon had probably rented their cars at Duluth International Airport. Glenn might have, too, though the car I thought he was driving hadn't had obvious Minnesota plates.

Our snooping had not brought Hope out of the house. I opened the door that led from the rear of the garage into the walled yard. "Let's check the back of the house."

We turned off our lights and stumbled out onto grass. Lights came on. Beside me, Olivia gasped.

I whispered, "Motion detectors."

The yard was small, and we could see all of it except behind the whimsical fairy-tale gardening shed toward the back and the section of the patio that was hidden by the sunroom jutting out behind the kitchen.

Together, the three of us went around the shed and shined our lights. No one was there. I swept my light over the vegetable garden and the shrub-and-flower borders. No one was in any of them, either.

From the middle of the yard, we could see the bedroom window. It was open, but the sheers were closed. Was Hope behind them, watching us?

I walked to the patio and called softly up toward the window, "Hope?"

The sheers didn't move, and Hope didn't answer.

Jocelyn and Olivia had come to the patio with me. Jocelyn murmured, "Heavy sleeper!"

With her fingernails, Olivia tapped out an uneven rhythm on top of the umbrella table. "Maybe this will startle her awake."

Something was odd about the hose hanging from its holder on the back of the house.

Beneath the hose's lowest loop, silvery metal reflected the patio lights back at me.

"What?"

I didn't realize I'd said it aloud until Jocelyn asked, "What what?"

"I found my missing coffee grinder."

Chapter 37

Jocelyn demanded, as if she didn't quite believe me, "You've found your missing coffee grinder with your hose?"

Olivia asked, "Who hoses off electrical appliances?"

I realized we'd been talking in tones that were only slightly softer than normal, and Hope had not responded. I bent closer to the coffee grinder. "No one who's innocent."

The grinder's lid was in the dirt beside the house's stone foundation. Careful not to touch anything, I waved my hand over the open grinder and inhaled. "Maybe it's my imagination, but it doesn't smell like coffee." I shined my phone's light into the vat where I usually poured coffee beans. "Maybe no one hosed it off. There are bits of something inside it. They're almost white, definitely not from coffee beans."

Crouching beside me, Jocelyn sniffed at the coffee grinder. "It's not your imagination, or else mine is doing the same thing."

I called Brent and described the coffee grinder partially hidden behind the hose.

From background noises, I could tell that Brent was in his car, using his phone hands-free. He said, "Vic's overseeing the investigation at the pond. Misty and Tyler haven't located

Glenn. I'm on my way to our Maple Street house to try to figure out what he and his wife are up to."

"You don't need a search warrant? Oh, of course you don't. You own half of the house. And I give you my permission for the other half, in case you need it."

He laughed. "Thanks. You and your fellow sleuths don't have to wait for me. Go home and give Dep some pats for me." He disconnected.

From the door leading into the sunroom, Olivia stage-whispered, "Come here! I think there's a fire."

Jocelyn and I jumped to our feet and ran to her.

A tiny flame flickered on something white on a loveseat cushion.

I punched the code into the sunroom's keyless entry and flung the screen and inner doors open. The flame bent as if trying to avoid the breeze, but it didn't go out. In two strides, I was beside it.

Missing its aluminum base, the bare wax bottom of a tealight candle was on a slanting stack of papers on the edge of a cushion.

Jocelyn and Olivia scrambled into the sunroom behind me and shined their lights on the candle. Melted wax pooled in the shallow basin surrounding the wick at the flame's base. Trying not to splash hot wax, I blew out the candle, and then I turned on lights in the sunroom and kitchen, I grabbed the first dish I came across in the still-messy kitchen, one of my delicate saucers, took it back to the sunroom, and carefully placed the extinguished candle on it. I set the saucer and candle on top of the half-height wall behind the loveseat.

The toe of my sandal touched something, and the candle's discarded cuplike base rolled away from me. I left it for Brent and other investigators.

Jocelyn picked up the papers. "You didn't spill a single drop of wax, Emily."

"Good."

"Not a single one. Three of them."

"That's okay, considering that we've disturbed the evidence."

Jocelyn joked, "Should we put it all back and take pictures?"

Olivia waved her phone at us. "I took a video."

Jocelyn sorted through the documents. "These were in the portfolio that was taken from your car, Emily. If my memory's correct, the only documents that were there before but are not here now are the marriage certificate and the two wills. Of course Glenn would take those and leave the incriminating employment documents here to catch fire and burn up."

"Along with, most likely, this house." I managed to sound calm, and not as furious as I felt. Trying to wake up Hope, I shouted her name. No answer.

Olivia asked, "Are you going to call Brent about the candle and the documents that Glenn must have wanted to destroy?"

"He'll be here soon. He would tell me to get out of the house. And I will, as soon as I'm sure that Hope isn't in danger in here somewhere. But you two, please go outside."

Jocelyn folded her arms. "I'm staying with you."

Olivia was as stubborn. "Me, too. And we'll be careful."

I knew that I could argue forever and not change their minds. "Let's stay together, then, and watch for burning candles, booby traps, or . . . or anything."

Turning on lights as we went, we looked around the kitchen, still piled with dirty dishes, and then the dining and living rooms. We even checked underneath couch cushions. We didn't find open flames, and we didn't find Hope. "Upstairs next?" I asked, switching on more lights.

We all trotted up toward the second floor.

Hope wasn't in the bedroom, and she wasn't in the guest room or in either of the rooms' tiny closets. She wasn't in the hall closet or the laundry room. She wasn't in the bathtub. And we didn't find any lit candles.

Jocelyn exclaimed, "Basement!" She charged down the stairs.

Leaving lights blazing, I followed her. All three of us hurried through the living and dining rooms. In the kitchen, instead of going into the sunroom in the back of the house, we turned right, down a hallway. On our left, windows looked out on the patio and flower gardens. On our right, we checked the inside of the pantry closet. Because of the many shelves, mostly emptied after Brent and I decided to rent the house, there was no room for a person. No one was in the coat closet that Alec and I had designed with air vents and internal fans to help dry garments hanging inside it.

Jocelyn paused with her hand on the doorknob of the closed basement door.

"Let me go first." I didn't know why I whispered. If Hope was in the house, she had to be in the basement. It was unfinished, its floor concrete, its foundation walls stone, and its ceiling bare joists and planks. They only place to lie down would be the floor. I doubted that she could be sleeping so peacefully down there that she would resent being awakened. I didn't want to think about the chest freezer.

Switches for the basement lights were beside the closed basement door.

I flicked on all of the switches.

Jocelyn pulled Olivia and me to stand with her where we'd be behind the door if someone on the other side opened it.

Holding perfectly still, I listened. I heard Jocelyn's and Olivia's shallow breaths behind me. No sounds came from the basement or the stairway to it.

I put my hand on the doorknob.

Chapter 38

Cringing at the squeaks of hinges, I eased the door open, inch by inch.

I heard nothing besides the shuffle of my sandals on the terra-cotta tiles as I tried to find a more comfortable position for my blistered feet.

With my hand still on the doorknob, I slipped around the edge of the door.

Nothing was out of place in the brightly lit stairwell.

Jocelyn murmured, "Want me to go first? Gymnastics moves can come in handy."

Izzy's black belt in karate had been no help to her when someone forced her car off the road and caused it to roll into a ditch. I merely said, "They can, but I'd better go first. I'm more familiar with these stairs and this basement." And I didn't want to send my assistants—and good friends—into possible danger.

Jocelyn glanced down the hallway toward the kitchen. "Then I'll stay here and watch your back."

"Backs," Olivia corrected her. "I'm going down, too."

I started down the stairs. I didn't try to be quiet, but I didn't run, either. I heard the soles of Olivia's sandals on the bare wooden steps behind me.

No one was at the foot of the stairs or to my left near the set tub, water heater, and furnace. The chest freezer hummed quietly. I opened it and found only a few frozen foods, including the bag of almond flour that I remembered leaving there, now unsealed.

I closed the freezer and went around the staircase and the wall on its far side. Near the rear wall of the storage area, a previous homeowner, possibly the one Alec and I had met when we first toured the house, had stored her canned garden produce on rough wooden planks. Those shelves were empty.

I turned around. Brent's and my locked filing cases lined part of the wall at the front of the house.

Hope's stiletto sandals were sticking out from the far side of the row of filing cabinets. I dashed to that mostly hidden corner.

Still wearing the black raw silk tunic and matching capris, but missing the ropes of gold chains, Hope was lying on her side. Her ankles were tied together, and her wrists were bound behind her back. One of my larger kitchen towels had been tied tightly around her mouth and knotted in back, just below her no longer sleek bun.

She didn't move, except for her eyes, so much like Izzy's. And while I didn't like Hope, compassion kicked in. I knelt and tugged at the knot at the back of Hope's head. "Who did this?"

The hazel eyes glared at me.

The back of her head was sticky. My hand and the gag came away bloody.

Hope croaked, "You did. And now you've brought an accomplice with a knife."

A knife? I turned my head. Olivia was sawing at the rope around Hope's ankles.

Olivia muttered, "The knots are too tight to untie. And I

don't mind sacrificing the rope. Neither of you has any other use for it, do you?"

I demanded, "Where did you get that knife?"

"From the kitchen. I grabbed it out of your knife block when we first ran in there. But it's serrated. I should have gotten a sharper one. This is taking forever, um . . ."

"Hope," I supplied. "Hope, this is Olivia. We're trying to help you."

"Sure. Like you helped me by tying me up?"

I worked at the knot on her wrists. It was also tight. "We didn't do this, Hope." I shut my mouth tight on the suggestion that Glenn—her husband—had knocked her out and tied her up and then had tried to burn down the house with her in it. I had no proof, for one thing. For another, she probably wouldn't believe me. And I didn't want to agitate her even more. I told her, "I'll call emergency. Your head's bleeding."

"Don't bother. Just get out. You have no right to be here. And what have you done with my phone?"

Olivia ignored her. "There, Hope. Your ankles are free, but they're going to hurt. I'll remove the other rope, now."

I sat back on my heels and pulled my phone out of my pocket.

Olivia hacked at the rope on Hope's wrists. Hope cursed us. I gave the emergency dispatcher the address and asked for an ambulance and the police. "And you might as well send the fire department, too, in case we didn't get the fire completely out." I set the phone down and asked Hope, "Where's Glenn?"

"I don't know, but he'll be back soon and rescue me from you two thugs."

Maybe it wasn't fair to ask a possibly concussed person questions that had nothing to do with her condition, but I persisted. "Do you know why my coffee grinder was outside?"

"I don't know anything about kitchens, let alone coffee grinders. I don't even like coffee."

I heard someone run lightly down the basement steps. At their foot, Jocelyn waved at us and whispered hoarsely, "Someone's unlocking the front door."

I realized I'd been hearing the beeps but hadn't consciously thought about what they meant.

Was Brent already here?

Jocelyn disappeared up the stairs, to go back to watching Olivia's and my backs, no doubt.

Olivia quietly exclaimed "There!" The rope fell from Hope's wrists.

Hope pushed herself to a sitting position.

Olivia put the knife down on the floor. "Stay still. You might have a concussion."

Hope rubbed her wrists. "Thanks to you and your friends. How many of you are there, anyway?"

She batted our hands away, kicked her shoes aside, and ran barefoot toward the basement stairs. Between wisps of hair that had escaped from her bun, rivulets of dried blood streaked the back of her neck. I hoped that her head wound had truly stopped bleeding and that it was only superficial. Olivia and I jumped up and followed her.

Someone was walking on the floor above us. Apparently, a man had just come into the living room. Brent, I thought, but I might merely have been imagining what I wanted to hear.

At the base of the steps, I looked up. Hope pushed Jocelyn aside and turned toward the kitchen. Her bare feet slapped down on the tiles.

I'd seldom seen Jocelyn look that startled. "What?"

I pelted up to the first floor. Olivia was right behind me.

Jocelyn tore after Hope. Olivia and I weren't far behind. I dashed into the kitchen and through the dining room, and then I stopped dead, nearly crashing into Jocelyn, who had also halted.

Someone had turned off the living room lights.

Enough light streamed in from the stairway and the dining room to see who had come inside, shut the door against the still-dark porch, and now stood in front of the door.

Not Brent.

Glenn. His arms were around Hope.

Chapter 39

Glenn demanded, "What are you doing here? Get out!" He was still in the white shirt and jeans, and now he wore a totally unwrinkled blue linen blazer over them. It wasn't buttoned. Because of the dim lighting, I couldn't see his pant legs or shoes well, but they weren't obviously muddy. He could have thrown Izzy into the pond without stepping into the mud or the water.

Hope leaned into him. "They attacked me. The tall one has a knife."

I turned around. Olivia held her hands up. They were empty. "No, I don't." Her face was about the same pink as the roses on the pretty, ruffled top she wore untucked over her jeans.

I remembered seeing her put my bread knife on the basement floor. I tried not to be obvious as I glanced toward where I'd seen the knife scabbard hanging at Glenn's hip. His blazer covered all but the very tip of the scabbard. There were no decorative circular cutouts on that part of it, so I couldn't tell if it was empty. Maybe he'd been sensible enough not to drive with a very sharp knife hanging at his side, especially when his trip plans had apparently included possibly ramming another car to force it off the road. Maybe he'd left the knife in my kitchen with the other dirty dishes.

Then I pictured the neat slash across Izzy's seat belt....

And I remembered the suitcase Jocelyn said Glenn had taken to his car. That suitcase had probably contained important things, like the marriage certificate and wills. And the expensive chef's knife?

He gave Hope a shove toward the front door. "Go get in my car. We'll escape these home invaders and call the cops."

I stood straighter. "Wait here. They're on their way. Along with an ambulance. Your . . . Hope's head is bleeding. She could have a concussion."

Glenn pushed Hope again. "Get going."

Behind me, Olivia stated with her new and admirable confidence, "She needs to see a doctor."

Glenn snapped, "I'll take her to one. Go ahead, Hope."

Hope opened the front door.

I edged around Jocelyn and turned on the lamp on the nearest end table. Beside me, Landon's napkin was still draped over the back of the couch. I ordered, "Wait, Hope. Glenn is the one who attacked you and left you bound and gagged in the basement, and then he started a fire to burn down the house with you inside."

Her hand on the edge of the door, Hope looked over her shoulder toward me. "He wouldn't do that. You attacked me." She sniffed. "And I don't even smell smoke."

Jocelyn told her, "Emily put the fire out. And you're lucky that she did."

Hope shook her head and then flinched. "You're making no sense. Glenn wouldn't start a fire and then come back."

Unless he returned to make certain that the candle burned down through the papers and set fire to the loveseat, and then to the entire house. Or he wanted to play the distressed victim desperate to rescue the woman he loved. "Wait here, Hope," I suggested. "The police will sort it out. You don't have to fear them."

"Except that one of them is your husband, Emma."

I didn't bother correcting her. "He's been at another crime scene. Someone forced Izzy off the road and then took her to a pond, dumped her into it, and left her to drown. The evidence points to your husband."

Hope narrowed her eyes. "How do you know he's my husband? We haven't told anyone."

Jocelyn demanded, "Why not? Did Glenn order you to keep it a secret?"

Hope's lower lip fell slightly, as if Jocelyn's guess was right.

I prodded, "And why would he do that? To keep your grandfather from suspecting that he was after your money? And that your will made Glenn your heir?" Apparently, Hope was paying some attention to me. She continued to stand in the open doorway with the screen door closed in front of her. I pressed. "And someone killed Adam Nofftry on the property Izzy was buying. Several years ago, Adam offered Glenn a job managing one of his restaurants, and Glenn gave up his own restaurant to take the job."

Glenn more or less confirmed my theory. "That has nothing to do with anything. Go, Hope."

She didn't budge.

I argued, "It has everything to do with everything, Glenn, if you became resentful about being fired and needing to hunt for another job or find funds to start another restaurant. Besides, you were fired for disobeying your employment agreement and serving almonds in one of Adam's restaurants. You either knew or figured out that Adam was allergic to almonds. Maybe you knew that Adam was fond of donuts. You sent Hope to buy donuts that you could copy, with added almonds. But she ran into a colleague in Deputy Donut and talked him out of the donuts he bought."

She glared at me. "I did not."

I backtracked, but only a little. "Glenn somehow got a box with some of those donuts, and he's an expert. All he had to do was taste our donuts, and he was able to copy them, but with a few changes that were toxic to Adam, like using almond flour instead of wheat flour. And then to add insult to injury, he used my coffee grinder to pulverize the kernels from inside peach pits, which can be poisonous, and added the ground-up peach pits to his replica donuts. He made mistakes, though. He didn't throw out the grinder. It's outside, where the police can collect it and analyze what's still inside it. Glenn also put cardamom in the donuts, which we hadn't done. My cat discovered the leftover donuts on the property Izzy was buying and became interested. My cat doesn't notice baked goods unless they have cardamom in them, and then she becomes obsessed. And Glenn took Adam's adrenaline autoinjector before Adam could save himself with it, but that autoinjector was later retrieved."

Glenn gave Hope another push. "That is all ridiculous speculation. And impossible. Who believes in a cardamom-sniffing cat or that a random autoinjector can be traced to anyone? Go get in the car, Hope, my car, not the one you're renting. She's making things up, blaming the innocent to cover up her own crime of selling poisoned donuts."

So . . . hoping to implicate his landlady—me—Glenn left the donuts and the Deputy Donut box where investigators would find them.

Hope reached for the screen door.

I didn't like the woman, but she was one of Izzy's few relatives, and I couldn't let her leave with a man who had murdered once and had also attempted to murder Izzy and Hope. "Wait, Hope. Do not get into Glenn's car. He had another motive for killing Adam in addition to revenge for having to start over with a new restaurant. Glenn killed Adam on property that Izzy was buying, and it was known that Adam was trying to prevent Izzy from purchasing that property. Glenn hoped that Izzy would be convicted of murdering Adam, and then your grandfather would certainly not change his will in her favor. But to make certain that Izzy would inherit nothing, Glenn shoved Izzy unconscious into a pond tonight. After you signed a will making Glenn your heir, how long did you expect to live?"

Hope glanced back at Glenn and repeated, "He wouldn't do that." This time, she sounded less sure. She pushed the screen door open and ran out onto the dark porch. Hearing her bare feet on the wooden steps, I could almost feel splinters piercing the soles of my own feet.

I wasn't surprised that Glenn didn't follow his wife. He stood blocking the front door. I took a couple of steps backward. Behind me, I heard Olivia and Jocelyn also retreating, slowly.

With the beginnings of a sneer twitching at his lips, Glenn moved forward. His pant legs and shoes were now in the light from the lamp I'd turned on, and I was almost certain from my quick glance at them that they were speckled with dried mud.

But I couldn't waste crucial moments examining his pant legs and shoes.

With one hand, he brushed aside the front edge of his blazer.

He yanked his undoubtedly sharp chef's knife out of its scabbard.

Chapter 40

I whispered over my shoulder to Olivia and Jocelyn, "Run!"

Squinting with menace, Glenn stepped toward me. My first thought was that he wouldn't risk damaging his carefully coddled knife by stabbing one of us or throwing it, but then I realized that Glenn was desperate. He had to silence all of us if he wanted to escape charges of murder and attempted murder. Plus, he might have already dulled that knife by slashing Izzy's seat belt.

I decided to brazen it out. "Hurting us won't help your case, Glenn. The police already have evidence against you. Don't make it worse for yourself."

Someone, either Olivia or Jocelyn, plucked at the back of my dress. I muttered, "Get out!"

Glenn raised the hand holding the knife.

I grabbed the nearest heavy object, the tall table lamp I'd lit when I ran into the room. My grandmother had been proud of the lamp's classic, solid brass base. It was, she'd claimed, a lamp that even she couldn't knock over. Grasping it near the top just beneath the shade, I yanked it off the table. The lamp was old, and the electrical wire leading into it must have weakened over time. The connection broke and cast the living room again into semi-darkness. Swinging that lamp as if it were a baseball bat, I was barely aware of footsteps in the dining room. Olivia and Jocelyn were supposed to be running away, but they seemed to be coming nearer. And the shoes sounded more substantial than Jocelyn's sneakers and Olivia's sandals.

I couldn't take time to think about who might be behind me. Focusing on saving us from Glenn's knife, I let go of that lamp, aiming its heavy base at the hand holding the knife.

There are good reasons why baseball bats don't have lampshades attached to their handles.

Acting as a sail, the shade altered the lamp's projection, and it missed Glenn's throwing arm. Out of the corner of my eye, I saw the knife fly out of his hand.

The lamp's base hit Glenn in the forehead, just above his nose.

The lamp and Glen thudded onto the floor. Delicate lightbulb glass tinkled over pine planks.

Calling, "Jocelyn, Olivia, are you all right?" I ran to Glenn, all of about four steps.

Jocelyn answered, "We're fine." But maybe she was losing her usual equilibrium. I could have sworn that I heard laughter in her voice.

Brent and Tyler ran in from the dining room and placed themselves between Glenn and me. I backed toward Olivia and Jocelyn, but only a little. All three of us stayed in the living room, close to the table that was now missing its lamp.

Vic let himself in through the front door. He knelt beside Glenn and picked up his wrist. "Unconscious. Strong pulse. I saw and heard enough to arrest him. Cuffs, please, Officer Tainwright." Vic pulled Glenn's hands behind his back and snapped on the handcuffs that Tyler gave him.

His eyes glinting with something like amusement, Tyler came to Olivia and patted her shoulder. "Maybe you should take that out of your waistband before someone gets hurt."

With a rueful grin, Olivia reached toward her back.

Tyler stopped her with a touch on her wrist. "Wait. I'll help. Stand still."

Seconds later, after a little lifting of her blouse in back and a lot of blushing, he set my bread knife on the table where the lamp had been. "Are you okay, Olivia? Did I scratch you?"

"I'm fine. If there are scrapes, it's my fault. Thanks for getting it out without scratching me more."

I stared at her. "You brought that up from the basement and kept it hidden from Glenn?"

"I thought it might come in handy. I wasn't going to use it unless I had to, and when I needed it, the serrations got caught in my waistband. Not that it would have done any good against that man's knife." She looked down at my grandmother's ruby-red velvet couch. "I suspect your bread knife did less damage to me and my jeans than that man's knife did to your couch."

Glenn's prized chef's knife was up to its hilt in a white linen napkin, pinning the napkin to the red velvet upholstery.

I shrugged. "I guess it's time for some reupholstering. That is, if we want to continue decorating with my grandmother's furniture." *And if we wanted to continue owning this house . . .*

From his kneeling position, Brent looked up at us. "I'm afraid I have to cancel my earlier offer to let you three go home. We'll need to talk to you while Tyler and Misty escort this man to the hospital to be examined before we take him in for questioning."

I agreed and then turned to Tyler. "Where's Misty?"

He nodded toward the front window. "Out on the lawn trying to calm a hysterical person."

I said, "We called an ambulance for the woman. I hope that's the siren I hear."

Brent stood. "Emily, Jocelyn, and Olivia, please go out back to the patio. Don't discuss this with one another, and we'll question you as soon as we can."

I asked him, "May we take water to drink? Tap water. I don't want anything that man might have touched, except glasses."

"Go ahead," Brent said, but he was watching Glenn and was obviously distracted by Glenn's signs of regaining consciousness.

Tyler, however, was gazing at Olivia. "Bread knife," he murmured.

Her face reddened again. "You're not going to let me live that down, are you, Tyler?"

His eyes warm, he smiled down at her upturned face. "Never."

Ah, romance, I thought.

Olivia, Jocelyn, and I trooped into the kitchen, ran tap water into glasses, and took them outside, past the dirty dishes and the extinguished candle on its delicate china saucer.

We sat at the patio table and sipped our water. We didn't talk much, partly because we obeyed Brent and didn't discuss the case, but mostly because we were tired. And I, for one, was silently going over the evening, thinking of what I would say to whichever officer questioned me. Vic, probably, I thought with a sigh.

And I was right. I told him everything that we hadn't discussed earlier, beginning with the dinner party and finding the portfolio of papers. I showed him the coffee grinder still partially hidden by the hose, the snuffed candle, and the wax-splattered documents that Glenn had tried to burn. "He'd set the candle and papers on a slant. Olivia has a video of it. I guess Glenn planned that the melted wax would drip away and not form a pool that could drown the flame. But he had other documents besides these in his portfolio. His marriage certificate and his and Hope's wills are probably in his car."

Brent questioned Olivia, and Misty returned from the hospital and took Jocelyn's statement.

Finally, we were free to go. I asked Misty how Hope was.

"She's being stitched up. She admitted that she lied about being with Glenn the entire afternoon and evening that Adam died, and that Glenn sent her out for donuts and instead of buying them, she cajoled—my word, not hers—some, including their box, from Landon. She didn't know that Glenn baked copycat donuts. She informed me that she never went near kitchens. She also denied that she had anything to do with Adam's actual eating of the donuts. Glenn went out for over an hour that afternoon, she thought, while she stayed home catching up with email from work. She said we couldn't arrest her because her grandfather would be angry, and she even turned on some tears." Misty could wear a very hard expression. "I basically told her that my heart was bleeding for her. She said she had nothing to do with the attack on Izzy. Somehow, she had the impression that Izzy had died tonight." Being one of my best friends did not stop Misty from glaring at me. She added, "I told her that Izzy was expected to live. Hope didn't seem as relieved as a normal person would be when told that a cousin had narrowly escaped death."

"I hope she's nowhere near Izzy in that hospital."

"She won't be. We've called in other officers. One will escort Hope from the hospital to one of our interrogation rooms."

"What about Glenn?"

"He's fine, except for a rather large goose egg on his forehead that he says you caused."

"Self-defense."

"Well done, too."

"I was trying to hit the hand holding the knife, but I missed, and the heaviest part of the lamp hit him in the face instead."

"I saw where the knife ended up. You might have ruined his aim, but he's strong, probably strong enough to subdue a man and force-feed him something, like tailor-made donuts. He threw that knife with plenty of force, and he could have damaged you severely. He's already in a cell and will probably remain in one for a very long time."

Before I left, through the garage, Brent caught me in a bear hug. "I probably won't be home until after you leave for work."

"Am I in trouble for assaulting Glenn?"

He shook his head. "Vic, Tyler, and I saw the tail end of the encounter. You were defending yourself and Olivia and Jocelyn. I'm sorry we didn't get there sooner." Holding me tighter, he sighed into my hair before he let me go. "You'd better get some sleep, if you can."

"And poor Dep has been alone since six thirty. She's going to sulk."

I took Jocelyn and Olivia to their homes, and then, eyes tired and dry but open, I drove back to Dep. She was on the couch where she'd been when I left. She didn't sulk. I picked her up. "You didn't miss me, did you? I bet you slept the entire time I was gone." She purred. I told her, "I'm glad you weren't with me."

"Mew."

I took her upstairs, cleaned and rebandaged my feet, and fell into bed.

Chapter 41

Brent wasn't awake yet when I groggily got up. I grabbed a quick breakfast and put my surprisingly cooperative cat into her carrier in my car. In cozy socks and sneakers, my feet barely hurt.

At work, Jocelyn and Olivia were already telling Tom about the night before.

He plopped a ball of risen dough onto our marble counter. "I'm glad you all survived."

"Piece of cake," Jocelyn told him. "Emily knocked him down with a lamp, and Olivia armed herself with a bread knife. But then she found a handsome police officer disarming."

Still feeling punchy, I giggled.

Olivia's fake glower dissolved into a smile.

Tom flattened the dough with an open palm. "And what did you do, Jocelyn, a forward roll right over him?"

"I covered my eyes and squeaked."

Tom forced a marble rolling pin across the dough. "I somehow can't see that."

Jocelyn picked up a tray of sugar bowls and creamers. "Emily acted faster than I could."

I confessed, "I was in her way."

Our customers didn't seem to notice that Olivia and I were

perhaps red-eyed and a little tired. Jocelyn, however, was her usual energetic self.

Olivia seemed to be watching the front door until I casually mentioned that Misty and Tyler were probably busy all morning, and since they finished the night shift at noon, they probably wouldn't come in for breaks that day.

Olivia blushed. "I know. And anyway, I'm meeting him for a late picnic dinner in the square before he heads back to work tonight."

"Are you bringing the picnic?"

"We'll have takeout from Frisky Pomegranate."

Jocelyn came along with pots of coffee for the Knitpickers and the retired men. She elbowed Olivia. "I'll try not to budge into your date this time."

"It's not exactly a date."

Heading back to the kitchen for plates of donuts, I said over my shoulder, "Call it whatever you want."

I took a short lunch break in our office with Dep, a plate of chickpea salad, some battered and deep-fried red and green peppers, and a bracing cup of the day's special aromatic and flavorful Kona coffee from Hawaii. I called the hospital and asked to speak to Izzy Korinth.

A woman told me, "We don't have anyone here by that name."

"Sorry, her full name is Isabella Korinth."

There was a pause, and then a tentative-sounding reply. "Can't help you."

Had Izzy been discharged, or was the operator following protocol about not giving out information about patients?

Although Izzy's phone had gone dead during the crash the night before and could have been irreparably damaged, I tried her number. It went straight to message. Hoping she would soon obtain a replacement phone, I said, "Hi, Izzy. I'm wondering how you are. Give me a call when you can."

At home that evening, Brent confirmed that Izzy was out of the hospital. "She's staying with her lawyer friends and recuperating, which probably includes getting a new phone and weeding the sisters' garden."

"Where's Glenn?"

"Off our hands. He's been transferred to the county jail. There should be a bail hearing tomorrow, but I don't expect him to get bail."

"How about Hope?"

"We probably can't make charges against her that will stick. She's back in New York or on the way. She hired someone to take her directly from our office all the way to Duluth International."

"She didn't drive herself in the car she rented?"

"She didn't want to wait until we released it. Both that car and the one Glenn rented will be returned to the agency after forensics finishes going through them. We did give her the gold necklace we found in the car he was driving. And we made copies of their marriage certificate and wills for evidence and gave her the originals."

"Where's Landon?"

"I don't have to keep tabs on him, but I believe he hasn't checked out of the B and B in Gooseleg where he's been staying since he drove down from Duluth."

I tried calling Izzy again.

No answer. I left her another message.

Brent reminded me, "Maybe she needs more time to heal, not only physically, but emotionally."

I agreed glumly. "Will you be talking to her soon?"

"Eventually, before Glenn's trial. We took her statement, what little she remembered, and she knows to contact us if she remembers anything else."

"It's sad, getting to know her again after all those years, and then losing her again."

Brent rubbed my back. "I know."

I flung my arms around him. "You're the best."

His laugh was low and warm. "I know that, too."

"You're impossible, but I suppose you're going to tell me that you know that, too."

He must have decided that kissing me was a better option. I didn't mind.

Chapter 42

By the following Monday morning, I still hadn't heard from Izzy. Deputy Donut was crowded. Sitting at their regular tables, the Knitpickers and retired men joked with one another.

Jerry Creavus came in, sat with the retired men, and effectively put an end to the fake bickering they enjoyed. He delivered monologues, giving them reasons why they should vote for him, although, since Adam's death, no one was running against him.

Or was someone about to? Ramona Schleehart came in by herself. She wore a TWIG T-shirt, but she didn't have any of her followers with her. She glared at Jerry and sat down with her back to him and almost touching him. I went to her table and asked what she'd like.

"Do you have organic fair-trade coffee?" Clearly expecting me to say that we didn't, she asked the question with a gotcha tone.

"Today's special coffee is an organic fair-trade medium roast from Timor. It's mild with a sweet finish."

"I'd like a mug of that." She said it almost grudgingly. "And are you still selling those peachy sour cream donuts?"

"Not quite. We've made basically the same recipe and added cardamom to it." Glenn's addition had made the donuts better,

I thought, though we still made ours with wheat flour, and we didn't add almond flour or ground-up peach pits.

"Bring me two to eat with the coffee."

"Glad to." I started toward the kitchen.

The front door swung open. Grinning hugely, Izzy danced in. She wore cutoffs, a blue T-shirt with green peppers printed on it, and sneakers. Her curls were even more unruly than mine. "Emily! Sorry for not answering your messages."

"That's okay. How are you?"

"Wonderful. Guess what happened this morning?"

I didn't want to make an incorrect guess. "What?"

"I closed on the property! It's all mine!"

I congratulated her. Jerry Creavus turned toward her. "Will you continue to allow people to hunt and fish there?"

Izzy made a sad face, but those hazel eyes sparkled with excitement. "I'm afraid not. It will be a working farm, and you know, greenhouses tend to be a little too fragile to withstand bullets or whatever. I hope you can find another place."

He waved his hand in a magnanimous gesture of dismissal. "Don't you worry about it. We have lots of other places. Did Emily give you my card? I wanted to arrange a meeting some evening."

Izzy looked at me.

I shook my head. "I haven't seen her since . . . I mean, I didn't get a chance."

Jerry puffed out his chest. "I thought I'd create a working group of young entrepreneurs to advise me as mayor. Emily can come, too, and bring donuts."

Izzy appeared to consider the idea. "Can I get back to you?"

Jerry laid his hand flat on the table. "You sure can. I look forward to seeing your business thrive and grow." He threw a triumphant look at Ramona.

Izzy obviously noticed. She asked Ramona, "Would you and other members of TWIG be able to tour the place with me? I'd like advice on which trees absolutely must stay, like if there are endangered or rare species there."

"They should all stay, but I'm sure that I can round up a few people to give you advice." Ramona's voice was gruff, but I thought I detected a suspicion of a smile battling with her usual frown.

Izzy followed me to the serving counter. Filling Jerry's and Ramona's orders took a little longer than usual because Olivia and Jocelyn joined us, and Izzy happily repeated her news. "And can I have a box of peachy sour cream donuts? I'll share them with my lawyers, the sisters who let me stay with them while I was recovering."

I again explained the change we'd made to the recipe. "Do you still want them, Izzy?"

"Absolutely!"

Finally, I took Ramona's and Jerry's orders to them.

I thought Izzy was about to leave, but she asked if she could visit Dep for a few minutes.

"Sure." I took Izzy to the office and shut us in.

Letting out anticipatory chirps, Dep ran down her ramp to greet us. Or maybe she was greeting the cardamom in the donuts in Izzy's box.

Izzy edged onto the couch, put the box behind her back, and lifted Dep, purring loudly and looking nearly boneless, onto her lap. Izzy stroked the little cat. "Emily, Hope asked me to collect her jewelry from your house and send it to her. In return, I can have whatever else she and Glenn left behind." She wrinkled her nose and let the corners of her mouth droop in revulsion. "When's a good time for me to come to your place and clear out Hope's things?"

"Brent and I will be there tidying this evening. The police have already picked up Glenn's phone, computer, and that expensive knife. And they packaged his other possessions for when he gets out. They also gave Hope the gold necklace they found in his rental car. As she must have told you, she hired someone to take her directly from the Fallingbrook police station to the airport in Duluth. We canceled the code we'd given Glenn for unlocking our doors, and she didn't want to stick around until the place was cleared as a crime scene. The police offered her the chance to go inside and get her things, but she didn't seem to want to visit the house with them watching her every move. The memories of her time there with Glenn, especially the night he attacked her and tried to kill her, would have to be painful." I lightened the mood with a guess that was only slightly less insulting than some of Hope's comments during the night of the dinner party. "Or maybe she was afraid she'd have to clean up the kitchen."

"Did you end up doing that?"

"Brent and I did, after the investigators finished. Hope told Brent she'd send someone for her things."

"That would be me, the snot-nosed, bratty cousin."

"Not to speak ill of your family, but she's the brat."

"Always was, always will be. See you this evening. Bye, Dep." I let Izzy and her box of donuts out the back door.

At the house on Maple Street that evening, the first thing Izzy noticed was Dep rolling invitingly on the couch. The second thing Izzy noticed was the hole in the couch's backrest. She pointed. "Did Hope puncture that with her stilettos?"

"Glenn did it with his chef's knife." I described the scene.

Izzy praised most of us who had been present that early morning but concluded with disgust, "My cousin-in-law is a real gem. Speaking of which, let's go see what gems Hope brought with her. Like maybe a wedding ring to go with that marriage certificate you said you found."

Dep helped us search. Hope hadn't brought much jewelry. None of the rings looked like wedding or engagement rings, but some of the jewelry did look, as the gold necklace had, valuable.

Izzy didn't want any of the beautiful and expensive clothes. "They'll fit you, too, Emily."

"I . . . no, thanks. How about giving them to charity?"

"I have a great idea. My lawyer friends help at a women's shelter. Someone's going to get a windfall of designer clothing."

We packaged the jewelry for Izzy to take to an insured courier, and then we put Hope's clothes and shoes into boxes, which involved lifting Dep out of the boxes each time we wanted to fold a garment into one.

When we finished, it was dark outside. Brent, Izzy, and I carried everything to Izzy's brand-new all-wheel-drive SUV, one that looked capable of climbing up into her property even before she had the driveway graded. "Courtesy of my grandfather," she told us. "Landon told him everything that happened, and Grampa sent me another huge check, with more to come. He's letting Hope keep her job, but he decided that her plans to lend a murderer money to open a restaurant so that, as Grampa says, 'he can poison more people' didn't pass muster. Maybe Grampa will change his mind, but for now, he says that Hope had better make good use of the money he gave her, because although she might inherit through her father, she's not inheriting anything directly from him."

I stowed a carton into the SUV's open rear hatch and inhaled that probably too-intoxicating new-car smell. "And are you inheriting?"

She shoved her box in with the others. "I don't know, and it doesn't matter. I'm going to make my greenhouse dream a reality. Best of all, though, I got my Grampa back, and my dad got his father back."

"How's Landon?"

"Back in New York. The money Grampa gave me and is promising me more of has turned into a nightmare. Landon informed me that after telling Grampa that I was the one who deserved to inherit, he—Landon, that is—can't continue to see me. He doesn't want to look like a gold digger."

Brent put an arm around me, and I patted Izzy's back. "I'm sorry, Izzy."

She looked straight at me. Tears might have glimmered in her eyes, but she raised her chin. "It's not over. I told him he's not allowed to make that decision by himself. It's our future and our decision. I'll use some of my newfound wealth to fly to New York as often as I have to, just to make him change his mind. And"—she waved her hand toward the north—"I'm naming the pond where he saved my life Mystery Pond in his honor. So, he has to come back. Oh, and when children come to tour, I'll hide treasures in Emily's Cave. See you two around." She got into her car.

Watching her drive away, Brent asked me, "Do you think she'll get what she wants?"

"I don't think it. I know it. By next summer, Landon will be wearing denim overalls and a straw hat and working in her greenhouses. And maybe they'll hold their wedding on that hillside and invite us."

We turned and faced the house. We'd replaced the porch lightbulb that Glenn had removed. It cast a warm glow over the old yellow bricks, the porch floorboards, and the antique door and screen. The entire effect, now that Hope and Glenn were gone, was again charming and welcoming.

However . . .

I slipped an arm around Brent. "You know what? This house contains a lot of memories, wonderful ones with Alec and wonderful ones with you. But I don't know about keeping it and continuing to rent it to other people. Maybe it's time to move on. We'll still have our memories."

My husband surrounded me in a gentle hug. "You don't have to decide right now."

"I don't have to decide by myself. Unlike Landon and his chivalrous notions, you and I will decide together."

And maybe it would depend on whether or not we started a family. I still wasn't pregnant. But, I reminded myself, I was a surprise late in my own parents' life. It could still happen. And to help the miracle along, I would find the courage to book an appointment with the clinic in Milwaukee.

I hugged Brent tighter and lifted my face toward his.

A bright light streaked across the part of the sky I could see between maple leaves. I leaned back and pointed. "Look!"

Brent managed to see it before it burned up. "A meteor," he said, and kissed me.

RECIPES

Baked Peachy Sour Cream Donuts

(Makes 10 donuts and/or cupcakes—cupcakes will be denser than normal cupcakes. For the baked donuts, you will need a nonstick donut baking pan. They have donut-shaped baking cavities.)

Vegetable oil for greasing the pan
½ cup 14 percent butterfat sour cream
1 extra-large egg, room temperature
½ teaspoon peach extract (lemon extract or almond extract can be substituted)
¼ cup vegetable oil
½ cup sugar
1 cup all-purpose flour
¼ teaspoon ground cardamom
½ teaspoon baking soda
1 medium to large fresh peach, pitted and small-diced (you don't need to peel it.)

Preheat oven to 350 degrees F. Lightly grease nonstick donut baking pan.

In one bowl, whisk together the sour cream, egg, peach or vanilla extract, vegetable oil, and sugar until well blended.

In a larger bowl, stir the flour, cardamom, and baking soda with a fork until well blended.

Pour the wet ingredients into the dry ingredients and mix well.

Stir in the diced peaches.

Spoon the batter into the donut-shaped cavities in the donut baking pan, filling them halfway.

Bake 12 to 15 minutes, until tops are golden and an inserted toothpick comes out clean.

Invert the pan on a cooling rack.

When the donuts have cooled, gently loosen them with a silicone spatula and remove.

Frost the rounded sides (the bottoms of the donuts when they were being baked) with Peachy Sour Cream Frosting (see page 295).

Optional: Decorate the tops with thin slices of fresh peach.

To vary: substitute diced fresh strawberries for the peaches and use lemon extract.

If you don't have a donut baking pan, bake as cupcakes in cupcake papers and pan for 15 to 20 minutes or until the tops are golden and an inserted toothpick comes out clean. Emily's home donut baking pan makes only 6 donuts, so Emily bakes the rest of the batter in cupcake papers in cupcake tins.

Peachy Sour Cream Frosting

(Frosts 6 to 10 donuts or cupcakes)

2 tablespoons unsalted butter, softened
1 cup powdered sugar, sifted or pushed through sieve
⅛ teaspoon peach extract (lemon or vanilla extract can be substituted)
¼ cup 14 percent butterfat sour cream

In the bowl of an electric mixer, cream the butter.
Beat the sugar into the butter until blended.
Stir in the peach extract
Stir in the sour cream

If the frosting is too thick, stir in more sour cream. If it's too thin, stir in more powdered sugar.

Store the frosting in the refrigerator until you're ready to use it. If any frosted donuts are left over, store them in the refrigerator.

Spiced-Tea Baked Donuts

Use the recipe for Baked Peachy Sour Cream Donuts, but omit the peaches. Instead of peach extract, add 1 teaspoon strongly brewed Darjeeling tea. In addition to the cardamom, add ⅛ teaspoon each of ground cinnamon, cloves, black pepper, ginger, and nutmeg—vary to taste.

Frost with Peachy Sour Cream Frosting, substituting ½ teaspoon strongly brewed Darjeeling tea for the peach extract. Sprinkle tops with cinnamon.

Chilled Sour Cream Peach Soup

(Serves 4)

4 large fresh peaches, sliced
1 tablespoon sugar
1 cup peach juice (orange or apple juice can be substituted)
2 tablespoons 14 percent butterfat sour cream (plain or vanilla Greek or Icelandic yogurt can be substituted)
Ground cardamom

In an electric blender, pulse the peaches, sugar, juice, and sour cream until well mixed.
Chill.
When ready to serve, place in bowls and sprinkle ground cardamom over each bowl.

Peach and Pinto Bean Salad

Because only a minimum amount of stovetop heat is used, this salad is a good one to prepare on a hot day as a main course. It is best when local peaches are in season. Where possible, use homegrown or local basil, peppers, and scallion, which will also be in season.

(Serves 3 as a main course, 6 or more as a side dish.)

⅓ cup pecans, toasted and chopped
1 lime
1 teaspoon finely chopped garlic—from a jar is fine, as it's milder than fresh garlic
½ teaspoon salt or to taste
2 tablespoons olive oil
Pinch of chili flakes or to taste
1 (19-ounce) can pinto beans, rinsed and drained
3 medium fresh peaches, pitted and cut into bite-sized pieces
1 head romaine lettuce, chopped
1 scallion, green part only, sliced on diagonal
1 handful fresh basil leaves, roughly torn or chopped
1 tablespoon mild red hot peppers or sweet pepper, finely chopped

Toast the pecans. In a dry frying pan, toast the pecans on medium-high, stirring continuously until they begin to brown lightly. Remove from the heat and the pan and set aside to cool.

Make the dressing. Zest and juice the lime and place the zest and the juice together in a small bowl. Add the garlic, salt, olive oil, and chili flakes. Whisk until combined.

Make the salad. Place the beans, peaches, lettuce, scallion top, chopped basil, and red pepper into a large bowl. Chop the toasted pecans and add. Drizzle the dressing over the salad. Toss and serve.

Broiled Peaches with Sour Cream

This recipe can be increased to serve many people, depending on how big your broiler is.

Fresh peaches
Unsalted butter, about 1/8 teaspoon per peach
Brown sugar, about 1/4 teaspoon per peach
Sour cream
Cinnamon
Fresh mint leaves (optional)

Halve the peaches, remove the pits, and put the halves, flat side up, on a baking tray. Place a small dab (about 1/8 teaspoon) of unsalted butter and 1/4 teaspoon brown sugar in each indentation. Place under the broiler for about 5 minutes.

Remove from the broiler, place peach halves in bowls, and top with a dollop of sour cream and a dash of cinnamon. Garnish with mint leaves and serve immediately.